DEMAIN PUBLISHING

Short Sharp Shocks!

Murder! Mystery! Mayhem!

Beats! Ballads! Blank Verse!

Weird! Wonderful! Other Worlds

Horror Novels & Novellas

Science Fiction Novels & Novellas

The 'A QUIET APOCALYPSE' Series

General Fiction

Science Fiction Collections

Horror Fiction Collections

Anthologies

Audios

Praise for *The Venus Complex*

"Wilde...is one of the finest purveyors of erotically charged horror around."
—Fangoria Magazine #320

"As intelligent and cultured as *Hannibal*, easily as disturbing as *American Psycho* and infinitely less reassuring than *Dexter*, this is a sexually-charged real life horror story that will definitely stay with you."
—Paul Kane, award-winning horror and fantasy writer

"Wilde's most recent offering is the wryly comic but no less grotesque thriller *The Venus Complex*, the sordid tale of mentally unbalanced art history professor Michael Friday, who moonlights as a sexual killer. The book has been garnering great reviews, firmly confirming the literary course that is now defining Wilde's life. Damaged people, ultraviolence, murder and explicit sex—what's not to love about her work?...She has developed a remarkable flair for the perverse and the poetic that echoes her mentor Clive Barker, but offers tales of inner hell and body terror told from a ferociously feminine point of view."
—Chris Alexander, Editor-in-Chief Fangoria Magazine, Issue #321

"*The Venus Complex* is an epistolary portrait of psychopathy as razor sharp as Jim Thompson's *The Killer Inside Me* or Hubert Selby Jr.'s *The Demon*. Disturbing, erotic and powerful."
—Jovanka Vuckovic, Filmmaker (*The Captured Bird, The Guest, Jacqueline Ess*)

"A novel by a female Cenobite that gives the world a smart, artistic, cynical, cultured serial killer who could give Hannibal Lecter a run for his money. On top of that, this is a poignant, funny, sexually-charged, hardcore critique of popular culture and a deconstruction of relationships, academia, and art."
—Gabino Iglesias, HorrorTalk

"Wilde expertly charts Michael's diabolical descent into voyeurism, stalking and murder in a transgressive tale that would make Patrick Bateman blush."
—Alan Kelly, Hell's Shelves, Rue Morgue Online

"Written in journal entry format, *The Venus Complex* is a quick, dirty little high-speed read, tense and shamefully exciting and almost impossible to put down. Imagine the hottest, horniest fuckbook in the Black Lace library spliced in with a Quantico serial killer profile report and you've got *The Venus Complex*. Read it and try NOT to squirm, either in ecstasy or horror. It simply cannot be done."
—Annie Riordan, Brutal As Hell

"I love dark crime, and this is by far the darkest story I've ever read. I felt guilty for enjoying it so much. *The Venus Complex* is tense and fast-paced, dizzying in its bold perversion. But like a serial killer obsessed with his next victim, I could not turn away...Barbie Wilde follows the tradition of Ellis's *American Psycho* and Oates's *Zombie* yet breaks new ground in the field of sadistic crime fiction. If you like the lurid and shocking, you'll love *The Venus Complex*. It's *Dexter*, without a moral code."
—Lee Howard, Midwest Book Review

"*The Venus Complex* is a deftly plotted and calculated work of terror. Like the painted

masterworks Michael Friday draws from to inspire his blood-fest, each verbal brushstroke falls on the page at the precise spot Barbie Wilde wants it."
—Blood E. Bastard, Horror News Network

"*The Venus Complex*, as the title suggests, is an erotically charged novel, and there are some passages that give the likes of Anais Nin and Alina Reyes a run for their money...Hitchcockian in its portrayal of murderous obsession."
—Jon Towlson, Starburst Magazine

"This is not a novel for the faint of heart and definitely NSFPT (Not Safe For Public Transport), but the skill with which it is written means that some of the darker imagery will haunt the reader long after they turn the final page."
—British Fantasy Society

"Welcome to the world of Michael Friday, an art historian turned serial killer who lays out the dark recesses of his soul for all to see in Barbie Wilde's deliciously dark erotic crime novel *The Venus Complex*. Those are some pretty major demons Michael is harbouring as we join him in his downward spiral via the musings of his private journal. Michael is not your every-day killer though, which gives *The Venus Complex* a delightful and refreshing edge. The culture of Hannibal Lecter, the forward planning of Dexter, and the wry wit of Holden Caulfield, Michael is all of this and more."
—The Gore-Splattered Corner

"Wilde's great triumph here is that she goes all the way with her man Friday, allowing his nasty flights of fancy full reign...But I think what I like most about this news story is that she kicked my ass so hard with her first novel. Turns out Barbie Wilde is even scarier

than we thought. And that is a terrible, beautiful thing."
—John Skipp (New York Times best-selling author for Fangoria Online)

"Shocking and explicit, Barbie Wilde's *The Venus Complex* is an intimate tour of Michael Friday's mind as he morphs from a misogynistic, hyper-intelligent university professor into a sexually-charged, calculating serial killer. Writ- ten in journal form, Friday reveals his most gory necrophilic fantasies, and then makes them a reality. Not for sensitive readers; after finishing this book you might never feel clean again."
—Jessa Sobczuk, The Grim Reader, Rue Morgue Magazine

"*The Venus Complex* is a compelling read and Barbie Wilde's confidence in the material shines—there are no first novel nerves here. Through her expertly controlled pacing, Michael's journey from nobody to serial killer is both believable and frightening. By allowing us to see aspects of ourselves in Michael, Barbie also shows us that his extreme fantasies may only be a couple of steps removed from our own, and that's the most frightening thing of all"
—Tom Elliot, Scream Magazine

"Entry by entry, Wilde guides the reader into Friday's world as he evolves not just into a stone-cold killer, but one who is highly charged, sexually. The scenes of eroticism begin as fantasies, but quickly sink into depraved vignettes that ignite the character and charge him further in his mission. What could easily be considered gratuitous is saved by Wilde's keen eye for detail of what excites the human libido and darker mote hidden in our vision...As Michael travels from victim to victim, seeking his transformation and

his freedom from both society's constraints and his own, the reader will find him or herself eagerly following, in a voyeuristic journey into a world of darkness that might just make one smirk in delight as he or she can almost feel him whisper his journals in an ear...A definitely different book but one which will undoubtedly find a big audience for those who are ready to cut open the ordinary and dig deeper...Recommended for adult readers of serial killer narratives, explicit violence, and erotic horror."
—The Monster Librarian

Other Works by Barbie Wilde

Sister Cilice
(From the Hellbound Hearts Anthology, 2009,
edited by Paul Kane and Marie O'Regan)

"Barbie Wilde's 'Sister Cilice' is devastatingly haunting, piercingly erotic and is one of the true stand-out stories of the anthology."
—All Things Horror

"Sick, but in delicious ways!"
—Doug 'Pinhead' Bradley, www.dougbradley.com

U for Uranophobia
(From the Phobophobia Anthology, 2011, edited by
Dean M. Drinkel)

"A very arty, grim, character study... a slow, steady drift into a heart of dark- ness climaxing with a buckling level of sex and violence and shock...It's like Von Trier's *Antichrist* and when reading it, I saw Charlotte Gainsbourg as Gaia..."
—Chris Alexander, editor-in-chief, Fangoria Magazine

Polyp
(From The Mammoth Book of Body Horror
Anthology, 2012, edited by Paul Kane and Marie
O'Regan)

"Barbie has created a brilliant twist on the creature feature genre. I really enjoyed how the tale went from being a very personal story into an apocalyptic cliff hanger."
—Ginger Nuts of Horror

Z is for Zulu Zombies
(From the Bestiarum Vocabulum Anthology and Gorezone #29, 2013, edited by Dean M. Drinkel)

"*Zulu Zombies* is pure Barbie Wilde; eccentric, bizarre, dark and frightening but laced with a inimitable, irreverent punk rock exuberance. It was an honor to reprint the tale in the blood-stained pages of Gorezone Magazine..."
— Chris Alexander, Editor-in-Chief, Fangoria and Gorezone, Filmmaker: *Blood for Irina, Queen of Blood*

Voices of the Damned Collection
Publishers Weekly Starred Review:
"In this impressive collection of short stories, actor Wilde (who played the Female Cenobite in the film classic *Hellbound: Hellraiser II*) reveals a world of beautiful fear. The most delightfully terrifying entries form the *Cilicium Trilogy*, which reveals the complex origin and destiny of Sister Cilice. This character-focused exploration is sensual in its brutality. In *Writer's Block*, Wilde combines the psychological torture of an unknown artist with the erotic egotism of fandom to create a fascinating sexual horror. She creates a dreadful family legacy in *Botophobia*, in which there are not merely skeletons in the closet but unworldly powers hidden in the basement. Wilde's mastery of shocking violence is given full rein in subjects ranging from reclusive self-imprisonment to the exploration of European nightmares. As much a chilling collection of frightful fiction as a delight for the darker senses, this is a satisfying triumph in a befitting, unforgiving, style. A starred review indicates a book of outstanding quality."

"...her work is so uncanny and fearless, it is a must have for any horror aficionado."
—filmmakers the Soska Sisters (*American Mary, Rabid, Festival of the Living Dead*)

"Raised from the dead, this phantasmagoria of tales offers well-written mini-nightmares that will traumatize, titillate, and stick in your mind long after you've closed the book."
—Fangoria Online

"...a brilliant, perfect horror collection spawned from the sick, twisted and beautiful mind of Barbie Wilde."
"Perfect & Perverse"
—A Girl's Guide to Horror

"This collection of eleven short stories confirms Wilde as a foremost author of erotic horror fiction..."
—Jon Towlson, Starburst magazine and author of *Subversive Horror Cinema: Countercultural Messages of Films from Frankenstein to the Present*

"This is nothing short of an absolutely stunning collection."
—DLS Reviews

"...hot sex and erotic horror, bizarre bloody situations, messed up fairy tales, humor and excellent writing."
"Seriously, Barbie Wilde's imagination is a place only the brave and twisted should enter."
"There's no other way to say it -- this collection KICKED ASS!"
—Horror After Dark

"...horrifically bloody, lascivious and wickedly shocking...if testosterone jumping erotica combined

with heart racing fear is your bag of horror then this is just what you're looking for..."
—Scream Horror Mag Online

"The themes of sex and death are inextricably linked, dripping a dark eroticism through many of the stories."
"Wilde has a strong voice. In a genre that is often dominated by male authors, she has taken on a leading role."
—Books of Blood

"Violence, pitch-black humour and yes, sex can be found in equal measure in her work, drawing complimentary comparisons to Clive Barker's early works in his seminal Books of Blood collections."
—Thoughts and Scribbles

THE VENUS COMPLEX
BY
BARBIE WILDE

DEMAIN PUBLISHING 2025

For further information, please visit:
WEB: www.demainpublishing.org
TWITTER: @DemainPubUk
FACEBOOK: Demain Publishing
INSTAGRAM: demainpublishing

ACKNOWLEDGEMENTS

Thanks to Eva, Paul Kane, Marie O'Regan, Tim Dry, Chris Alexander and Georg.

And thanks to author Colin Wilson for his books on serial killers, especially *Order of Assassins: The Psychology of Murder* and *A Criminal History of Mankind*.

For Georg

CONTENTS

INTRODUCTION

By Paul Kane

I first met Barbie Wilde back in December 2006. I was having a launch for my book *The Hellraiser Films and Their Legacy* at a British Fantasy Society Open Night at Ye Olde Cock Tavern in London. I'd invited as many people associated with the mythos as possible, in particular the four Cenobites themselves: Doug 'Pinhead' Bradley, Nick 'Chatterer' Vince, Simon 'Butterball' Bamford (who couldn't make it that time, but who I met later on) and, of course, 'Female Cenobite' from *Hellbound: Hellraiser II*, Barbie, who brought her partner Georg along too. All thoroughly nice people and about as far from demonic sadomasochists as you can get.

I remember it being a fantastic event, a bit of a dream come true for this *Hellraiser* fan actually. And, during the course of the evening, as the drink flowed, I got chatting to Barbie. Of course, I knew her as an accomplished actress, TV presenter and dancer (she was one of the founder members of SHOCK), but what I didn't know was that, like Nick Vince, she also wrote fiction.

Not long after that, Barbie sent me some samples of her work, which I happily read and was bowled over by. It led directly to myself and my wife Marie using her for the *Hellraiser*-inspired anthology from Simon & Schuster, *Hellbound Hearts* (for which she delivered one of the most popular and controversial entries, 'Sister Cilice') and, more recently, *The Mammoth Book of Body Horror* from

Constable & Robinson (her tale 'Polyp' is a perfect example of the sub-genre, described by one reviewer as "a wonderfully disgusting story that's a brilliant twist on the creature feature genre"; Clive Barker would be very proud, I think). She has also gone on to appear in other anthologies, such as *Phobophobia* and *Mutation Nation*, steadily building a name for herself in the writing world.

I'm proud to say I was one of the first people to get a preview of this, her debut novel: *The Venus Complex*. Proud and very lucky...Because, when I sat down to read what had popped into my inbox, I had no idea what ride it would take me on. Like so many other examples these days—Mo Hayder springs to mind—Barbie blurs the genre lines between crime and horror, but also delivers a serial killer thriller that stands out from the crowd. She does what the best exponents of this field also do, she gets inside the head of the killer...and 'encourages' us to enter it as well.

His fixations and the way he selects his victims are—without giving too much away—unique. Delivered in first person, all his intimate moments are recorded in journal form. And the most frightening thing about him is what surely disturbs us about the serial killer in general: he hides in plain sight. He could be your neighbour, your friend, your lover...Like Thomas Harris' Lecter—before his capture, obviously—Professor Michael Friday might even be teaching your kids at University. Yet, like Jeff Lindsay's creation, Dexter, he has his own dark side. Perhaps the darkest of them all; one that compels him to act out his warped fantasies. At the same time, Michael just wants to be someone, not a 'nobody'. He's the perfect dichotomy, in fact. Trying to find his place in the world, experiencing conflicting emotions. At one point he agonisingly comments: "It's a miracle that I am as sane as I am," then asks us: "I am sane, aren't I?" It's the kind of thing an actor might do as an aside in a Shakespearean tragedy...

Barbie effortlessly puts herself in Michael's position, so effortlessly that within the first few pages—the first few paragraphs—you forget that you're reading fiction at all. This could happen, this could be real. And isn't that at the heart of good horror and crime writing? That's not to say the writing isn't top notch; quite the opposite, actually. It's incredibly skilled.

Barbie manages to pull off something that's very rare in fiction; she delivers poetic and lyrical lines, deep hidden meanings, that we appreciate even more fully on repeated readings, without once throwing us out of the narrative. On the contrary, we're compelled to read more, to find out what Michael's up to next.

Like Bret Easton Ellis in *American Psycho*, Barbie also offers up a commentary on contemporary life, which touches on everything from MTV attention spans to apathy about sexual partners.

There's also black humour to be found here, as evidenced when Michael's watching a report about a serial killer who got caught: "My advice to him would have been: don't take up a new profession unless you decide that you're going to do it properly...What a jerk."

But I'll say no more about the book you hold in your hands and are probably now desperate to read. As desperate as I was when Barbie originally sent it to me...and I wasn't disappointed.

I'll just end by saying, like Lecter, Bateman, Dexter, I feel certain that Michael Friday will soon be added to the list of famous fictional serial killers we all seem to be simultaneous terrified of and fascinated by, perhaps because it's the 'safe' way of touching that darkness I was talking about earlier.

And I'm also sure that we'll be seeing many more terrific novels from Barbie Wilde in the future. Enjoy the ride.

Paul Kane
Derbyshire
www.shadow-writer.co.uk

THE VENUS COMPLEX

It was another dank spring day in Syracuse, New York. It was raining intermittently, the drops falling down from the heavens like God's indifferent spittle.

Michael's head was aching with one of his periodic migraines and the whiteness of the paper almost blinded him. He blinked and made a conscious effort to stare at the page—willing something, anything, to come to mind. He stared so long and so hard that he began to focus on the shadows of the dead cells floating across the retinas of his eyes. What were they called again? Floaters, that was it. He lost himself in the act of following them on their tiny darting journeys. He remembered visiting the ophthalmologist to ask if there was anything that could be done about the damn things. The doctor said that there was a procedure to get rid of the Muscae volitantes, as he called them, but it was a bit tricky. It involved piercing the eyeball and sucking out the gel, the vitreous humor. Then they would filter out the micro-debris (…through what? a muslin bag? a tea strainer?) before squirting the gel back into the eye with a syringe. It all sounded highly unpleasant.

Michael decided against the procedure. He resolved to peacefully coexist with his little pals—the dead cell inhabitants of his eyeballs. Maybe he should give them names. Make friends. They would be the only friends he had.

No. That would be too weird. Where was he? This wasn't the exercise, was it?

Write something. His shrink, Dr. Cordess (or "Dr. Clueless" as Michael liked to call him), advised him to start a journal so he could, "vent his anger." He concentrated on the keys of his dad's old typewriter. Michael remembered all the essays and term papers he had written on the damn thing—even his Art History dissertation. All long before computers were in vogue. For some reason, he preferred the idea of going back to using the typewriter: pounding his thoughts out on the keys, and at the same time, symbolically thumping on his long-lost father's fat face. He liked the concept of pure thought flowing down upon the page without revision or editing. Pure thought. Perhaps better to say, impure thought.

Something had to come out of his damaged brain. He squeezed his eyes shut until the floaters became swirling icy pinpricks of light and then he opened his eyes and focused on the page. That was better...and Michael began to write:

ENTRY 1

I haven't told anyone what really happened that night. I suppose if someone ever reads this, they might try to get me arrested for vehicular manslaughter or whatever the charge might be, but I don't care.

I've been thinking about it and, in my opinion, the worst combination in a relationship is when a guy still powerfully desires his wife physically, but hates her as a person. That was the case with Angie. She had a wonderful body and knew how to use it, but, personality-wise, she made Attila the Hun look like Sponge Bob Square Pants.

The night of the Accident, we'd been driving back from a Halloween dinner party. I'd had a couple of drinks, but nothing too excessive. I wanted to stay alert because I was convinced that Angie was having an affair with one of my best friends, Charlie Landru. That evening, I looked for secret signs between them, but they were very discreet. Of course, Charlie's vapid and pretty wife, Tammy, was in attendance, which would dampen down any overt displays of affection. But I knew—I just knew—that Angela was screwing Charlie.

The drive home started off in silence, then Angie tried to make small talk. God, how I hate meaningless chatter. So, I cut her short. "Do you want to tell me who you are fucking, or should I just guess?" I asked.

Well, that shut her up—for about two seconds.

The argument began: vicious, nasty...the usual dance. Then came the full confession. I had been right. It had been Landru, and Charlie had been a better lover than I could ever hope to be...blah, blah, blah. That was that. Angela was leaving me.

"You can't leave me," I said, and she laughed.

"Can't I?" she asked. "Just watch me, you worm."

I can never remember what the trigger had been: her laughter or being called a worm, but I reacted instantly.

I jammed my foot down on the gas and turned the wheel sharply to the right—heading straight for a copse of sugar maples. Angela started screaming and it was like music to my ears—a fucking symphony. At that moment, I didn't give a damn and, God, was it liberating. I turned to her briefly and the vision of her face illuminated by the dashboard lights—mouth open, eyes bulging—burned itself on my brain. We were heading for a large tree. Angie— arms waving wildly like a demented crab—was scrabbling at the steering wheel, but to no avail, as I was holding her back with my hand firmly placed on her chest. Just seconds before impact, my hand dropped down and undid Angela's seat belt. "Bye, bye, honey," I managed to blurt out, and then we hit the tree with the force of a freight train. I remember her flying through the windshield before what felt like an atomic bomb exploded in my brain. So many bright colors, it was beautiful. Then oblivion.

I woke up briefly. Red was the dominant color now. Red was everywhere: in my eyes, on the windshield, drenching my shirt. I somehow managed to crawl out of the car, despite feeling indescribable. I was bleeding from a wound in my head, my legs weren't working so well and something had gone very wrong internally, I could feel it. I looked around and tried to see where Angela had gone, but it was as if she had flown out of my life like a witch on a broomstick. That imagery struck me as funny and I started to laugh, but that was a big mistake. It hurt like hell.

I reached into my pocket for my cell phone. Amazingly, it was still working. I dialed 911 and then remembered nothing until I woke up in Crouse Memorial three days later.

I didn't feel any guilt. I was relieved to get rid of Angela and I'd avoided the possibility of an extremely messy divorce. No one ever suspected the Accident to be anything other than just that: an accident. Of course, Angie's money was an added bonus, not that I'm the mercenary type. My only regret was writing off my car, a 1968 Mustang GT that always started—no small thing in a classic car.

No, the agony was in surviving. Surviving the Accident to undergo the torture of physiotherapy. All those sadistic, so-called angels of mercy tormenting me every day with their good-natured cruelty. God, how I hate nurses. Nowadays, even spotting a woman in a white dress is liable to send me off into a silent rage of anger.

Fuck, fuck, fuck them all.

ENTRY 2

I feel a lot better today. Writing about the Accident helped, I'm sure. I slept like a baby the whole night through and didn't wake up once. No nasty dreams either.

Anger vented successfully, Doctor, for now anyway.

ENTRY 3

When I came home four weeks ago (aptly on April Fool's Day), my housekeeper, Mrs. Tochlovski, was waiting for me—arms open wide as if she wanted to clasp me to her enormous bosom. I had missed the old girl. She was the only person to faithfully visit me in the hospital; bringing chocolates that were so sweet they made my teeth ache, magazines more suitable to a beauty salon than to a bored and broken art historian, and the occasional kielbasa to keep me warm at night.

Mrs. T. had made sure that no one had touched anything and my house looked like *The Mary Celeste*—the crew having absconded, leaving no forwarding address. I was surprised that tumbleweeds weren't rolling down the hallways as I passed through them. Just six months ago, Angie and I had gone off to dinner at the Landru's place and never returned. Or at least, Angie hadn't.

During the last month, I'm sure that I would have cheerfully murdered my physiotherapist, Sandy Dudstein, if Mrs. T. hadn't been there to restrain me with her benign and calming influence. Now that I am supposedly on the mend, Mrs. T. only comes in twice a week and "The Dud" was given her marching orders three days ago. After barely having a minute to myself after all that time in hospital, with nurses and doctors fussing over me every second, it is blissful to be alone at last.

Yesterday, I went for my first walk outside by myself since the Accident. I felt a bit shaky, but it wasn't as traumatic as I thought it would be. I wandered around in the woods behind my house, so no one could spot me from the road. The spring sunshine warmed my face. The sky was a shade of violent blue and the leaves of the elm trees were the color of emeralds: mysterious and jewel-like. I think that I must have suffered more brain damage than I previously thought, because I am sure that the colors of the world look much more saturated and intense to me than they were before the Accident. It is as if I am living in a painting by Vincent Van Gogh and, frankly, his over-rated and over-priced daubs always made me feel queasy.

As I walked, or rather tottered around, I felt unbelievably self-conscious, as if the whole world was checking up on my progress. What a mess I am. I wish I had never survived the Accident. What's the point when you have to live like this? The doctors said that I would make a full recovery, but they lie. I'll always have the scars—perhaps not on my body (all that expensive cosmetic surgery had to count for something), but in my mind. Still, I feel more energetic. Writing doesn't tire me out so much today.

ENTRY 4

I was thinking about work. About whether I should try to set a date for going back; to have some kind of goal to shoot for. I used to like teaching, but now the thought of it revolts me. Tutoring the brats of affluent businessmen in the History of Art seems to be such a totally pointless exercise. Talk about pearls before swine.

Maybe I'll drive over to the University and take a stroll around the campus. No, I'll wait until I am stronger. Next week. I will do it next week. I don't want all the students staring at the crippled guy.

Until then, I am going to start working out in the gym in my basement. I have to get back into shape. I am sure that it will alleviate my depression. The doctors said that if I did some mild exercise the limp would go in time. Hell, maybe having a romantic limp will make me look Byronic. With my luck, more likely moronic.

ENTRY 5

I haven't written anything for a week. I just decided to concentrate on my body, such as it is. I worked out for as long as I could each day and the difference in my energy levels is amazing, although I thought that I was going to pass out in the beginning. I just wish that I could exercise my mind. I still feel mentally sluggish and deeply depressed. I hate my life. I'd like to shed my skin and turn into something else.

Saw Dr. Clueless again on Monday. I wish that I didn't hate him so much and I wish I felt that going to him and paying a small fortune in fees was going to do some good somehow. Actually, hate is the wrong word. I don't hate him. I just don't think anything of him. He is neuter, nothing, zip, zilch.

Psychiatrists are so full of shit. Who can truly understand the workings of the human mind? It is all fruitless speculation. Theorems and suppositions. I can't even be bothered to remember whether Dr. Clueless is Freudian or Jungian, or whatever. It is a farce. He can't help me. No one can. But the doctors are insisting that I go to him, and so, like the good little boy that I am, I go, even though I cannot relate to him on any level. But truth be told, I can't relate to anyone anymore. It's as if I've been cut off from humanity. I feel like I'm living under a glass jar being stared at by entomologists; like a bug on a plate. I have never been more isolated in my life and that is saying something.

Still, at least I am communicating, if you can call it that, with another living creature, even if that creature is just a psychiatrist. I called a couple of my old friends the other evening and attempted to have a conversation, tried to make contact. It felt so stilted, so artificial. Were these people really ever my friends? What has happened to me? What has happened to them? I couldn't care less what they thought or felt.

Maybe there was one good idea that Dr. Clueless had and that was to suggest writing this journal. I've spent my life bottling things up inside me, being a man, big boys don't cry, etc., etc., etc. Never bothering to get in touch with my feelings, and all that warm and fuzzy New Age bullshit. But all that I've been really doing is playing the part of a man. What I really am, I don't know and I don't know if anyone will ever know. One thing is for certain; Dr. Clueless will never figure it out.

I think that I will go out of town for a few days. Syracuse is stifling me. I don't know why I stayed here in the first place—godforsaken upstate New York. What a hellhole. You freeze your ass off in the winter, die of heat prostration in the summer and, on top of everything, it is dull as ditch water. And will they ever fix the potholes in this jerkwater berg? Maybe I'll go down to New York City for a few days when I am stronger. Catch a few shows. No, I hate the theater, what am I thinking? Hey, maybe I'll go to one of those lap-dancing clubs. Try and get a hard-on. Ha, ha, what a joke. Everything is a joke.

We are just toys in the hands of a prankster God.

Anyway, all the best sleaze joints have been chased out of Manhattan and the last thing I need is a night in Brooklyn.

ENTRY 6

I had a very disturbing dream last night.

I am in a large industrial-sized kitchen with huge chrome fittings. It is late at night and I am alone. I open an immense stainless-steel refrigerator and the body of a young woman falls out of it. She is dead. She is naked except for a pair of white panties. Her skin is blue with the cold, but she is still very beautiful.

I panic, thinking that if I call the police, they will suspect that I've killed her, so I try to stuff the body back into the refrigerator. Of course, a dead body is hard to handle and I'm not having much luck putting her back. Then, something happens. I just manage to place the body in the refrigerator so it stays put and the girl's legs swing open. I stand back and stare at this beautiful, dead, blue-skinned woman with her legs wide apart and I become aroused.

I look around and I see that I am still by myself. I carefully pull the girl out of the refrigerator and lay her out on the shiny, black, tiled floor and stare at her some more. She is so beautiful, so exposed. She is all mine.

I get undressed. I pull off her panties. I kneel at the head of the body and put my hands on her breasts. They are cool and smooth and firm. Her nipples are erect, permanently. Her mouth is open in an "oh" of surprise, like an inflatable sex doll. I get more excited. I look down and I see that I have an erection, the first since my Accident.

I pinch her nipples and it's almost as if there is a direct connection from her nipples to my cock. I lean forward and touch her, caressing her surprisingly pliable limbs. (No Rigor Mortis in my dream.) I move her legs farther apart, as wide as they can go. I open her mouth a bit more and put my cock between her lips and then I start pumping. I can feel her stiff, velvety tongue against my penis. I put my face between her legs and I suck her cold pussy. I remember thinking that it still tasted sweet, even though she was dead. I pump and pump, and suck and suck, and it feels like nothing I have ever experienced before in my life.

Then I come.

The orgasm was so profound that I woke up moaning in ecstasy. I had come in my dream and all over my sheets, but I didn't care. I reveled in it. I grabbed the sheets and pumped them some more, exulting in the sticky wetness of them. My orgasm seemed to last forever.

When it was over, I turned on the light and felt disgusted with myself. I cleaned up, changed the sheets and tried to get back to sleep, but the memories of my dream kept coming back to me in little jolts, like electric shocks.

The more I thought about the beautiful, blue-skinned, fridge girl, the more sexed up I got until I had to masturbate. And so I came again.

They were the first sexual feelings that I've had since the Accident and they had to be about a dead girl.

What does this mean? I'd ask Dr. Clueless, if I had any anticipation of him coming back with a coherent answer.

Maybe it just means that I have become some sick, sad fuck.

ENTRY 7

I have decided to coin a new phrase. You've heard of road rage? Parking rage? Air rage? Well, how about world rage?

It's not that I hate the world exactly. It's just that the things in it—people, for example—constantly put me into such a condition of unrelenting wrath that it is a triumph for me to go through the day without contemplating killing someone.

My rage is focused mostly on the world of men and mankind in general. Women, with the exception of my dear departed wife and nurses and Mother and the Dudstein bitch and women drivers and those dim bimbos on TV, are such vulnerable little things. They are creative beings and all they want to do is to nest and have babies. Men, on the other hand, are only creative when they are being destructive. Just glancing at the headlines of a newspaper is enough to kill the whole day for me. The absurdity of this farce makes me nauseous.

Take this one, for instance: South Africa has the highest death rate from AIDS on the planet. So, what are they doing about it? Well, first their ex-President said that he didn't think HIV causes AIDS a few years ago, which wasn't very helpful. Then he said the West should give Africa more money, as if the whole damn continent wasn't in enough debt as it is. Then—get this—then the government goes out and buys some more attack helicopters and jet planes because, let's face it, medicines and condoms are not sexy, but jet fighters...wow! Why fork out a load of dough to try and save your people from a hideous disease when you can spend it on arms instead? After all, those sick and dead people need protection from THE ENEMY, whomever THE ENEMY might be.

I'm not making this up. Why doesn't this kind of news enrage more people? Don't they care? Folks all over the world are asking America for cash, saying, "You MUST help us. You are richer and stronger than us. Give us money now to help our starving/ailing/war-stricken people."

So, out of "white" guilt, or "colonial" guilt, or "Catholic" guilt, or "filthy rich" guilt, or whatever damn guilt you want to use, we hand over billions of dollars and what happens? More Swiss banks accounts— already stuffed with the ill-gotten gains of a thousand dictators—swell up and more Leaders' Wives go on shopping trips to Paris. It makes me sick. And we, poor bumbling assholes that we are, fall for it every time. Why? Because, we desperately want to be loved. America wants to be loved and be regarded as special, and, like some dweeby high school kid with braces on her teeth and good grades, doesn't understand why nobody wants to take her to the prom.

People who don't live here couldn't possibly love or appreciate America like we do, because they are jealous. They envy our lifestyle, our freedom, our opportunities and the undeniable fact that America is the most powerful country in the world. Even the poorest person in America can grow up to be President. Take our ex-Prez Clinton. Look at the shit hole he came from, but, because he was smart, he made good. Well, sort of.

I only used South Africa as an example, because I'm not racist. I can cheerfully say that I hate everyone. That kind of thing happens all over the world and it doesn't matter if you are black, white, yellow or puce. The ones in power will fuck you up the ass if they can; it's in their nature. That's why I despise humans so much. They are so predictable.

The sad thing is if I ever held a position of power in the grand scheme of things, I would probably act exactly the same. I am just as predictable as the rest of the sheep.

ENTRY 8

This morning, I decided to start up my computer for the first time in months. I attempted to read the book about 18th Century Art History that I was writing before the Accident. I couldn't bear to glance at more than a few pages. There doesn't seem to be any point in continuing. "Fuck Art, Let's Fuck," as my students say. I wish.

Here I am, the proud owner of a vast library of books about the history of art and they have become useless to me. It is as if I have lost all understanding of what any of it means. I suppose the figurative works still say something to me, but there doesn't seem to be an emotional response anymore, which is odd.

When I look at modern art, non-representational art, it is like gazing at the scrawls of a two-year old. There is nothing there for me, nothing. I feel that something vital has vanished from my brain, something that I desperately needed to have inside me to survive in this dreary world. It, whatever "it" was, has gone missing and with it my capacity to enjoy beauty. If a person doesn't have that anymore, what is the point of life?

Wanting something to do, I did some surfing on the Internet. I used to think that it was a total waste of time, but now I can see why people get hooked. Battling my baser instincts, I decided not to hit the porno sites. I just checked the news. Some serial killer had been caught in Spokane, Washington, of all places. He had murdered a string of prostitutes. Why? They never seem to discover the motivations of these people. Why do they do it? Is it a power trip? Or does it turn them on to kill women? Does it give them some sexual high? I suppose I should understand, since I was instrumental in my wife's death, but an erection was the last thing on my mind when I was hurtling towards that maple tree. Anyway, what I did wasn't murder, was it? When you want to die as well as the other person? That has to be included in that weird kind of Jim Jones - poisoned Kool-Aid – "Hey, let's all go together!" - kind of thing.

The news is so depressing, yet I seem to be addicted to it. I watch CNN in the morning, *ABC World News* at night and cruise the NY Times and the ever-so-venerable BBC on the Internet. The news is either all bad, or pathetic little human-interest stories that would warm the cockles of my heart if I had any left.

ENTRY 9

I had a dream about my mother last night. I guess it was because yesterday was her birthday, May 27th. She would have been seventy-four if she'd been alive today.

Mother is in her tiny powder-blue bedroom in her apartment in Montreal where she finally ended up after her surreal travels around North America. I am sitting in a chair about two feet away, talking to her. She is wearing a thin, nylon, girlishly pink nightgown, so insubstantial that it doesn't leave much to the imagination. As always, Mother is complaining that she has been sick and that I have been neglecting her. She does look terrible, like the wrath of God. Then she says, "Do you want to see what my illness has done to me?" To my horror, she gets out of bed and opens up her nightdress, revealing her aged, emaciated body.

I woke up in a hurry from that one. Not a pleasant dream. Not a pleasant memory, because it was an actual incident from my past. It happened just before she died.

Mother had been an artist all her life and, to her way of thinking, there wasn't anything unpleasant or unnatural about showing off the human body. She would never have understood the effect something like that would have on someone, especially her son.

The vision of my ancient, wrinkled and nude Mother will stay with me for all time...

ENTRY 10

My existence has become almost nauseating. I have become so stultified in my behavior patterns that I am no longer living my life; I am just experiencing events. Sometimes hours go by and all I do is sit on the couch and listen to the clock ticking on the mantelpiece. I am not aware of thinking of anything. I just sit and listen. Listen to the ticking. It is oddly soothing.

Then I come to—that is the only way to describe it—and I realize that the whole day has passed me by and I didn't even notice. I wasn't aware. The sun traveled across the sky, the birds were happily chirping away outside and all I heard was the ticking of the clock. Yet my mind never registered the fact that the ticking was time passing. It was just ticking. There was no emotional or cognitive resonance. Just ticking.

It is as if I am turning into something. Something dead. I am becoming a mechanical man, a robot. I have this eerie feeling that if I make one wrong move, someone is going to come along, switch off the juice and that will be the end of it all. No more me. I will be still and cold and I won't be able to think of anything. I will be a big fat zero. In many ways that would be a relief.

ENTRY 11

My emotions are teetering between being completely anesthetized or being in a state of utter irritation with the world.

Ordinary people's hypocrisy is mind numbing. I read today that some born-again Christians bombed another abortion clinic. They killed a couple of doctors and nurses in yet another misguided attempt to save the lives of a few unformed tadpoles that haven't even shed their tails yet. I would have thought that the Sixth Commandment directing the faithful not to kill would also apply to atomizing doctors and nurses, and not just to the elimination of unborn fetuses.

So here is a knotty conundrum: why is it okay with the brethren to execute men on Death Row (something they all seem to enthusiastically support), but it isn't okay to scrape an inconvenient sack of cells from a woman's uterus? I just don't understand. Actually, who am I kidding? I understand all right. Giving someone on Death Row a lethal injection isn't done from any moral perspective. It is done from the age-old standpoint of Vengeance with a capital "V." It has nothing to do with justice and everything to do with revenge. We Americans are supposed to be living in the most civilized country in the world, but we are still sending criminals into the arena to fight the lions. Except now we strap them to a table or a chair and don't give them a chance to defend themselves.

Last week, I was reading a book about ancient Rome. One of the intellectuals of the city was complaining that all Rome's citizens ever cared about was food and entertainment, entertainment meaning the mayhem and violence of the Coliseum. How little things have changed in the last two thousand years.

ENTRY 12

Today I didn't do anything except play Solitaire on the computer. I couldn't believe it when I finally bestirred myself to look at the clock. All those hours wasted that I will never get back again. Not that I have a particularly fulfilling life at the moment, but I didn't bother to work out and I completely forgot to take a shower.

I just sat and stared at the computer screen for hours. My eyes were dry and scratchy and my hand ached because I was using the mouse so relentlessly. I was totally engrossed in the game and I began to feel that somehow there was a greater meaning to it all. If I could only win a certain number of times, then everything would come together in my life. Everything would fall into place.

It scared me. I suddenly realized that it would be very easy for me to spiral further down into the pit and give up caring about anything.

I don't want to do that. I have to find something for my mind to work on, but what? I don't have the energy or the will to learn anything new. I seem to be just hanging around, waiting for SOMETHING to happen.

My greatest fear is to end up being insignificant, a complete irrelevancy. To not even make a scratch on the surface of life. To have lived and died without doing something of note. That is the great UNKNOWN that we face. Not anything as prosaic as dying. But dying in obscurity, surely that is the worst. Perhaps that's why people strap bombs around their waists and blow themselves into infinity. Better to die for a cause and be known as a hero than to live a pathetic life just eating, working, fucking and dying.

Maybe that is why all those little nobodies throughout the world keep on having babies, in the vain hope that one day their inferior genes may come together and produce an anomaly: a truly great and significant human being. Sometimes it happens. Take Beethoven, for example. His family was totally nondescript. His parents were poor alcoholics. Supposedly, the legend goes that many of his siblings were deaf or retarded in some way. Yet against all odds, a genius popped out of his mother's tired, dried-up womb. You never know.

I want to be SOMEBODY. I don't want to be a big NOBODY.

ENTRY 13

I read somewhere that Rasputin, that wily old con artist and buddy of the last Czar of Russia, was of the opinion that he had reached a higher spiritual plane than most other mortals. He had become so holy that he was utterly without sin. Rasputin thought he had come up with a dandy way of generously transferring his sinless state to others. All he had to do was fuck them and then they would also become without sin. This in some way explains this unwashed peasant's immense popularity with high society ladies. You have to admit that it's an ingenuous tactic for maneuvering a woman into bed: "Make love to me, baby, and you will be first in line to get into Heaven and shake St. Peter's hand. Sleep with me, and all your sins will be washed away."

It is similar to a benighted idea that is still the rage in South Africa. The neighborhood witch doctors advise AIDS sufferers to rape virgins as a cure for their affliction. This is what is known as magical thinking. Deep down, you realize that this improbable course of action won't work, but you're willing to give it a try because...hey, you never know. Maybe the asshole with the beard and the weird staring eyes is right and God is on his side. Perhaps the local quack is more tuned in to health problems than the WHO doctor with the painful injections and all those stupid pills that no one can remember to take. So much easier to fuck and hope for redemption or a cure than to actually take responsibility for your life and your actions. To use your noggin and think. To actually DO something about it.

I need to DO something about my life, or I'll be no better than those poor ignorant slobs in Russia or South Africa. I'll fall into a bottomless pit, or turn into a mechanical man, or become a dribbling idiot in the corner playing Solitaire until the end of Eternity. Either that, or I'll be walking into my local McDonald's or post office to work a little magic of my own. And it won't involve any thinking either.

ENTRY 14

I woke up this morning and looked at all the things in my house and had a powerful urge to redecorate. So much of this place screams "Angie," that if I had the energy, I would toss out the lot. Maybe that's why I am depressed all the time. I am surrounded by the miasma of HER. Angie's presence is everywhere, haunting me. Of course, why hadn't I spotted it before? The bitch is still bugging me from beyond the grave. Now, that makes sense.

Everything in this house reeks of someone with "perfect taste." It is as if they couldn't be bothered to put some personality into it, they just skimmed through Better Homes and Gardens and did a paint-by-numbers job of decorating the place.

The only room in the house that I wouldn't let her touch was my den. No soothing pastels and French Provincial allowed in there. My desk is from Mexico, an enormous monster of dark wood and metal bands, ancient and full of secrets. It cost more to ship it up to Syracuse than it did to buy. Right over the desk is a large, ornately framed print of one of my favorite paintings, *Judith Beheading Holofernes*, by Artemisia Gentileschi (1620).

Artemisia was greatly influenced in the use of chiaroscuro by Caravaggio, so the effects of light and shade are striking. I love the look of grim determination on her face as a surprisingly muscular Judith robustly hacks off Holofernes' head. The blood spurts from his neck like a miniature Old Faithful while Judith's devoted maid stands by her side and gives her a hand by holding the old goat down. I always preferred Artemisia's version to Caravaggio's depiction of the same subject. Although it is also gory in the extreme, his Judith's expression is hilariously prim, as if she was gutting a particularly unpleasant fish rather than actually decapitating someone.

There are other prints on the walls, reflecting my eccentric taste in the arts. A particular favorite is a photograph of the statue of *The Ecstasy of St. Teresa* by the 17th century Italian master, Gianlorenzo Bernini. My fascination with that particular piece goes back to my childhood, when Mother would encourage me to watch reruns of *Civilisation: A Personal View by Kenneth Clark* on the PBS Channel. One night, he was enlightening us about the St. Teresa sculpture and I was struck even at my tender age at how the artist had made the ecstasy of the saint so sexual. She lies there exposed: head back, mouth open, eyes shut, ready and willing. There is an angel armed with an arrow tantalizing her bosom with the point. Any minute, she will be penetrated by the barb and the look on her face is one of rapturous anticipation.

St. Teresa gave me my first hard-on, bless her. Fortunately, Mother didn't notice. She might have put it down to an excess of religious mania and sent me off to the local kiddy shrink.

Maybe when I am feeling more energetic, I will get rid of all of Angie's overstuffed sofas and dried flower arrangements, the cunningly distressed pseudo antiques and the bland modern paintings of nothing in particular and I'll really go to town. I'll buy the furniture I want to sit in and be comfortable in. Lots of expensive leather sofas. Leather is so sensual, so smooth, so cool. Just like the breasts of my blue-skinned, fridge-dream girl.

ENTRY 15

I had another dream last night. I don't like these dreams. They disturb me and they excite me, and I am particularly disturbed by the fact that they excite me.

I am swimming underwater in a deep, crystal-clear, turquoise pool. The water is blood temperature and I can barely feel it against my naked skin. The light is filtering down from the surface and I have the most compelling sense of well-being and peace. I have no trouble breathing underwater, which is bizarre I guess, but it seemed natural at the time.

I keep on swimming and start to notice that the water is becoming murky. It takes me a while, but I soon realize that there is blood in the water. At the same time, I see an indistinct shape in the distance. I am not alone. Is it a shark? I am concerned, but curiously unafraid.

I decide to investigate. As I get closer, I can see that the shape is a naked woman frantically swimming away from me. I gain on her. I want to tell her that she has nothing to fear from me.

She seems to sense that there is no escape and she turns around to confront me. She doesn't have any problem breathing underwater either, by the way, and when she speaks to me, I don't have any difficulty understanding her.

She puts her hand out to stop me and says, "Please don't hurt me."

For a moment, I am puzzled. Why would she think I was going to hurt her? Then, almost subliminally, I notice that I am holding something. I look down and see an enormous carving knife in my hand. The sunlight is glinting off the blade and it looks like an implement of sacrifice.

I look back at her and she is beautifully terrified. She looks so scared and so sexy.

She says, "Kill me if you have to, but, please, fuck me first."

I am happy to oblige.

She comes close and puts her arms around me. I kiss her. I have the knife pressed into her back and I can tell that she is turned on. I can remember every sensation: the softness of her skin, the taste of her lips, her dark hair surrounding her face like a cloud.

The combination of sex and death is so powerful, so fundamental. Eros and Thanatos.

I enter her and as I am making love to her, I hold the knife to her throat. She arches her back and her legs encircle my waist and her pelvis is humping away. She spreads her arms out, effortlessly floating and completely helpless, giving herself to me. Her mouth is wide open and she is silently screaming with pleasure. A ray of sunlight embraces her like a spotlight. It is the most beautiful image I have ever seen.

My knife gently travels down to her chest and I delicately touch her nipples with the point. She is getting more excited and at the moment of her orgasm, she thrusts herself forward and skewers herself on my blade. She screams and screams, but I can hear her now. Screams of pleasure and pain. I stick my tongue down her throat and taste blood. I come while her dying body is convulsing on my cock. Blood billows around us and we sink down into the black depths of the pool, still coming, still fucking, a trail of blood in our wake.

I woke up sweating after that one. Sweating and with a huge erection. Another dream about a dead woman. I am going to have to get laid soon, or I am not going to be responsible for my actions. I masturbated, thinking about the knife slipping in between the swimming girl's voluptuous breasts and coming out her back, her mouth open and screaming, her body bucking in its death throes, and I came easily.

I think I know what triggered my dream. I was watching the Discovery Channel that evening and saw a documentary about the ancient Mayans of Central America. A light-hearted bunch, they would periodically throw young virgins into a deep sacrificial pool in the jungle to placate one of their many bloodthirsty gods. Some divers explored the pool and found hundreds of skulls at the bottom.

Nice.

The following program was about sharks, so put two and two together and you get one screwed-up dream. Sometimes I wish that I did have some respect for psychiatrists because I am sure that Dr. Cordess would have had a field day with that particular nightmare.

As I swim in the shark-infested waters of my subconscious, what demons do I meet?

ENTRY 16

One of my neighbors came over today. The bell scared the shit out of me. I nearly didn't answer, but then I thought, "what the hell," and opened the door. It was Mrs. Donnalson from down the road. Nice enough woman, I guess, but Angie knew her better than I did. She was a typical resident of Manlius, the prosperous little village just outside Syracuse where I live. In her forties but well-preserved, upper middle class, professional, attractive in kind of a prim, schoolmarm sort of way. She had this cute habit of nervously tugging the skirt of her snazzy little suit down over her knees, like they were the crown jewels or something.

We sat and talked. She even brought me a cake, for God's sake. Mrs. Donnalson told me that she was shocked by the Accident and Angie's unfortunate death. She apologized for not visiting me in the hospital, but her husband had to have a hernia operation, which was closely followed by the death of her father. I'm not sure that I believed her excuses, but what did I care?

Then Mrs. Donnalson mentioned something that I thought was quite funny. She said that one of the reasons that it took so long for her to come over on her own was that my house disturbed her.

"How exactly does it disturb you?" I asked.

She said, "Honestly, Michael, why do you live in this hideous gray barn? It doesn't even have any windows facing the road. It looks so creepy."

I laughed. Made some excuse about my abode's other advantages, but the real reason was that even before the Accident I was always searching for increased separation from the crowd—enhanced privacy. The very idea of other people driving past my house and being able to see me going about my business bothered me much more than the concept of having no windows facing the street. The way I look at it, at least I am not as weird as the guy who built the damn thing.

The conversation proceeded along amiably enough, and then something perverse transpired. I began to fantasize about dear Mrs. Donnalson. This is peculiar, because I've never been sexually attracted to her before, but I think that I am just desperate for a fuck. (See: previously reported dreams, not involving Mother.) I knew that she was married, so I didn't try to hit on her, not that I would have had the confidence to do so anyway. We just chatted mindlessly and I imagined her without any clothes on, lying on my couch with her legs spread open, fondling her breasts with one hand and playing with herself with the other. It was a very amusing way to spend an hour or so.

After a while I noticed that she had turned a bright shade of pink. She made her excuses and left hurriedly. I saw her to the door and as I turned to go back to the kitchen, I happened to glance down and notice that I had an embarrassingly large bulge in my pants. Somehow, I don't think that Mrs. Donnalson will be back in a hurry.

Well, I must be making progress. At least I am fantasizing about a living female for a change.

ENTRY 17

I couldn't be bothered to go out at all today. It was one of those cloudy, miasma-filled, early July days, not helped by the accompanying clammy humidity. The air of Syracuse in the summer months seems to have less oxygen in it, giving it an atmosphere as thick as Mexico City's, but minus the Mariachi bands. I was gulping air like a guppy and getting no sustenance from it.

So I stayed inside and browsed through some old art magazines that I hadn't bother getting rid of. I came across one from 1999 that featured an article on the contemporary art exhibition at the Royal Academy in London, England entitled, *Apocalypse: Beauty and Horror in Contemporary Art*. It featured a photo of an alarmingly realistic wax statue of Pope John Paul II being pranged by a meteor. The piece was by the Italian artist Maurizio Cattelan and it was called *The Ninth Hour*.

I couldn't stop laughing.

I'm sure that this statue must have caused an outcry, but perhaps not as vociferous as the one that followed the *Sensation* exhibition at the Brooklyn Academy the same year. I remember that the portrait of an African Virgin Mary executed in elephant dung by British artist Chris Ofili was a personal favorite of mine. It was that painting in particular that had sent the good Mayor of New York ballistic.

Frankly, in my opinion, all these conceptual artists are full of shit—no pun intended—from Hirst on down, but no one listens to me, do they?

The Brits were much more sanguine about the squashed Pope. They don't have the albatross of Catholic guilt hanging around their necks. They also don't suffer from an irony deficiency, like most Americans.

I cut out the photo of *The Ninth Hour* and taped it to the wall above my desk. Every time I feel a bit depressed, I look up and laugh my head off.

The venerable Pope: the greatest confidence trickster of all. The only accurate thing Karl Marx ever said was that religion was the opiate of the people. (Did Marx say that, or was it Lenin? What does it matter? They were both sublime tricksters themselves, supplanting one religion for another. They just disguised it as a political system.)

Religion allows people to hope for a better life in heaven when there is no heaven. There is no hell. Heaven and hell are here, now, on this planet. Experience them while you can, because when we finally shuffle off that mortal coil, all we are going face is a big, black NOTHING.

We are utterly expendable beings on this planet, yet religion fools us into believing that we are unique and that someone is looking after us. Religions try to justify and explain the horrendous cruelty and viciousness of the world, but how do you explain the unexplainable? How can we understand the torture and death of one child, let alone the genocide of a nation? If we are made in God's image, then he must be a cruel God who fashioned the world to a cruel design.

Religion is the greatest weapon that man has ever invented. It is nothing but an endless rationalization of chaos. Most of the world's population lives in such dire poverty that if they didn't believe in an afterlife, then they would probably pull their own heads off right now. Believing in an afterlife is the only way to endure such desperate misery.

All religion does is allow the powers that be to screw you, while promising the gullible populace so-called redemption. The amount of money and art and power that the Church has squirreled away in the catacombs of the Vatican would astound the general populace if only they were permitted to know about it. But when was the last time the Roman Catholic Church had to account to anyone, let alone file an income tax return?

I'll never forget visiting a famous monastery church on the outskirts of Mexico City. The architecture and artwork were fabulous, the gilt ornamentation baroque in the extreme. A rich Mexican friend who had accompanied me asked me what I thought of it all, no doubt expecting a response full of praise for the beauty of the place. All I could say was, "If it was up to me, I'd melt all this stuff down and give it to the poor." The shock on the guy's face was something to behold. What did he know (or care) about the grinding poverty of his own people? I was surprised at myself for my vehement response. I was an Art Historian after all, and it wasn't as if I had suddenly and miraculously metamorphosed into a Socialist. It was just that at that particular moment, I found all that blatant display of wealth ostentatious in the extreme.

But nothing will change. The rich get richer, the poor get poorer: nothing truer was ever said. The wealthy and powerful play by their own rules, while we work like drones hoping for some crumbs from their table.

ENTRY 18

Last night I spent a mindless evening in front of the TV, channel hopping. I despair of the human race, I really do, when I look at a screen filled with morons, delivering meaningless pap to the unschooled masses. Talk about lowest common denominator. I watched about thirty seconds of a rerun of *Friends*. This used to be America's favorite sitcom? Not one of those actors had anything going on behind the eyes. Every one of them looked totally brain-dead. If I had a Kalashnikov, I would put all of them out of their overpaid misery right now. And the so-called music on Youtube? Don't get me started. Nothing seems to have any spark, originality or intelligence involved in it. The songs aren't even songs any more. (Shit, I am starting to sound like my father.) Honestly, would anyone really mind if Britney Spears or Justin Bieber got involved in some unfortunate accident? Tell the truth and shame the devil.

It terrifies me that children are watching this pointless twaddle, but we all know that this generation is going to grow up to be more vicious and stupid than any of the previous ones. Look at Columbine, Arkansas, Oregon, Virginia Tech, North Illinois, Ohio. All those boys with guns strutting around with their *cojones* bulging and shooting the shit out of their math teachers before putting a bullet into their own tiny brains, just because THEY WEREN'T POPULAR. Poor babies. Hey, there is an interesting dating tactic: "You don't want to go to the prom with me, you bitch? Die motherfucker!"

Too many pointlessly violent movies, that's what I say. Maybe the families of the victims should sue Hollywood, instead of blaming the school principal, poor bastard. That's great, isn't it? Your kid gets murdered at school and what do you do? Have a litigation fest. Sue the principal, sue the police for not noticing the kids were weird, sue the parents of the little murdering sons of bitches for not realizing that their children were disaffected losers. Sue the world. Hell, why not sue God? It is ultimately his fault at the end of the line.

Perhaps I should make a drastic career change and become a professional assassin. I could start with targeting television executives and movie producers. That would get them worried. I'd demand that they start putting out some decent programming, or else. Maybe I should become politically motivated, make a difference and kill people who really deserve to die. Unfortunately, the list would be endless.

I wish Charles Gibson was still anchoring *ABC World News*. I liked him. He seemed to be the only intelligent person on the tube. So measured, so grave when the situation called for it, then so twinklesome when he described some humorous news item. But aren't they all like that, newsmen and women? I wonder if they go to some special News Anchor Training School. They all have the same head movements, scintillating smiles and flawless complexions. They look perfect, even the older ones, like Barbie and Ken dolls. I bet that they're robots, just like *The Stepford Wives*. Now that would make perfect sense.

Perhaps the whole world of television is populated by artificial intelligence life forms, like Data in *Star Trek: The Next Generation*. It might even extend beyond entertainment. Maybe all of American society is living in a vast robotic recreation park, à la *Westworld*, and Yul Brynner is on his way to kick our butts if we get out of line.

This is not so farfetched as it sounds. It would explain our current crop of politicians, anyway.

Whew, the flights of fancy my mind takes when I allow it free rein. I should stop watching so much television. It is rotting my brain. I know that something is.

ENTRY 19

I was sitting in my den today, going through old family photograph albums. I have no idea why I was doing this. Maybe I had some vague notion of gathering up and burning every picture I could find of Angie as some kind of final purification rite.

Flicking through one album, I came upon a snapshot of yours truly when I was around sixteen. I was standing in front of an old Pontiac Catalina and looking as sullen and rebellious and sex-starved as only an adolescent can.

Then a long-forgotten incident from that time popped unbidden into my brain. Like any other young guy of my age, I was obsessed with music. I used to go to a little record store a few blocks away from our house that was managed by an unpleasant-looking individual called Earl Saville. Earl wore a beard, but no mustache; a tonsorial affectation that I find both irritating and disconcerting even to this day.

One day I was in the shop, wistfully looking at some vinyl that I couldn't afford. Three little girls came in, all around thirteen—slender and graceful as young swans. It was summer and they were wearing tiny, brightly colored shorts and tops. They perused the records, picked out their favorites and brought them over to Earl. He looked over their selections, smiled and waved them out the door. Giggling their thanks, they left. Earl then turned to me and said, "You know, kid, one thing's for sure: little girls' pussies are the sweetest of all!" I asked him how he would know. He said, "Them little darlings and me got a great deal. They spread their legs for me and let me suck their pussies and I give them whatever records they want."

Half of me was utterly repelled by what he said; the other half contained an unsettling mixture of jealousy and curiosity. I had certainly never tasted female pussy of any age at that point. The thought of doing it to a little girl was so forbidden that I felt sinful even contemplating it, but I was intrigued. The girls seemed quite happy with the arrangement. None of them looked uncomfortable or nervous while they were in the store or when they were talking to Earl. On the contrary, they treated him as they would a favorite uncle. Who can fathom a young girl's mind? At that age, I guess records were more important to them than keeping their knees together. They hadn't yet learned the value of the precious treasure that nestled between their thighs.

I made my excuses and left the shop, never to return. No one ever squealed on Earl and as far as I can remember, he died peacefully in his sleep at a grand old age.

What made me think of that now? And what possessed Earl to take me into his confidence at that particular moment? He couldn't have known that I wouldn't spill the beans. Was he boasting? Lying? Worse still, did he recognize a kindred spirit?

When I was a couple of years older, I was so desperate for sex that I used to drive around in my car, just looking at girls walking along the sidewalk. I would fantasize about kidnapping them, as I couldn't imagine any girl going with me of her own free will. I even put ropes in the trunk of the car for the purpose of tying the girls up if I ever caught one. Fortunately—or unfortunately, depending on your point of view—I never worked up the nerve.

I don't think people realize how frantic some young men feel about women at that age. Guys want sex all the time. They are obsessed by it and it appears that all girls want to do is to keep it from them. The female of the species seems to hold all the cards. She has the power to say, "No," and she also possesses the frightful capacity to reduce a guy to a quivering mass just by a condescending glance. What's a shy, hopeless guy supposed to do? Masturbate and fantasize, that's what. But how much of that can you do before the fantasies become darker and more aggressive? Not only do you dream of having sex with a girl, you dream of totally dominating her. You dream of making her your slave. You are tired of being a nerd. You want to be a sheik with a harem of willing women to do your bidding. You don't want rejection, only grateful acceptance and adoration. You dream of women in chains— golden chains—strapped to a bed, naked and willing, begging you to fuck them. The dark dreams start to become the only ones that can turn you on. Normal sexual fantasies don't hack it anymore. The only thoughts that get you hard are the ones that are about violence and domination.

When I was a kid, I used to buy detective magazines and masturbate to the illustrations of women tied up and looking frightened. I'd draw nooses around their necks and dream of them being strung up by their ankles, hands tied behind their backs. Their legs would be wide open and I could just stand there with their pussies at mouth level and suck them while they writhed and screamed with pleasure. Then I would take out my cock and they would suck me off while I was still giving it to them. Wow, that one worked fast. I'd better stop soon and do something about it.

I hated my wife with a passion at the end of our relationship, but, in a small corner of my soul, I am profoundly grateful that I met her when I did. After all, meeting someone you can have sex with unblocks the pressure valves clogged up with disappointment. If I hadn't, I am sure that something bad would have happened to someone.

ENTRY 20

I can't seem to stop watching the boob tube, so aptly named. It is becoming a compulsion, even though I can't stand anything on it.

I caught a program called *The FBI Files* on the Discovery Channel the other night. It told the true story of a homicidal maniac who ran around Wisconsin or some other godforsaken part of the country back in 1986. He murdered kids, adults, black and white, male and female, whatever. He wasn't fussy. This guy became enraged because he had to make an appearance in court, so he killed a little girl, then grabbed his girlfriend and hightailed it out of town. For some reason, perhaps because his girlfriend was in on it, the killer easily approached people on the street. He would then inveigle his way into their homes, kill them, and then motorvate on over to his next crime scene. He was stupid, sloppy and didn't even bother to use gloves. Yet the FBI and the police were always fumbling away a few steps behind him, can you believe it? They even broadcast his face on TV, probably nationwide, but people still invited the killer into their houses. The only reason the cops caught him was that he and his bimbo were dumb enough to return to his hometown. The couple just sat there in a public park eating peanut butter sandwiches until the police moseyed on in and slapped the cuffs on them.

Jesus, I didn't know whether to laugh or cry. Now, where do I begin? Let's take the serial killer first. My advice to him would have been: don't take up a new profession unless you decide that you're going to do it properly. Read up on the subject and inform yourself about the risks. Fingerprint detection has been around for over a hundred years now, so why not wear gloves? Also, keep away from kids. Nothing sickens me more than child killers. What is the possible challenge in murdering a little kid? None whatsoever. What a jerk.

Next, the police. Why did it take them so long to bring the bastard down? Honestly, with the trail that guy was leaving, my blind grandmother could have caught him sooner. It just goes to show how untouchable serial killers are. Since they have no connection with their victims, they are almost impossible to trace.

Finally, the victims. Could someone please tell me what would possess people to let TOTAL STRANGERS into their homes, and even give them dinner, for goodness' sake? Okay, he had a woman with him and, for some bizarre reason, most of the general public have a hard time getting their heads around the idea that women kill, but they can and do. (Remember Aileen Wuornos?) Folks need to get more paranoid. As far as I am concerned, I am coming to the conclusion that it might be sensible to regard every stranger as a potential serial killer. Even some of my friends are suspect. I just imagine that everyone has the same sick fantasies that I do. Then I'm not surprised when horrible things happen.

ENTRY 21

After months of procrastination, I finally went through some of Angie's stuff today, sorting it all out for a major run to the Salvation Army. Her mother had offered to do it when I was in hospital, but, for some perverse reason, I wanted to do the job myself. After all, I was responsible for her untimely demise and I wanted the satisfaction of throwing away all her precious designer clothes and knickknacks. Boy, I'm glad it was her cash that she was spending. If I thought that she used my hard-earned money to buy that crap, I would have driven my car into that tree years earlier.

Of course, some items brought back memories, good and bad.

I was on the way to becoming a major weirdo when we encountered each other at University. Lord knows what she saw in me: a quiet, manageable guy, I guess, and unbelievably grateful for the small sexual favors that she granted me. I was also unimpressed with her wealth, which she appreciated. It must be difficult if you are a woman with means. You never know if a man is there for you or your cash. I was also penniless, which she loved. I think Angie married me simply to irritate her parents, who were rooting for some major player from Yale or Harvard with a bankroll of his own. Ironically, I always liked her folks and they ended up liking me. They had worked hard for their money and knew its value. Angie just wanted to shop 'til she dropped.

In Angie, I saw a good-looking girl, confident in some ways, totally insecure in others. I was obsessed with art; she attended the classes because she thought it was an easy way to get a degree. She was smart and sassy, but this couldn't make up for her lack of intellectual substance.

How such a fun-loving couple ended up being the Syracuse equivalent of Edward Albee's George and Martha is something that I don't want to even begin to record in detail here. In short, it all came down to her ambition to be married to a man who was a Somebody and me not giving a damn. She wound up being profoundly disappointed by me and I suppose a divorce was inevitable in the long run. I guess the thing that made it difficult for her was that she might have to give me a chunk of her considerable fortune. That must have really galled her—like a pebble in her expensive Manilo Blahnick shoe.

Sex was great in the beginning. We were both enthusiastic and she was quite adventurous in allowing me to live out some of my milder bondage fantasies, but that soon stopped when she got bored. But the thing that really soured our marriage was the whole baby thing. We spent thousands on In Vitro Fertilization, but it just didn't take. She even wanted us to adopt at one point, but I put my foot down. Deep inside my soul, I knew that I was unsuitable father material and I didn't want to take the chance of screwing up some poor bastard who wasn't even mine.

So things got more and more bitter, until our existence was just excruciating. She started seeing old Charlie and even though I suppose I was relieved in some odd way, it infuriated me all the same. Why do people put each other through such endurance tests? Why tolerate all those years of irritation and loathing? Was the money so important to her? To me? I should have bailed out years ago. I might have ended up happily ensconced with some unchallenging little grad student and she might have finally found her Wall Street magnate.

No use in thinking about what might have been. We suffered each other to the breaking point and then something snapped. She ended up dead and I ended up a basket case.

Great.

ENTRY 22

The fall semester is about to begin and I have made my decision. I am not going back to teach at the University. Professor Mandelson understood and he said any time that I wanted to come back, even part-time, he would be happy to have me.

I just can't face it. I don't feel confident enough to look in the mirror, let alone confront a classroom full of demanding students. It's not as if I need to work anymore. Angie's money has taken care of that.

I have to find something to do, though, or I will probably go crazy. Just working out and watching television isn't enough. I need a project, or a job, something that can fulfill me. But what?

ENTRY 23

Something happened today.

I decided to go to the campus this morning to check things out, even though I wasn't ready to start teaching again. I just had an urge to see the University, to get a whiff of the place and to ascertain if I could work up the enthusiasm to eventually go back to my job. I went to my office, but, of course, they had given it to someone else. Jeff is a nice guy and wanted to talk, but I immediately felt claustrophobic. He told me where my stuff was, but I couldn't be bothered to go over to ADMIN and field more questions. I wandered around, feeling utterly detached. Everything looked odd and out of place. The students that knew me said "Hello" and were pleased to see me, but I felt like I was playing a bit part in my own life.

I went outside and sat on a bench in the Quad and watched the world go by. It was a pleasant September day, not raining for once. I looked at the kids bustling past: so full of energy and love and excitement about the lives they had stretching out in front of them; so confident that nothing bad was ever going to happen to them; so immortal. The fools.

Then I saw her. She was obviously a teacher, maybe from the School of Medicine or Chemistry. (She was wearing a white lab coat.) She was walking across the campus with a gaggle of students in tow, but to my eyes, she and I were the only people in the universe. It was as if some clever movie director had created a special lighting effect just for her. She seemed illuminated from within. Funnily enough, she wasn't my usual type at all. I normally go for medium-to-tall brunettes, but she was petite and blonde, with a hidden sensuality. It was her face that arrested me. Her face made time stop for me. I could barely breathe. She was smiling, laughing...she seemed full of brightness and promise.

An idea like a thunderbolt struck my brain. This would be the woman to save me, to bring me back to the world. This woman was my soul mate, I knew it.

I fell in love with her right then and there. Hit smack dab in the heart with Cupid's poisoned arrow. Crazy, I know, but let's face it, I am not exactly Mr. Stability at the moment.

For the first time in months, I felt a stirring in my inner being. Something was coming alive again. It felt good. It felt exciting. However, underneath it all, there was a dark shadow. I wanted this woman and I wanted her right now, but I knew that I could never possess her. I could never approach her in the state I was in. My self-confidence was at rock bottom. But instead of experiencing despair, as I would have felt before the Accident, my world rage boiled up again. Not towards her, but towards everyone else. Towards every living creature on the whole goddamned planet. My self-loathing at this point was only matched by my utter animosity towards everything else.

If I had the power, I would have blasted the entire Earth to smithereens. It was as if a helmet of anger had clamped down on my head, the visor coloring my world a deep, blood red.

However, I controlled myself. I forced the rage back inside. I decided that there is always hope. Hope springs eternal. Hope, that last will o 'the wisp that Pandora trapped in her famous box.

I followed my soul mate the best I could and do you know where we ended up? Oh, irony of ironies: the Psychology Department! Trust me to become instantly smitten by a woman whose profession I loathed. I went inside and limped around, trying not to draw too much attention to myself, but I needn't have worried. I was the Invisible Man. No one took any notice of me. Then I bumbled right past her office. I saw her in there, deep in conversation with a student.

Her name was on the door. It is Elene...sorry, Doctor Elene Sheppard. I wonder how she pronounces her first name. Is it Elaine, or Ellen, or Aileen, or Elena? I have decided that it is pronounced like Elaine (with the emphasis on the last syllable) until further notice.

Now I have a face for the women in my dreams. No, hold on. Is that a good idea? The women in my dreams are always dead or dying. I don't want anything to happen to Elene.

Tomorrow I will find out where she lives.

Now, I have a Project! Something to get me going in the mornings; something to think about; to take me out of myself. I am going to find out everything about Elene. I will know where she likes to go out for dinner; who are her friends; where she shops; who she is dating...

Ah, yes. A girl like that would have a boyfriend, wouldn't she? On the other hand, professional woman, early thirties...perhaps not. So many women want their independence these days and she looked the type. A strong-minded girl who walks her own path.

She had a lovely voice. Very melodious. Not the typical Upstate nasal whine, thank God. Great legs, too. Well-defined calf muscles. Of course, all the girls of Syracuse have amazing calf muscles because of the abundance of hills in this damn town.

I am going to enjoy this.

ENTRY 24

It has taken me nearly a week, but now I'm an expert on Elene. It was easy obtaining the info from the Administration Building. I was discreet as well, telling Mrs. Johannson that I needed to get some information from my own files. I went just before lunchtime, so she left me in the Records Room on my own. I had no idea that I had such a knack for devious behavior.

Elene is thirty-two years old and she was born in Spokane, Washington. (That's an interesting coincidence. Isn't that where the serial killer came from on the news a little while ago?) She went to the University of Washington for her Bachelor's Degree in Psychology. Elene then went on to the California School of Professional Psychology in Fresno for her Master's and subsequently her Doctorate in Forensic Psychology. She shares an office downtown with some other shrinks, but she spends most of her time teaching at Syracuse University. (Why didn't I ever spot her when I was working there?) Occasionally, she helps out the police if they have a case involving some psycho. She also counsels prisoners at the Correctional Facility in Jamesville.

Elene lives in a modest, turn-of-the-century house on Euclid Avenue, five minutes from the campus. She drives a metallic gray Ford Taurus with black interiors. She likes to go to Phoebe's on Genesee Street for lunch on Tuesdays and Fridays.

Elene doesn't seem to have that many friends. She works all the time.

The only man that I saw her with all week was a tall guy with well-defined features. A real lady-killer type, he looked like Tommy Lee Jones meets Sam Shepard on a dark night. I decided to follow him after they had dinner together at Kahunaville in the Carousel Center, of all places. He must be on a peanut salary. If you're going to take a girl like Elene out to dinner, take her to Pascal's or at a pinch, Salario's.

So I tailed Tommy Lee Shepard to the Public Safety Building on State Street. I am hazarding the opinion that he might be an officer of the law. He certainly looked like a cop—bad suit, tired shoes and all.

Anyway, they only saw each other once and they spent most of the time arguing. He dropped her home and didn't come in, so maybe they are just working on a case together.

That's all the news that's fit to print. Not bad for an amateur detective. I was amazed at how unobservant people are when they are whirling around in their own little worlds. They never look around when they are walking down the street or strolling through a mall. I always look behind me. Constantly. Hell, I'm not paranoid, I KNOW everyone is against me.

Now, a strategy must be worked out. How to meet Elene?

I need to make contact soon. My dreams are now becoming so bizarre that I am afraid to write them down. I need a dose of human contact or something terrible might happen. I am so sexually frustrated that I am masturbating all the time.

I came across this web site the other day called The Serial Killer Hit List and I read the biography of Albert De Salvo, the Boston Strangler. He claimed that he raped at least two thousand women. TWO THOUSAND. He had three or four orgasms a day, sometimes one right after the other. He was unbelievably over-sexed, to the point of it interfering with his everyday existence. (That's obvious, otherwise why go out raping and murdering? "His compulsions made him do it, your Honor.")

Before the Accident, I wasn't particularly sexed up, as the dire state of my marriage had placed me in a state of sexual lethargy. Since the Accident, as the days go by, I seem to be more and more obsessed by sex. I fantasize about girls all the time. The other day, I even fantasized about the late Angie. I imagined dragging her lifeless body out of the wreckage of our car and giving her the fuck of the century. I ripped off her ridiculously expensive clothes and I fucked her in her mouth, her cunt and her ass. Fantasizing about fucking my dead wife up the ass (something she would never had stood for in life, by the way) was enormously satisfying. It's giving me a hard-on just remembering it.

I can't meet Elene in this state. I have to do something about this. If I met her now, I would either disintegrate into a drooling wreck, or tear her clothes off and screw her right then and there on the floor of the staff canteen. Hey, that's a good one. I might work on that one later.

Maybe I should go to a prostitute.

ENTRY 25

I went to see Dr. Clueless again. I told him that I wasn't getting any benefit from our sessions and that I wanted to quit. Boy, did he look worried. So would I, if I got his fees. He said that I should continue treatment; that he had only just scratched the surface. He said that he didn't have a full picture of my background yet. He wanted to know more about my childhood, about dear old mom and pop.

As if I would tell him.

I said that I found it difficult to relate to him and that I probably would communicate better with a woman doctor. I asked him if he could recommend anyone. Dr. Clueless came up with a few names, none I recognized. I said that since I was considering going back to my job at the University, it might be more convenient if my counselor was teaching there. Bingo! He eventually mentioned Elene's name. I said that I had heard of her. He said her expertise was more on the forensic end of Psychology, but she was also an experienced counselor. He would give her a call, see if she was willing to take on my case, and arrange a meeting.

All of a sudden, I had very warm feelings for Doctor Cordess, especially since I was never going to have to see him again. I was suitably grateful, wrote a big check and left.

I am going to meet Elene! Of course, this is a rather awkward way of choreographing a love affair. I know shrinks have rules about messing around with patients, but I figure I could make contact—and then decide not to consult her. I could ask her out to dinner later.

Would I be able to deal with that? Would I be able to have a decent conversation with Elene? I don't know. I guess that I will have to cross that bridge when I come to it.

ENTRY 26

Still no word from Dr. Clueless about the possible appointment with Elene.

I had nothing better to do today, so I spent the morning hanging around the campus. I stopped off at ADMIN and picked up a schedule of psychology courses, so I would know where Elene was located at all times.

I walked back towards my car. I'd parked it on Marshall Street, not coincidentally around the corner from Huntington Hall, where Elene worked. I spotted her coming out of the building and I thought, "Hell, why not?" So I followed her. It was so easy. I felt like sending her a note advising her to be more aware. It was Tuesday, so I knew that she was heading to Phoebe's for lunch.

Together, we strolled down University Avenue until we got to Genesee Street. It was comforting to know that Elene is such a creature of habit.

I have tried to avoid following her too much, simply because I don't want to get noticed, but also to space out the enjoyment. I loved watching Elene move. I liked lingering over her legs and ass as she walked down the hill. She reached back to smooth down her hair and I imagined that her hand was my hand. That I was the one touching her soft, silky hair. Then I had to bring myself up short. It's not safe fantasizing about someone when you are walking down a busy sidewalk. I could just see myself ambling in front of a bus, while my eyes were glued to her damn calf muscles.

We arrived at Phoebe's, but I didn't follow Elene in. I went down the block and had a quick sandwich at Goldie's Delicatessen. Then I walked back to Marshall Street, got in my car and drove home.

I have to pace myself with all this following business. Oh, who am I kidding? This stalking business. Stalking, that is exactly what I am doing. At least I can fool myself that I am not hurting anyone. Elene couldn't care less. After all, ignorance is bliss. As long as she doesn't realize that I am following her, what harm is being done?

ENTRY 27

I can't believe it, but I found a book by Elene on the Internet! It wasn't on Amazon.com, but a smaller, more obscure forensic psychology web site. It is called *Death In My Pocket: Inside The Minds Of Serial Killers*. My cup runneth over! I ordered it directly from the web site. The chances of my finding it somewhere else were minuscule because, unfortunately for Elene, it was out of print. Since it's such a popular subject, I didn't think books about serial killers could go out of print, but I guess that's the book biz.

ENTRY 28

Elene's book arrived today. I'm afraid to say that after reading a few chapters, I can see why it didn't race up the New York Times Bestseller List. It is a starkly clinical look at such a juicy topic. Still, I was fascinated by Elene's take on the subject. I feel like I have been given a key to the door into her mind. Now I will be able to understand her more fully through her work.

One passage at the beginning struck me. Elene was explaining how some killers and psychopaths regarded themselves as different than the rest of us. They were similar to poets and artists in that way. They saw themselves as outsiders—not belonging to the rest of the human race...

"To be an outsider means that these individuals perceive the human race as we really are. Outsiders rise above the mundane, everyday realities of life that inevitably wear us down. They have a bird's eye view (or even a God's eye view) of the human condition. If one views life from such a perspective, then it is easy to say, 'What's the use? What's the use of the job, the mortgage, the kids? What does it all add up to in the end, but a lot of heartache?' To the outsider, it means nothing. Hence his feelings of uselessness and detachment, coupled with a compulsive sense of superiority. That kind of combination can only lead to frustration and we all know where frustration can lead to...

"To have these feelings of superiority and no release for them—no talent to channel them—must be supremely disconcerting. Unlike the poet or the artist, who have their talents to comfort them, a man on the outside with homicidal tendencies has nothing to fall back on. To feel like a god, to have the lofty detachment of a god and yet to be bereft of power. How does one confront these feelings? How does one deal with the anger that this condition would engender? To the potential serial killer, the natural and logical way to achieve that kind of godlike power is to take someone's life. To move amongst the sheep and pluck a victim as randomly as any other act of Nature—touching down on a soul like a tornado touches down on some God-fearing trailer park in Florida."

When I read the preceding passage, I wondered if I were an outsider. Someone who is condemned to sit at a shadowy side table in the Restaurant of Life and observe the rest of humanity getting on with things. On the other hand, maybe being an outsider isn't such a terrible thing. To be a member of the herd is so demeaning, so humiliating, so normal.

I want.

I want, I need, to make a difference somehow. I cannot bear this dullness I feel, this unrelenting boredom with my existence. Maybe I should go out and kill someone. It would be the ultimate transgression, the ultimate high. The ultimate.

ENTRY 29

Elene doesn't have time to see me. Dr. Cuntface said that he could recommend someone else, but I told him that I didn't have the time at the moment and that I would get in touch later.

I am not taking this personally.

I am not taking this personally.

I AM NOT TAKING THIS PERSONALLY.

Elene doesn't even know me. She doesn't know who I am. She just didn't have the time to take on a new patient.

I should have realized that. I can see how busy she is. I don't blame her in the slightest. I don't blame her, really.

I am very disappointed.

My wonderful plan is in tatters.

What do I do now?

Fuck, FUCK, **FUCK!**

ENTRY 30

I got drunk last night. Angry drunk. On tequila, which is as close as you can get to being high on alcohol. I carefully went around the house and systematically smashed everything that reminded me of Angie. Then I went into my den and finally ripped out all the photographs of her in our albums and threw them on the fire. After that, I found all the pictures of my father that I had left and ripped them up and tossed them on the merry blaze as well. I was surprised to see how many I had, but Mother had refused to get rid of them and I inadvertently inherited them.

The old bastard. I looked carefully at each photo before I destroyed it, bringing back the memory of the time and place when it had been taken. There's dear old Dad with his movie star looks, wearing swimming trunks and lounging in a lawn chair, cool as Cary Grant. There he is with Uncle Danny, both of them leaning on a 1962 turquoise and white Chevy Impala Coupe, looking sporty and daring. (Nice Uncle Danny, my mother's brother, tried to sodomize me when I was eleven. I only escaped because he couldn't get it up. He told me never to tell anyone because if I did, then God would punish my mother. Uncle Danny was a real charmer.)

My father dumped us when I was ten years old. One day, he just upped and left. No note, no word of explanation, no good-byes. Mother was devastated, but she gritted her teeth and went back to teaching art. We survived somehow. After all, it wasn't as if Dad had been some tremendous breadwinner or anything. As a matter of fact, I was always hazy about what he actually did for a living. Something in sales, I think. It was years later that my mother admitted to me that he was an unrepentant serial adulterer. He went off my mother after she got religion. I guess he finally said, "Fuck this!" and disappeared with one of his floozies to a warmer and happier clime. Mother did have the occasional boyfriend after that, but no one was like dear old Dad. She never allowed a word against him.

I wonder where he is now? That's a lie. Fuck him. I hope he's rotting somewhere, poor and lonely. How dare he leave me with HER? My mother and Uncle Danny. What a great combo. The irresponsible artist who didn't have a clue about raising a child and the sodomizing pederast uncle. It's a miracle that I am as sane as I am.

I am sane, aren't I?

ENTRY 31

I woke up this morning and decided to go to New York City. If I am going to go to a prostitute then I am going to pick up one down there. I know a few places where the girls aren't too bad. They are not street girls—more like call girls. Very discreet. They demand that their customers wear condoms, which suits me down to the ground because catching AIDS would not exactly brighten up my day.

Even if I don't get up the nerve to get some relief, then a change of scene would be good for me. A change is as good as a rest, they say.

I called up Darlene, my travel agent, and asked her to book the flight and hotel. I will stay at the Larchmont in the Village, a very quiet little Bed and Breakfast on West 11th Street. I have the money to stay at the Sheraton, but I don't think that I could stand being at a big hotel. I don't want to negotiate the gauntlet of a huge lobby every day, dodging obsequious staff and roving packs of gawking tourists.

ENTRY 32

Watching television is now making me physically ill. What are we the people supposed to do when confronted with the likes of Jerry Springer and his guests? There they are in all their glory, "ordinary people" trotting out their miserable little lives. I suppose we are meant to sit and wonder. Or are we meant to sit and feel nauseous? Who cares about these nonentities and their penny-anti problems? "MY HUSBAND RAN OFF WITH MY SIXTEEN-YEAR-OLD BABY-SITTER!"

Who truly gives a shit? And who can blame the poor sad clod of a husband when you see the blimp-like wife appear from backstage? What is it with the large proportion of American women? They get married, say "to hell with it" and then proceed to gain sixty pounds, give or take a few ounces. It's repulsive. Yet does hubby ever ask why? "Why does my wife now resemble the *Hindenburg*?" Could it be possible that she piled on the pounds so she could repel all boarders, i.e., her paunchy, balding loser of a mate?

And what about the sixteen-year-old? What in God's name is going on in her bean brain? What would possess a groovy young thing like her to run off with the aforementioned has-been? Well, she is like any other example of today's feckless youth, with an intellect just this side of plankton. She probably thinks that screwing an older man gives her some cachet; that it makes her "cool." Maybe the dim teen imagines that she's Catherine Zeta Jones to his Michael Douglas. Yeah, and I'm Brad Pitt. Maybe she thinks that he will "teach" her something. Yeah, sure. He will teach her how to suck his wizened cock for two minutes until he spasmodically has a half-orgasm while he dreams of wifey's pot roast.

Springer's guests and audience are all so shriekingly common that I can only stand to watch ten seconds of these diabolical shows at one time. Just seeing the subject matter of that day's program is enough to make me gag: "MY SON IS A TRANSVESTITE!" or "MY FIVE-YEAR-OLD LIKES BEAUTY PAGEANTS AND HE IS A BOY!" I am just waiting for "MY HAMSTER LIKES IT UP THE ASS AND SO DOES MY HUSBAND!" to make my life complete.

Yes, I only need to see the title and then take in the baying crowd—with Jerry goading them on like some demented master of ceremonies at the Roman Coliseum—and my gorge rises.

It's a shame that there isn't an UGLY button on the television remote control, like the mute button. If anything offensive appears on the screen, just press the UGLY button and "shazam!"—only the truly beautiful will be left to pirouette in front of our bedazzled eyes. Trouble is, that would eradicate 95% of today's television content. All that would remain would be the girls of the *Baywatch* reruns—they must have waxed their bikini lines every day, you never see a whisper (I've checked with a magnifying glass right up against the TV screen, so I should know)—and Charlize Theron.

To be brutally honest, ordinary people should be put out of their misery as soon as humanly possible. How ludicrous to think that by spilling the sordid details of their mundane lives on nationwide TV that they will somehow become as famous as, say, the unfortunately named, asparagus-thin Gwyneth Paltrow or hunkier-than-thou Tom Cruise. We admire celebrities for their slim figures and cleanness of limb, their brighter-than-bright smiles and sparkling lives. There is no comparison between these glittering stars of the Hollywood firmament and the circus chimps that we see on display on the Springer show.

I saw Jerry Springer being interviewed once and he said, "If you don't like the show, you don't have to watch it." But that is an oversimplification of the problem. This kind of stuff is a disease. It is a pestilence. A plague of tasteless, low common denominator-type of programming that is rotting the collective brain of the nation. It isn't just Jerry, it's Leeza and Ricki and Sally and Maury and Oprah. It's *Survivor* and *Who Wants to Marry a Millionaire?* and *Temptation Island* and *American Idol*. It's a virus out of control, an Ebola of the mind.

Someone should be held responsible.

ENTRY 33

I spent the weekend in New York City and did nothing. I couldn't get up the nerve to phone a call girl. I left my hotel room only to eat and see movies. I saw six movies. When I wasn't eating and watching movies, I was gazing with dead eyes at the television.

It would have been a complete waste of time and money, but something happened. That THING that I have been waiting for finally arrived in my head and now I have to decide what to do about it. It was quite extraordinary.

My world rage came out and metamorphosed into something else. Something that doesn't have a direction yet, but will soon, I feel it.

Yesterday, Sunday afternoon, I was standing on a street corner in the Upper East Side, waiting for the green WALK sign. As I stepped off the sidewalk, police motorcycles appeared and the cops waved the pedestrians back. Then two limos whizzed past through the red lights. The occupants were fat, complacent, diplomat types.

Now, what really burned me was that these guys broke the law with the help of the law, just because they were VIPs. By the way, I'm only assuming that they were diplomats. There weren't any little flags on the cars or anything. They just looked smug enough to fill the brief.

Why did I get so angry? Was it because I was a white man being forced back on the sidewalk by two carloads of self-satisfied looking Africans? Yes, these guys were black and somehow I just knew that they weren't Afro-Americans. I don't think that race had anything to do with it. No, what infuriated me way beyond any logical level was that I knew that they knew that they were better than me. They were off to do important business—much more important than anything in my life. I was part of the crowd of "little people" and they were part of the ruling class— those fortunate few who could command the attention of the police and get the cops to do their bidding. It messed my head up. Right then and there, I decided that I didn't want to be a little person anymore—drugged into submission by the elite on lethal doses of TV, the lottery and basketball games. The scraps they throw us to keep the population manageable.

When I flew home that night, I threw away my television set.

All the news I need I can get from the papers and the glorious Internet, spiritual home to potential nutcases everywhere. I have decided to go on a media diet: no TV, no sports, no playing the lottery. It's tough giving up "24-Hour Breaking News!"—but I'm sure that I'll survive.

I know now that I need to slim down my flabby mental processes. I have to stop playing around in my fantasies and stand up to be counted. I need to make a difference. I am forty already and my life is splintering away into a million inconsequential pieces meaning fuck all. I haven't made a dent in the impervious shell of life in general. I want to feel powerful again, like you do when you are twenty-one and have the world in your pocket.

I need a cause.

I have to think about this deeply. I have to make some choices. I know that this is all going to revolve around Elene somehow. She has to notice me. I want contact. I need her.

What am I willing to do to feel powerful again? What am I going to do?

I can't answer these questions now, but I somehow feel that they will be answered for me soon enough. There is something bubbling away beneath the surface of my mind, a dark shadow of an idea. It is swimming with the sharks of my unconscious.

ENTRY 34

Fucking Christmas is already on its merry way. Halloween isn't even here yet and the Carousel Center has outfitted its so-called "Christmas Shoppe" so all the sad little shits can buy their Xmas cards early. Of course, if you were really wretched, you would have already bought your cards in last year's after-Christmas sales. The other day, one of my more sad-sack neighbors, Wilbur Cartwright, said to me, "Isn't it a shame how commercialized Christmas has become, Michael?" I was astounded he had said this to me, because:

A. Did he really think I gave a flying fuck?

B. Did he really think he had said something original?

C. Did he really think that I cared what he thought about in the first place?

Christmas long ago lost any meaning to just about anyone. I once knew a couple at the University who were both atheists. Keith and Lucy Burgess were their names. (Now why would I remember that useless piece of information? I should throw my head away.) Anyway, Keith and Lucy were Botany teachers or some damn thing and not only were they atheists, they taught their kids to be atheists, too. When anyone ever said, "Oh, my God," they would always answer back sassily, "You called?"—as if they were Jackie Mason or something, and had just said the most hilarious joke in the world.

Now you think that these people would eschew the trappings of an originally pagan festival celebrating the birth of a nonexistent Son of God, wouldn't you, but, no, they went Christmas Crazy every year. They sent out hundreds of Christmas cards to people, accompanied by a newsletter lovingly penned by Lucy, detailing all their boring little escapades of the previous year. The package was topped off by a slew of nauseating pix of their little darlings. While these abominations were being perpetrated on their innocent friends, Lucy and Keith carefully preserved their objectivity by choosing to say "Season's Greetings" instead of "Merry Christmas" on their cards. Excuse me, but why send them at all if you don't believe in the damn thing? They bought the tree and loads of presents for the kids and took tons of mawkish photographs on Christmas morning with the children screaming and opening presents. Of course, the day was topped off with an enormous turkey dinner with all the trimmings—finally ending with the family going to bed with distended stomachs, so they could happily fart themselves to sleep.

When I asked Keith why he put himself through all that shit when he wasn't a believer, he said, "Well, gee, it's for the kids."

I see, so the little stinkers can squeeze even more gifts and money and food out of the already shriveled husk of Daddy's bank account. Christmas was tailor-made for smart people and children to leech off the gullible. It is also designed to make us feel good about ourselves for about five minutes, until cruel reality hits on New Year's Day. We have a blissful week when the homeless are fed and sheltered before they are tossed back out on the streets; the kids are temporarily sated with toys and candy; Mommy is too exhausted from all the present wrapping and cooking to complain; and Daddy is just too pooped to pop after assembling the tree and wrestling with the Christmas lights.

Everyone is too fat and tired to make a fuss, so for a brief time the Western World is as content as it will ever be. Of course, two thirds of the world's population has never heard of Jesus Christ and couldn't care less, so the contentment level is only confined to a small segment of the population, but then who truly gives a damn? So what if half of the world's population has never made a telephone call—let alone used a computer. Unfortunately, those Third World folks wouldn't have a whole lot to say to you even if they could afford fifty cents in the first place. What have they got to phone up and chat about that isn't mind-numbingly depressing anyway?

What about, "Hello, Yankee Running Dog, I have just harvested two acres of rice today, but since I have to hand every grain over to the State, my family is starving to death."

Or maybe, "Hi, Imperialistic Oppressor, my mother just died of AIDS, just like my dad three months ago. What should I do? I am only ten years old. By the way, my country's President has just canceled elections while he and his fat wife go on a holiday to Barbados."

Or perhaps, "Gosh, Tool of the Zionists, someone just shot me with an AK47. Please advise."

Merry Fucking Christmas to all and to all a good night. We can sit here plump and happy and dream of snow drops and sugar plum fairies while the rest of the world starves and dies and suffers, mostly because of the gross stupidity of their benighted leaders and our casual indifference. Meanwhile we can kid ourselves that we are content, knowing full well that our lives are meaningless, while we work ourselves to death like drones for our ungrateful children, for our slimy bosses, for the military industrial complex, for the ever-present tax man and for the great society in which we live.

I just love Christmas, yes I do. Can't wait.

ENTRY 35

A week has passed since I last wrote anything in my journal.

I have been working out and carefully sticking to my diet. I still have a drink now and then, but I am cutting out wheat and dairy products. I feel extremely clear.

I have not seen Elene. That is the punishment I gave myself for being so stupid and lazy since the Accident. I don't deserve to see her yet. When I make the final decision about what I am going to do, then I will allow myself a visitation.

I am going out to pick up a prostitute. No matter how many cold showers I take and no matter how much I exhaust myself with exercise, I cannot get sex off my mind. I am sure that this will help, because I must be calm and clear when I decide what to do about Elene.

Sex with a prostitute means nothing. It is not as if I am being unfaithful to Elene. After all, she is a psychologist. She would be the first person to understand a man's natural urges.

ENTRY 36

Yesterday was Halloween. Exactly a year ago, I drove our car into a tree and killed my wife, killing something inside myself at the same time.

Last night, I dreamt that I was in hospital, with my arms and legs in casts suspended by ropes, helpless. I urgently wanted to shit, but couldn't.

I call for the nurse to get me a bedpan. When she comes in, I see to my horror that it is Angie. She is dressed up in a nurse's outfit and looks great, but all I care about is the bedpan. Angie tells me that the hospital has run out of bedpans and that I just have to shit in my pajamas. I refuse, ordering her to go to McDonald's and buy me a bedpan. (Why McDonald's, I'll never know. Perhaps I subliminally associate their food with crap.) Anyway, Angie refuses to get me a bedpan. She explains to me that if she sucks my cock, then she can suck the shit out of me that way.

Jesus, even I am amazed at the weirdness of this dream as I am writing it down.

I tell her to go ahead. She smiles and I see with horror that all her teeth are filed into nasty little points. I start to struggle, trying desperately to get out of the bed, but I can't move. She comes towards me and removes the bed covers. She exposes my cock, innocently standing at attention, waiting to be gobbled into that frightful mouth. Angie goes down on me and for a while it feels great. She is sucking away quite enthusiastically. Then I hear this horrifying sound, a CRUNCH. She stands up smiling, with my cock still in her mouth. I look down and see that where my penis used to be, an enormous vagina has appeared. I start screaming and Angie takes my cock out of her mouth and tells me to shut up. She hikes up her skirt and screws my cock into her vagina. Then she gets on top of me and fucks me with MY OWN COCK.

The surreal thing is that I could distinctly feel myself inside myself and—in spite of everything—it felt good. Then Angie starts to kiss me with her blood-smeared lips and I get worried that she is going to bite off my tongue next.

I woke up screaming from that one.

Call Dr. Freud. I've got an emergency!

That's it. Tonight I am finding a prostitute and getting laid. I need some relief, pronto.

ENTRY 37

I did a bad thing tonight.

It was bad, but it was good too, because the act showed me what I have to do. It showed me the path I have to take.

First of all, I want to say that I didn't go out with the intention of hurting anyone. I didn't mean to kill her, but my desires have become so overwhelming that it almost wasn't me out there tonight. I suppose I knew deep down that something was wrong, but I didn't want to think about it. Well, now I have to face up to something even darker than my fantasies.

I drove to an area that I knew was frequented by street girls and I looked around. Even in a backwater like Syracuse, there were still some foxy prostitutes to choose from. I zeroed in on a little girl, a little catlike girl, standing around on South Salina Street. God, she was pretty. I drove alongside her. She sized me up. I had gone out of my way to look like a normal, nerdy guy. I figured the glasses, the gray suit, the affable demeanor would all add up to equal a non-threatening individual.

She asked me if I wanted a date. I said yes.

She got in my car. I asked her, "How much?"

She said, "Fifty bucks for full sex."

I said, "I'll give you $200 if you do what I want." I could see the mental processes going overtime. "Was this guy a creep, or a pervert, or what? How much danger am I in?" She sized me up again.

"Hey," she's thinking, "this is a nice guy. He is so well-dressed. This could be his first time with a working girl. He is okay."

She was so right on many counts, so wrong on the crucial ones.

I let her take me to a motel that she knew by the Interstate. She got the key. She knew the guy at the reception desk and he never saw my car or me. This was to protect her as much as her client. But in the end, it was to my advantage.

We went to the room. A woefully drab place that reminded me of all the fleabags that my parents and I used to stay in during our periodic wanderings across the glorious US of A, before Daddy left us high and dry. I said to her, this little cat-like being, "You know, I've never done any bondage. If I pay you $300, will you let me tie you up?"

Well, she looked worried, but she thought of the $300 and she looked at me, Mr. Solid Citizen. I'm sure that it was the glasses. They added an air of respectability.

Anyway, she acquiesced. I had to pay her up front. She allowed me to tie her to the bed. I had brought some of Angie's old scarves especially for the occasion.

I was just beside myself. Pretty girl, half-naked, tied to the bed. She had to be half-naked. That was very important. She was still wearing her bra, panties, garter belt and stockings. She got a bit disturbed by me just staring at her and she started making little noises of protest, so I ripped off her panties and stuffed them in her mouth.

"It's okay," I told her. "Don't worry. I'm not going to hurt you." That calmed her down a bit. I started to kiss her. Her body. I pulled her bra up and sucked her nipples. She made some encouraging sounds. Her nipples got hard and erect. I was getting her hot, I could tell.

I stopped and stood up with my cock in my hand and just looked at her. All of a sudden, I got this feeling of utter—clarity—is the only way I can describe it. Cold and clear like spring water. I didn't care about this girl. She meant nothing to me, but I wanted to fuck her. She was totally helpless. God, the feeling of power it gave me.

Then a voice popped into my head and said, "Kill her. Fuck her and kill her and fuck her again." It was so loud that I looked over my shoulder to see who was there. But there was no one. It was just my friendly, neighborhood, inner demon talking.

I was still looking at her and SHE KNEW. She must have seen the change in my eyes...yes, indeed, she knew what I was thinking...and she started to...well, writhe is the best word for it. Don't women realize that when they writhe, it makes men more excited?

Seeing this girl in terror of me absolutely aroused me. I remembered the swimming girl in the crystal pool, looking scared and sexy. Why are women so ravishing when they are frightened? My cock was so hard that it was almost painful. Oh, it was beautiful. The cat-like girl knew she was going to die. And I knew that I was going to kill her. But I was determined to make her come, before she went. That was the challenge. That was the art.

I got completely undressed. I put on a condom. Then I thought, "Hold on a minute, make this LAST." So I didn't fuck her then and there. I went down on her. I spread her legs wide and I stuck my tongue up her pussy as far as it could go. I licked her from her clit to her anus. Talk about writhe. Writhe and shine, baby. It was like honey in there. She started to pump away and I made her climax. I didn't think she was faking it, but by God, it didn't matter, nothing mattered at that moment, because I made her come in spades. It was like Niagara Falls in there.

Okay. It was my turn. Her panties were still stuffed in her mouth. I took them out and I kissed her. I knew prostitutes hated to be kissed. I thrust my tongue down her throat and she was making noises as if she liked it. Did I believe her? I disengaged. I stuffed her panties back in her mouth. She got panicky and started to wriggle around again. That just got me even more excited, if that was possible.

I made sure the condom was still on and I fucked her. I penetrated her and she was screaming behind the gag. God, the rush of power. I fucked her and fucked her. I made her come again. I did. A prostitute. I mean what is the chance of that? These girls must fuck a thousand guys a year. But I made her come. And as she came, at the peak of her orgasm, I took her by her smooth soft throat. I squeezed very gently and I could see in her eyes that it was heightening her pleasure. Her pelvis was pounding into mine, faster and faster. I had to wait and make sure that she was at the height. That was the utter science of the act. My little work of art. I pressed harder against her throat. I ripped the gag out and I strangled her. I could see in her eyes that it was the best sex that she ever had. Then I kissed her and I stole her last breath. Was it sweet? It was the sweetest! Her tongue was sticking right out and I sucked it in. The best. It was the best.

The moment she died, she came, I came. Total bliss. The feeling of control. It was an epiphany. Yes, I shall use that biblical phrase. I knew right then and there what I was made for.

I rested for a while. I felt good about what I had done, even though I knew it was a bad thing. The experience had been beyond satisfaction. I lay next to her and caressed her body. I kissed her all over and thanked her for giving me such a wonderful time. I gently untied her. Then, I arranged her body in the same position as the blue-skinned refrigerator girl in my dream, with her legs wide open. I stood up and looked at her for what seemed to be a long time.

I stared at her open pussy as if I would find the meaning of the universe in there if I looked hard enough. I started to feel like I had in my dream and I became aroused again. I looked at her—beautiful, quiet, dead, mine—and I knew that I had to do more.

I also realized that I had to be careful. I removed the used condom, wrapped it in toilet paper and put it in my jacket pocket. I put on a new one. I placed a pillow under her lovely ass, then I fucked my pretty little cat-like girl one more time and if anything, it was more exciting and fulfilling than the first time.

I possessed her totally, utterly, without argument.

Afterwards, I cleaned up thoroughly and left nothing behind. I stole the bottom sheet off the bed. I even took the money I gave her, although for some absurd reason, it made me feel guilty. After all, she had taken care of me so beautifully. I filled the bathtub and washed her. I tenderly sponged away the traces of my presence from her body (paying special attention to her mouth and vagina) and then carefully dried her and put her back in the bed.

As I was looking at her for the last time, an image flashed into my head. It was gone in an instant. I desperately wanted to recapture it, because I knew that somehow it was very important. So I sat there on the edge of the bed and took in every detail of the girl's body: the position of the limbs, the way her hair tumbled over the pillow and hung over the bed, the expression of her face. After about ten minutes, it came to me. My little cat-like girl reminded me of an obscure painting by French expressionist Henri Ottmann called *The Sleeping Courtesan* (1920). I only had to arrange her arms above her so that her hands cradled her head to make the picture complete.

I allowed myself ten more minutes just to stare at her perfection.

I carefully covered her up with a clean sheet from the closet before I left the room. I didn't want policemen to gaze at her in all her naked glory and get turned on. I wanted her to know that she belonged to me, only me, forever. My pretty little cat-like girl.

It was so easy to escape. Sad to say, but who really cares about the death of a prostitute? The police hardly bother to investigate hooker murders. Society considers that kind of woman so expendable.

So, I did a bad thing, but the bad thing had a good result. It has given me a direction. I know now what my purpose is. I know what I am made for. I know how I can get to meet Elene. This will take a lot of planning and research. I don't want to get caught. I don't want to have some documentary made about me so people can say, "What a dummy. Look at all the mistakes he made. He deserved to get caught."

So much work to do and so little time to do it in.

ENTRY 38

I woke up this morning and, for a split second, I thought it had all been a dream. Then I read last night's entry and realized that it had really happened. I had DONE SOMETHING. I felt no guilt, which was strange. It was almost as if it was just another dream, just another fantasy, hurting no one.

I checked the papers. There was no mention of a murder in a motel by the Interstate. It was as if the whole thing had never happened.

As I read (and reread) my entry from last night, I got aroused. I seem to be possessed by powerful sexual urges over which I have no control. Somehow, I have to find the strength to discipline myself. My brain is overheating with desire and I need it cold and clear to plan my strategy.

And I thought stalking Elene was going to be fun. This is going to be even better. This will be my life's work, the culmination of all those years of depression, frustration, fear, weakness, anger and hate. It will be glorious.

I am going to create a serial killer. That should get Elene's notice.

ENTRY 39

Father, it has been a month since my last confession and, like the good little boy that I am, I have spent the time industriously researching my new Project.

First, in the comfort of my own home, I surfed the Net. I downloaded and read the biographies of over a hundred serial killers, courtesy of The Serial Killer Hit List web site and others. Then I moseyed on over to Amazon.com, where I was able to find out which books would help me most on my quest.

It is interesting to see how many sites are dedicated to crime in general, and murder in particular. At the end of the week, I copied all my personal files to a portable hard drive and then wiped my internal hard drive. I memorized and destroyed my notes. During my surfing, I made sure that the sites themselves would not be able to place tracer cookies on my hard drive. Even so, I erased all temporary Internet files that might have accumulated, as well as any stray cookies before I reformatted my hard drive, just to be on the safe side.

At the weekend, I went to New York City again and visited a few bookstores around Manhattan. I bought the books that I required, always with cash and never too many from one shop to cause comment.

The books I bought were all solid research material that included professional guides to homicide detection, serial killer profiling manuals and books detailing the psychology and methodology of psychopaths. Finally, I bought quite a few books on the serial killer poster boy himself, Theodore Robert Bundy, Esquire. Ted was one of a small percentage of highly intelligent serial killers and he also did his research well before he began his personal project of death. I also bought one very good textbook on Forensic Psychology, but, as I suspected, it was virtually indecipherable.

I read solidly for three weeks. I kept to my diet and worked out, but every other waking moment was reserved for my research.

It was fascinating.

Little fun details stand out, like the alarming fact that many serial killers used Volkswagen Beetles as their stalking cars (either that or vans). You wouldn't catch me dead in a Beetle, let me tell you. If I can't go out and stalk girls in my late, lamented wife's BMW, then I'm not going. Ha, Ha, Ha.

However, I've decided to obtain a car that is more unobtrusive. Maybe even a couple of cars. That would confuse the police. Price is no object in pursuit of my dream.

I made a list of all the large, popular nightclubs and bars in town.

More people equal more camouflage. I figured that I should target so-called "medium risk" females. Party girls who aren't prostitutes, but who are willing to take a risk with the occasional mysterious stranger. (Aren't most women?) I rejected prostitutes as prey because I didn't want to be seen in red light districts. I assumed that places like that would have a fairly regular police presence. Also, killing prostitutes is so easy. It's like shooting fish in a barrel. I felt in need of a challenge. Pretty ladies, in their late twenties/early thirties, professionals who like to work hard and play hard. Girls like my late wife for instance. Medium height, good-looking brunettes/dark blondes with fair skin. Serial killers normally pick victims for a "goodness of fit." That is the extraordinary phrase the FBI use: the "fit" being women who remind the killer of his ex-wife, or his mother, or his sister. In other words, a woman with whom the serial killer came into conflict often. And why should I be any different? Of course, the difference is that serial killers rarely kill the actual object of their ire (or even desire), while I did, but that's a minor detail.

I read with interest all the breakthroughs with DNA testing and thanked my lucky stars that I cleaned up so thoroughly at my first crime scene. Even so, according to Locard's Principle, I probably took something of the scene away with me (as well as the sweet memories), and I presumably left something behind, but there is no point in crying over spilled milk now. It is just very important to be aware of all the dangers and pitfalls.

While I was in New York, I also bought a box of heavy-duty surgical gloves (thin ones can leave behind finger prints), a lot of Trojan condoms (America's most popular brand), and some magic markers in assorted colors.

I also purchased a brand-new Oreck vacuum cleaner. I chose it because (according to the commercials) it was widely used in hotels across the globe because of its power, maneuverability, compact shape and lightness. It would easily fit in the trunk of my car.

THIS IS THE PLAN

I will visit various nightclubs and bars in Syracuse and target ten victims. After stalking them and checking out their lifestyles, I will choose five women who will be my ultimate targets. Then, the fun will begin.

I will pick up and murder a girl every other Friday night. After I kill her, I will paint her body with unusual designs (still to be decided upon). I got that idea from The Tamiami Strangler. He painted a message on the body of his third victim and his calligraphy was so artistic that I was quite struck by it. Decorating the bodies of my victims would make my crimes a little out of the ordinary, with a touch of the outré. I don't want to go as far as Richard Ramirez (AKA The Nightstalker) and pop my victims' eyeballs onto a dinner plate. Torture is out and mutilation is disgusting. I want to enjoy this, so strangulation and decoration are the only methods of operation that I can contemplate.

I am hoping that by painting intriguing and mysterious designs on my victims, I may be asked to assist the investigation. After all, who knows more about arcane art in this town than I do? In all probability, Elene will be asked to consult on the cases, so I am hoping that this will be my entrance into a world of fun, murder and romance.

I can't explain how alive I feel, how exhilarated. My self-confidence has grown. Not as far as approaching Elene in a normal manner is concerned, of course, but it seems that in every other aspect of my life I feel more in control. It is wonderful. A miracle.

I look back at my earlier entries and read the thoughts of a dead man. Well, I am dead no longer. The flowers of evil are blossoming into full bloom.

There are many things I have to sort out yet, but I feel that events are progressing in the right direction. What I will have to do before I start is to find a safe place to hide my diary. If someone found it and read it, it would be incriminating, to say the least. But I can't burn it. I can't get rid of it. I need to write everything down. It has a calming effect on my mind.

If Elene only knew what I was going through for her. Boy, is she going to get a surprise.

ENTRY 40

I went out and bought a new, wide-screen, LCD television today. I realized that my incipient burst of enthusiasm about my so-called media diet had waned and if I was smart, I'd keep tuned to the local news to find out what was happening in the world. Not that the radio, the newspapers and the Internet didn't give me enough information, but suddenly I felt disconnected without a TV.

It was also a great vehicle for venting my stress. I even invested in several "TV Bricks" to throw at offending programs. Nothing like a cheerful evening in front of the idiot box to reaffirm my conviction that the world is ruled by imbeciles.

ENTRY 41

I was glancing through one of my particularly grisly and humorless research books and was fascinated to read about the psychology of evil and malignant narcissism. Mentally healthy "good" people just naturally submit themselves to some kind of higher authority, like God, or their conscience (which many religious people believe is some kind of inner light from God), while the "evil" ones just merrily follow their own will, their own impulses and desires, without feeling guilty at all. How delicious is that?

Why should I submit my will to anyone, be they God, or the police, or the government? What if I don't believe in a religion, or truth, or whatever? Did any of the illustrious men of history that we all venerate with such fervor submit their wills to a higher authority? Did Alexander the Great worry about who he was going to offend when he conquered half the known world? Did Julius Caesar? Did Napoleon, or Wellington, or Churchill, or Eisenhower, or any of the so-called great generals and leaders who are the subjects of innumerable TV shows and whose lives are written about ad nauseam in countless books?

We admire those who can make a ruthless decision; those who can lead us; those who can make the tough call without hesitation. People have always equated strength with ruthlessness, because most of us are inhibited by our conscience.

Well, not me. Not anymore. I may not have the military genius of a Caesar or a Napoleon. I may not have whatever it takes to send thousands to their deaths in battle, or order countless civilians firebombed into ashes, or condemn millions of people to eke out a miserable existence in Gulags or concentration camps. But I do know that I have the will to do something. Something artistic. Something creative. Something about death. I have proved it. I have the will and the power and the intelligence to succeed in my Project.

I have an ideal and I will continue to work towards that ideal. My ideal's name is Elene, but it won't be I who will be the one doing the submitting. My ideal will submit to me.

ENTRY 42

I have picked the lucky contestants in my game of death. Five beautiful women will soon be the fortunate ones to have the privilege of dying at my hands. Not one of the girls had a clue that someone was watching over their lives. I was peering down a microscope at my pretty little specimens and they were as unaware of me as a strain of bacteria would be of an observing scientist. (I read somewhere that we all carry around five pounds of bacteria in our bodies. It doesn't bear thinking about.)

AND THE WINNERS ARE:

Tamsin Kearney: Age 27, 5'6", slim build, single, Caucasian, dark blonde hair. Works as a legal secretary at Bourke, Cox, and Lucas, Attorneys at Law. Lives at 430 Onondaga Avenue. Tamsin likes aerobic classes, going to the movies, fast cars and faster guys. I saw her in action at Trexx, the gay disco in downtown Syracuse that caters to all walks of life. She is a real party animal, but only on weekends. Monday mornings, she is up with the lark and working hard. Her other favorite haunts are The Liquid Lounge and Club Mirage.

Katrin Franklin: Age 29, 5'7", shapely, divorced, Caucasian, brunette. Works as dental hygienist at the Edelstein Clinic near the U. Lives at 503 Ackerman Avenue. (Close to Elene!) Katrin likes going to the gym and doing a bit of amateur dramatics at the Salt City Playhouse. Doesn't go out that much, but when she does, whoa mamma! She likes Awful Al's Cigar Bar and Charades.

Susie Morton: Age 30, 5'5", slim build with a superb butt, single, Caucasian, brunette. Works as a personal assistant at Collins, Randell and Wynn

Stockbrokers in downtown Syracuse. Lives at 44302 Salina Street. Susie likes going to dinner with her girlfriends at the weekend, then heading off to the nearest singles bar to pick up a guy for the night. Aren't these girls worried about AIDS and other STDs? I'm concerned about the chances they take, honestly. She goes to Sh-Boom's in Liverpool and Viva Debris Comedy Club.

Nancy Staniak: Age 31, 5'6", athletic build, single, Caucasian, brunette. Works as a beautician at the Base Cutz Hair Salon. Lives at 56777 Genesee Street. Nancy cheerfully fulfills every cliché one has ever heard about hairdressers. Likes eating, drinking to excess (yet again, only at the weekends—each one of my girls has a highly developed sense of responsibility), and exercising—aerobic and the other kind. She frequents Nibsy's Pub and Styleen's Rhythm Palace.

Kim Marie Eyler: Age 29, 5'8", slim build, divorced, Caucasian, dark blonde, assistant accountant at Simon, Lang and Aronson, Chartered Accountants. Lives at 3543 Sanger Street. Kim Marie is a bit of a dark horse, but she is a beauty. Goes out a lot with her friends, but seems lonely. I am sure that she will be suitably grateful when I pick her up on the night of her Date With Destiny. She goes to the bar at the Sheraton or the Turning Stone Casino Bar in Verona.

I didn't choose anyone who worked at the University. You don't shit in your own nest. Too risky.

None of my ladies have any connection with each other. This is an important factor, as my acts must appear random. They all live in their own places that are set back from the road to give them (and me) privacy. None of them live close to me, which is also a crucial factor. The typical serial killer's first victim is frequently located in the so-called "Comfort Zone," an area where he feels at home. The police often target the first Victim's neighborhood and workplace, because it is possible that the killer might have observed her there before he struck. I won't be making that mistake.

There is a special indefinable quality about my girls. All have an obvious spark, but there is also an air of vulnerability about them that singles them out. There was a certain something about each one of my targets that attracted me to them. It hung around them like a cloud of perfume. What it was, I don't know. I'm not sure that I ascribe to the theory of the "born victim', but I am sure that it was a combination of certain genetic factors, plus a basic unawareness of potential dangers plus, perhaps, a whiff of desperation. Since my ladies were all close to or past thirty, single or divorced, it might explain an over-eagerness to please.

As a lion sniffs out a weak member of the herd and marks it for its prey, so I single out my victims for my Project. My sweet, little troupe of goddesses will soon be joining all the other beauties in The Victim of a Serial Killer Hall of Fame.

ENTRY 43

I have been working out, keeping to my diet and discreetly following my ladies. A couple of times a week, I indulge myself and follow Elene.

She sees the police guy every Thursday. I don't understand why they keep going out, because they always end up squabbling.

I visited the Chamber of Commerce and picked up a schedule of events for the year. One of the traits of a serial killer is that he is fluid in his tactics. At first, I had wanted to keep to a rigid timetable—killing a girl precisely every two weeks—but taking all the various elements into consideration it is wiser to be more adaptable.

I plan to make my move whenever there is a convention or a conference in town, or when there is a "Big Game" or some other event at the University. An influx of strangers into town gives me more protection, more camouflage. I checked out some of my victims' hang-out during the week and they were virtually deserted, so doing the deed at the weekend is still the best option. I have to be careful not to draw too much attention to myself. I already feel overexposed. Also, I have decided to go back to teaching. It will be a strain, but I think the cover will be helpful.

A couple of weeks ago, one of my neighbors said, "Oh Michael, you must be feeling better. I never see your car in the driveway!" That worried me. My absence from the house had been noticed. I am not working, so my neighbors are wondering what I am up to, the nosy bastards. That is the hazard of living in such an isolated place. Perhaps I should move to an apartment in town.

Last week, I went to that haven of anonymity, New York City, to buy a second-hand car with cash. It is a medium-sized, silver gray, 2005 Dodge Neon sedan with no distinguishing features. I drove the car back upstate and parked it in a space that I have rented for cash in advance under an assumed name at a parking garage near Hancock Airport. Lots of traffic around there, so hopefully my comings and goings won't be noticed.

I have gone over everything in my mind a hundred times. My fear is that my confidence will desert me at a critical moment. Then, I had a bit of a revelation. Serial killers often do practice runs, so why shouldn't I do the same? I'll go out one night at random and see if I can just pick up a girl and buy her drinks. Then the next time, I will choose a different girl, buy her drinks, drive her home and give her a peck on the cheek. Then the next time...hold on, I don't want to get a reputation as the town Lothario. One trial run is all that I will allow myself.

This is a game. A game of wits with my prey and I cannot be thrown by any untoward circumstances such as rejection, for example. I must not take any rebuff personally. I also must not display any anger, anything that might frighten off the pretty gazelles. A cool, calm attitude, keen observation, unobtrusive stalking, passionate seduction, and then the final *coup de grâce*. That's all it takes...I can't wait to begin.

ENTRY 44

Tonight is the night for my practice run. I have selected the girl. She was one of the initial ten that I whittled down to five, so I was already aware of her lifestyle patterns. Her name is Carol Kurland. She is 28, 5'5", slim, dark brown hair, single. She works for a small desktop publishing firm that is located downtown. She likes going to the ballet and the Syracuse Symphony. Carol is a bit dull, which is why I rejected her, but she is quite faithful about going out every Friday night with her friends.

MY PREPARATIONS

1. I took a long luxurious bath. I normally take showers, but I needed to relax. I thought things out and imagined different scenarios, even ones where I just came home and did nothing. I tried to prepare my mind for every eventuality.

2. I picked out what I was going to wear very carefully. It was important to look well-dressed, but not flashy or conspicuous. I chose gray and black as my color combination. I combed my hair in a different way, so it covered the small scar on the left side of my forehead. (The one obvious physical reminder of my Accident.) I was wearing a pair of tinted glasses that hid the color of my eyes. After a lot of hard work, my body was in good shape and my limp had finally disappeared. The doctors had done a fairly competent job at patching me up after all.

I looked at myself in the mirror and was shocked. I looked okay. I had barely given the mirror a glance in the past few months because my self-loathing was at such a crisis point, but now there was something different about the intriguingly nondescript guy looking back at me. I remembered what that something was: purpose! Yes, I had a purpose and, boy, does that add a spring to the step of any man.

I put my raincoat on. Nestled in the copious inside pockets was a pair of surgical gloves, several condoms and some indelible magic markers in red, black and blue. I placed the vacuum cleaner in the trunk of my car, with a few large strong garbage bags.

I will continue my entry on my return...

LATER

The evening went well.

I drove to the airport and picked up my stalking car and transferred all my equipment. Then I went to Regina's near Armory Square, where I was confident that I would find Carol. I left my raincoat in the car. I parked down the block and around the corner from the actual premises.

Regina's was dimly lit, which comforted me. There was a huge aquarium behind the bar and the place was heaving with young, well-dressed professionals. Large chandeliers hung from the ceiling and the walls were painted blood red. Vermilion couches with pink throw cushions were dotted about the place. It was like being in a noisy Baroque womb.

Carol was there at the bar surrounded by a gaggle of friends. She was with them, yet slightly outside the group, like a vulnerable deer at the edge of a herd. The background music was quite loud, so approaching her was problematic. It isn't easy to execute a subtle pick up if you are shouting, so I just hung back and observed her for a while. I leaned casually on the bar and asked the bartender for a vodka martini with just a whisper of vermouth, shaken not stirred, two olives. As the ice-cold vodka slipped down my throat, I had an immediate hit of warmth and well-being. I just had to take things slow and easy.

I watched Carol. She was a little livelier than the last time I had seen her, but I could tell that she was bored. She kept looking around, trying to make eye contact with various guys, but they ignored her for some reason. She was attractive, but she lacked some spark, some elusive sensual quality.

I smiled and thought, "Don't do anything. If it is meant to be, Carol will come to you." At that very moment, she spotted me. She caught me smiling at her. She smiled back. I turned away and feigned embarrassment. I took a drink, looked at the fish in the tank, counted to ten and then looked up again, over my glasses in a sneaky kind of way. She was still looking at me and still smiling.

Contact.

I held up my martini and mouthed, "Would you like a drink?" She nodded enthusiastically and moved away from her friends. They didn't notice her leaving.

Excellent.

She came over and introduced herself. I told her my name was John Smith. She laughed and said that with a pseudonym like that, I must be married. I said, "No, I just have the most boring name in the world. Did you know that there are twenty-six John Smiths in the Syracuse telephone book?"

She thought that was funny.

I can't be bothered to record every word of our conversation. Suffice it to say that I was as amusing as I could muster. I kept an eye on her friends, but they were totally absorbed in themselves. I suggested that perhaps we should go someplace quieter. Carol agreed wholeheartedly.

We left. No one noticed us. We walked around the corner to The Manhattan Lounge, which was busy but at least the noise level was tolerable. We managed to arrive just as some people were leaving, so we were able to grab the sofa near the window.

More desultory conversation ensued. Carol was no brain surgeon, but she was a sweet girl. She was so easy-going, I was sure that I could have wrangled an invitation to her bed. I even contemplated starting my Grand Project tonight as I had all my supplies with me, but I rejected the idea. I hadn't decided on what form my paintings would take and, as lovely as Carol was, she just didn't excite me. She didn't fit the ideal image in my mind, so the thought of trying to seduce her didn't appeal.

An hour later I took her home and gently kissed her on the cheek. She gave me her telephone number and looked hopeful. I drove to the airport, switched cars and toddled off home, very content with my progress.

It would have been so easy to snuff out Carol's life, but I chose not to do it. The whole evening gave me an enormous boost of confidence. A little voice inside my head said, "Hey, if you feel this good about yourself, why not try to arrange an 'accidental meeting' with Elene. Try and date her legitimately."

The idea made me feel instantly let down and—let's face it—disappointed. I have to admit that I am really looking forward to starting The Project. I want that rush of power again, like the first time with my little cat-like girl. I know that at this stage, I can't feel that way with Elene.

I don't want to lose sight of the ultimate purpose of the whole plan, of course, but the prospect of feeling so godlike again made abandoning The Project unthinkable at this point.

ENTRY 45

I know that human beings dream every night, but for the past few months I can only seem to remember the ones involving sex. Obviously, my body didn't understand why I refused to seduce a willing and beautiful young woman last night and decided to punish me by contriving yet another libidinous dream-fest.

I am back in the dingy motel room with the little cat-like prostitute. I have just killed her and I am untying her. I enter her and every detail of the second time I screwed her when she was dead is reproduced flawlessly. I am just about to come when she suddenly comes to life like a young tigress. She flips me over onto my back with her legs like a female Bruce Lee. Now she is on top, riding me, and I can see that she is close to orgasm, as am I. She is hitting me and screaming, "You bastard, you killed me!" I keep telling her to keep it down as the neighbors might hear. Then she reaches out, grabs me by the throat with both hands and starts to squeeze. Oh, boy, the sensation is terrific. In my dream point of view, I am on my back looking up at her and every perception is magnified. I can even feel her breath on my face. I am close to blacking out and then I come. She comes too. While she is in the throes of orgasm, I grab her by the throat. There we are, both trying to murder each other, both coming, both with our tongues sticking out to the max. I bring her down as I feel her grip loosening and I kiss her. I can almost feel her tongue in my mouth now as I write this. I kiss her and strangle her and fuck her and I relive in my dream the whole experience of sucking out her last breath.

I woke up in drenched sheets again. Shouldn't wet dreams stop once you are out of adolescence?

I lay there panting for a long time, hardly able to get my breath. Against my will, my mind started fantasizing about Elene, that she was the one I was fucking, that she was the one on top, strangling me. So predictable, but I started to masturbate and I came again.

I have tried not to think of Elene in that way, but it was inevitable that she would enter into my darker fantasies. I thought that she was purer than that. Elene was supposed to be the undefiled and bright love object, but, no, she has fallen into the video nasty vault in the basement of my mind for all time now, along with the others. In a crazy way, it is a relief.

This wouldn't have happened if I had taken Carol last night. It would have been so effortless. All these poor little girls wandering around nightclubs searching for Mr. Right. Don't they realize that Mr. Right doesn't go to nightclubs? He is at home getting his shut-eye so he has the energy to be a nice guy in the morning.

Can't they see that I am not a nice guy? Don't they have any defensive radar that shouts: "Beware, sicko ahead?" Don't they notice the pictures in my mind projecting onto my forehead like some Saturday Afternoon Creature Feature? My fantasies are now so intense that I am surprised that people don't recoil from me on the street.

I guess they can't see into the depths of my blackened soul. They can't see what is going on in my head. Thank goodness, or I wouldn't be sitting here now.

My dream world is now so powerful that everyday life is a pale shadow. My fantasies are so pervasive that they seem to be slipping into reality and out again, like watching two televisions at the same time.

Last night, I wasn't ready, but the next time I will be.

I want this.

ENTRY 46

Last week was taken up with more research, about art this time, not murder. My extensive library of art history books was very helpful, as well as the numerous gallery sites on the Web.

There are going to be two threads of artistry flowing through my work. The first will be the unusual positions of the body. I have chosen to pose each of my ladies to mirror one of five portraits of Venus, the Goddess of Love.

The Paintings Are:
1. *Venus of Urbino* (Tiziano Vecellio AKA Titian, 1538)
2. *An Allegory of Venus and Cupid (Agnolo Bronzino, 1550)*
3. *The Sleep of Venus* (Marie-Françoise-Constance Mayer-Lamartinière, 1806)
4. *The Birth of Venus* (Sandro Botticelli, 1485-86)
5. *Sleeping Venus* (Paul Delvaux, 1947)

I thought that the choice of the Goddess of Love was quite apt. I have decided that, in addition to the capture of my ultimate love object, my Project should have the dual purpose of creating new stars in the serial killer firmament.

I have an alternate painting if I get bored near the culmination of The Project and it is an exception to the mythic subjects that I have previously chosen. I was arrested by the model's pose in Caravaggio's lost masterpiece *Mary Magdalene in Ecstasy* (1610). She was so sensual in her rapturous state that I felt that I had to include it in my little gallery. I am a big fan of Caravaggio and I think it is rather endearing that he preferred painting Mary Magdalene to Venus any day, as he had an affinity for prostitutes. I can understand that.

Now, here's an interesting problem. The images that I paint on my victims must be quick and simple to execute, yet at the same time strange and puzzling to the authorities. What to choose? For a while—having admired the scribblings of the Tamiami Strangler so much—I considered the idea of artfully writing some literature on my beauties' bodies. I thought that the beautifully sinister poems of the decadent French poet, Baudelaire, might be appropriate, since he had such a gloriously warped mind. His poems were all about the ephemerality of life, the finality of death, the lure of evil and the yawning abyss that is love, but I am in two minds about it. The sentiment is nice, but are poems too pretentious?

The other possibility is using the symbolic objects displayed in each of my chosen paintings. For example, in Botticelli's *The Birth of Venus*, the most obvious item is the scallop shell on which the goddess is standing. There are also the gold-hearted roses that fall from the lips of the spirits of the wind, Zephyr and Chloris. However, I don't want the girls to end up looking like Maori warriors. Whatever I choose, it will have to be beautiful and simple. Also, I am not the best of artists. "Those who can—do, those who can't—teach," as George Bernard Shaw so rightly said. I don't want to spend hours working on something that turns out to look like the finger paintings of a toddler. That is not the effect I am looking for. I want my art to shock and disturb.

ENTRY 47

I was puttering through my library and came across a book about alchemy. The symbols in the book were quite arcane and have the added element of being in the realm of the occult. Anything to do with the occult will bound to concern the authorities. I can just hear them now: "Oh, no, a Satanist is killing our lovely local girls!" People have a tendency to become hysterical about the occult and hence not think too clearly or logically about motive. I am not saying that the police will simply freak out and call for a priest, but any seeds of confusion that I can sow will be to my advantage.

If I mix a touch of alchemy with a soupçon of Baudelaire poetry and add my classical Venus poses, then we just might have something here.

I have a little leeway before The Project begins in earnest, so I have ample time to decide and then practice my handiwork. There is a conference of software designers in town soon, God help us, so when the hordes descend, the wolf in sheep's clothing can safely infiltrate the flock.

ENTRY 48

The more research I do into the mysteries of alchemy, the more comparisons I find relating to my Venus Project.

Most people assume that the basic aims of alchemy were to transform base metals such as lead or copper into silver or gold. They think of alchemy as a pseudo-science, an esoteric predecessor of chemistry whose precepts were lost in the mists of time. The whole idea of changing base metal into gold seems ludicrous to modern minds. The elements on the Periodic Chart are immutable, aren't they? Well, scientists may have thought that a while ago, but the use of atomic power proves that we can alter elements. Humans have a frightening capacity for altering the planet, species by species, rock by rock. Soon, no molecule will be safe from the marauding hordes of scientists wanting to change its DNA, or modify its gene pool, or clone it, or bombard it with fusion or fission. We are cloning sheep, creating glow-in-the-dark kittens and developing human ears on mice (one of THE most disturbing images of recent times), so who is to say that in a few years' time, we won't be turning lead into gold?

The vital principle of alchemy that most people miss is that it wasn't only about changing lead into gold. It was also about the attainment of the perfection and purification of the alchemist's soul. It was about finding the mysterious Elixir that would prolong life. It was all about TRANSFORMATION.

Now, that's the word that leapt off the page and struck me right between the eyes.

As I was leaving my lovely little cat-like girl, the thing that struck me was how transformed she had become. No longer the sad street whore, she had metamorphosed into a goddess. She was beautiful beyond compare, as well as being ALL MINE, FOREVER. She will always be a goddess in my mind.

It all fits so wonderfully. I chose images of the Goddess of Love to be my templates without even realizing how meaningful it will turn out to be. Meaningful for me and for Elene.

ENTRY 49

The 13th century alchemist and magician Albertus Magnus devised the following rules and conditions that the alchemist should observe in his pursuit. I find the parallels with the rules that I will be following in my own Project of Transformation quite startling:

First. The alchemist should be discreet and silent, revealing to no one the result of his operation. *(This is just common sense. Most serial killers keep their mouths shut, for good reason.)*

Second. He should reside in a private house in an isolated situation. *(My home in Manlius is made to order.)*

Third. He should choose his days and hours for labor with discretion. (Thanks to the Chamber of Commerce schedule, I have chosen the nights for my labor in advance.)

Fourth. He should have patience, diligence, and perseverance. *(Got them in spades.)*

Fifth. He should perform according to fixed rules. (I am following the tried and tested rules of the best killers in the business.)

Sixth. He should use only vessels of glass or glazed earthenware. *(Well, there had to be something that didn't fit.)*

Seventh. He should be sufficiently rich to bear the expenses of his art. *(Thanks to darling departed Angie, I have no financial worries.)*

Eighth. He should avoid having anything to do with princes and noblemen. *(I'll make a leap of thought here and say that Albertus was advising his compatriots to stay away from those in authority, which, needless to say, I will.)*

The more I read about alchemy the less I understand, but it is compelling stuff. Carl Jung studied it for ten years before he could make any sense of it. In the final analysis (the pun is intended), Jung felt that alchemy had more to do with the psychological transformation of the soul than any material change. But he would say that, wouldn't he?

I have to watch it, though, because I can see myself getting so caught up with my research into alchemy that The Venus Project's starting date will pass and I would have blown it. And that wouldn't do. That wouldn't do at all.

ENTRY 50

Tonight I went out with the express purpose of killing someone. I succeeded and it felt so good.

Everything went according to plan. I prepared myself in the identical way as the practice run, even down to the change in hairstyle and the tinted glasses. I switched cars and headed over to The Liquid Lounge to pick up Tamsin. I arrived in plenty of time. I found myself a good position at the bar to observe and ordered my usual vodka martini. I felt very good about myself. Confident. Untouchable. It is as if an obscene and twisted God of Serial Killers gave me redemption and protection.

I think it is because I have a secret that no one knows about and no one will ever know about. Even now, that secret gives me power and I feel unstoppable.

Tamsin arrived, looking radiant in a jade green dress that highlighted her fair complexion. My loins stirred just looking at her, but I had to remain in control. I waited for the moment to make my move.

Tamsin had a couple of drinks and then went on to the dance floor. She danced beautifully, gracefully, unlike most of her contemporaries. She was dancing by herself with none of the self-consciousness that would normally make such an act attention-seeking. She made lots of eye contact with the men on the floor. Her dress rode up her thighs. She looked good enough to eat.

I decided to take the bull by the horns. If she turned me down, I could always move on to another candidate. I walked up to her, did a little bow and took her by the hand. She was startled, but amused. We moved around sizing each other up. The only dance that I had ever learned was the salsa, so I began to do some simple steps and she laughingly followed. This lasted for about ten minutes, then I gestured to the bar. She nodded.

The dance of death had begun.

We ordered. We drank. We talked. I pretended to be a software salesman with the conference. Tamsin said that she only knew basic stuff about computers. I told her that the last thing I wanted to do was talk shop. I just wanted to listen to her. She liked that, as I knew she would. Most women assume that men only want to talk about themselves and they would be right. However, since I wanted something out of Tamsin—her life—I was willing to forgo the usual thrill of spouting off about myself to hear all about her. And how trivial her life was. So small, so mundane, so dull. How could she bear living it? However, I endured, because I knew that the evening would end with a bang.

During our conversation, I kept a discreet eye on the crowd surrounding us. No one seemed very interested. They were all too involved in themselves.

I bought more drinks. I had to make sure that my victims were fairly inebriated. I have observed that women are more vulnerable and open to suggestion when they are drunk. Strange men look much more interesting and handsome. Potential risks are ignored. Female sexual energy is also at a higher-than-normal level.

After about forty minutes, I said that I had to leave, because I had a breakfast meeting in the morning. Tamsin looked disappointed. I told her that I would love to give her a lift home. Even though it was quite early, she said yes.

No one took any notice when we left.

We drove to her place. We chatted and laughed and it was very pleasant. For one millisecond I considered not doing it, but then I caught a glimpse of those divine legs and thought, "Don't be stupid. She is yours for the taking, if you want her."

I escorted Tamsin to the front door of her house. I asked her if I could kiss her goodnight. She seemed touched at my gentlemanly good manners. She said yes. I took off my glasses and put them carefully in my pocket. Then I kissed her lips very gently, sensually, not forcing it, taking my time. I could tell she liked it. I placed my hand behind her head, caressing her hair. She liked that, too. Then I was a bit more forceful and tongued her. She really liked that. We kissed for a long time, and then I stopped myself.

I said, "Tamsin, I have to go now." She looked sad and asked why. I said, "Let's just say that I better go before I reach the point of no return."

She acted coy and said, "What's the point of no return?"

I said, "You know what I mean."

Tamsin said, "No, I don't."

So I take her hand and put it between my legs on my hardening penis. "That point of no return," I say.

Tamsin smiles. It is a smile full of promise.

"Maybe I've reached the point of no return myself," she says.

She takes my hand, guides it under her coat and puts it on her right breast. Her head goes back and she sighs deeply. Then she kisses me, sticking her tongue in my mouth as far as it can go. I am almost taken aback. Girls nowadays seem to know what they want and they aren't afraid to ask for it.

Tamsin says, "Let's go inside, it's freezing out here."

I say, "This is crazy, we hardly know each other."

She smiles again and says, "That's what makes it so exciting."

We go inside. I have achieved the entry of her premises in less than ninety minutes from the moment of meeting her.

Tamsin shuts the door and I take off my coat and hang it up. When I turn around, she already has her dress off—can you believe it? I say, "Hold on, girl, I like to do some things myself." She laughs.

She is wearing a silk jade green panties and bra set, to match her dress.

I put both my hands on her breasts and push her up against the front door, just rough enough to be exciting. Then I tug her bra straps down to expose her breasts, soft snowy little bundles that feel so warm and alive under my hands. She tells me to stop, all the while lifting her arms above her head, giving herself to me. I pinch her left nipple hard and she squeaks a bit, but I shut her up by kissing her. I continue to twist her left nipple while my other hand searches for and finds her pussy. She opens up her legs a bit. I push aside the damp silk of her panties and stick my middle finger deep inside her. It's hot and wet in there. She likes what I am doing. She wiggles around appreciatively.

I quit kissing her. "Where's your bedroom?" I whisper.

Tamsin takes my hands away from her body and leads me to her bedroom at the back of the house.

The room is dominated by a large American Colonial-style four-poster bed. The perfect frame for my painting. She asks me if I want a glass of wine. I say, "No, I just want to suck your pussy."

She laughs again. She's a happy girl, laughing her way to oblivion.

She throws off the covers and lies down on the bed on her stomach with her ass in the air. She still has on her panties and her jade green bra is pulled down around her waist.

I walk over to her. She is peeking up at me over her shoulder. I say, "Take off your bra and panties."

She says, "Take them off yourself."

I unhook her bra and toss it carefully over to where I hung my jacket on a chair. She turns over and I peel off her panties. She helps me by lifting up her glorious ass. I throw the panties by the chair as well.

Tamsin is now totally naked except for her stockings, garter belt and stilettos.

She asks, "Why don't you get undressed?"

I say, "Not yet. I just want to look at you. You're so beautiful. Your body is perfect."

I tell her to touch herself. I tell her that it turns me on. She smiles and fondles her breasts.

I say, "That's not what I mean. Spread your legs and touch your pussy. Put your fingers deep inside. Make yourself come. I love watching beautiful women masturbate."

So she starts to pull herself while I get undressed and put on a condom. Then I just stare at her and take my hardening cock in my hand and start to masturbate. I can tell that she is getting more and more excited. She likes me looking at her. She's using both hands now and she's losing it, not paying any attention to me while she pleasures herself. She is close to coming when I grab her hands and pull them away. She protests, but I just push her legs apart and dive right in there, sucking her pussy. She stops complaining and starts moaning. It doesn't take long for her to have an orgasm.

She lies there, recovering. I get up and lie next to her. I suck her nipples and stick my fingers inside her and massage her clit until she comes again. She is wide open and ready for me now.

She says urgently, "I want you inside me."

I say, "Not yet." I turn her over and kiss the back of her neck. I kiss her all the way down her spine and she is loving it. While I kiss her, she opens her legs and I finger fuck her from behind. I get to her ass and spread her cheeks. She gets nervous and says no. I say, "Okay, no problem."

Then I lie down on my back and ask her to sit on my face. She happily complies and lowers her juicy pussy right down on my waiting tongue. I have my hands on her breasts, tweaking her nipples and she undulates and shudders and comes again. At the height of her orgasm, I take my right hand away from her breast and stick my finger right up her ass. She says, "You mustn't, no, stop, please, oh God," and then comes even harder.

She falls back down on the bed, spent. I pull her around into the position I want. It is like playing with a rag doll. I grab a pillow and stick it under her ass so her pelvis is up high. I guide myself in and she is moaning sweet and low.

I start to pump and at the same time I suck her nipples, hard. I resist the temptation to bite them, because I know that's how they got Ted Bundy in the end, with bite mark evidence. So I am fucking Tamsin and I whisper in her ear, "You have to tell me when you are coming, okay? Promise?"

She is grunting with each slam of my cock, but she nods and groans, "Yes."

She lifts her legs way up and grabs her ankles. Wow, what a sight! Her head is thrashing from side to side and I can barely see her face because her hair is all over the place. She is screaming, "Oh God, oh God!" with every thrust, over and over.

"Come one more time, come!" I think. I am so close that it is torture, but I can't come, not until she has.

She lets go of her legs and wraps them around my waist. I am driving into her like a piston and then she comes. Her pelvis lunges up into mine and she shrieks, "I'm coming, baby, I'm coming."

That's my cue.

Like a viper I grab her throat tight. Tamsin tries to buck me off, like a wild mustang trying to throw a wrangler, but she doesn't have a chance. I take her so fast, so hard that she is almost immediately close to blackout, although she is still coming because I can feel her pussy grabbing my cock convulsively.

I tighten my grip and her tongue comes out. Stick out that tongue, baby. God, I love that. Then I experiment and loosen my hold. She gasps for air, her chest heaving, breasts wobbling, arms flailing. Tamsin can't talk, but if she could, I am sure that she would have cursed me out. I wonder if she has time for a moment of regret. If only she hadn't let me inside her house. But it doesn't matter. Nothing matters but the moment.

I am still fucking her and I tighten up my grip. I look into her eyes and she is begging me, she is begging me for more, I know it. I press harder and her tongue comes out again and I kiss her again. Her hands are weakly beating against my back, but there is no stopping me. I can feel her juddering underneath me and I know that she is still coming. Her legs are frantically pummeling my ass in her last struggle for air. Then I finish her off and come myself. Spectacularly. For minutes it seems, I pound into her body as her life force ebbs away; as her arms and legs slowly fall back down on the bed. I hold her down and as I am kissing her, I suck her soul deep into my lungs.

I drink in her very essence.

It seemed to last for hours, but the whole thing only took twenty minutes.

I rested for a while on top of her and when I recovered some of my energy, I kissed her and fondled her cooling body. I told Tamsin that she was the best. Even better than the little cat-like girl and that's saying something.

I looked up at the clock. I had plenty of time left.

I kissed her quiet lips. I sucked her sweet pussy again. It was still hot and moist. Delicious. I stood up and looked upon her eternally silent beauty and got hard again. I put on a new condom and entered her and fucked her again, this time slowly, luxuriously. I didn't have to wait until she came, but I took my time. I looked into her tranquil, frozen face and thought that I had never seen anything so beautiful. It was heartbreaking how lovely she was, much more beautiful in death than she ever was in life. She did everything I wanted. She was wonderful.

After it was over, I put on my surgical gloves and went to work. I took her into the bathroom and immersed her in a tub of warm water. I made sure that her fingernails were clear of any skin evidence in case she had managed to scratch my back. I cleansed her mouth and vagina thoroughly, and then I carefully dried her. I even blow-dried her hair.

I stripped the bed down and put the sheets in garbage bags. Then I laid her out on a fresh sheet on the bed and began Tamsin's transformation into a work of art.

I was nearly moved to tears when I left, she was so beautiful. I almost didn't want to leave her and, for one irrational moment, I thought about taking her with me. But I knew that would be madness. She couldn't last forever. Already, her limbs were becoming stiff. Rigor Mortis was setting in.

Before I left, I showered, dried myself, put on a new pair of gloves, and then cleaned up the bathroom, including the drain trap. I turned on the taps and kept the water running, so any evidence I may have missed would eventually flow away. I put the towels that I used in the garbage bags as well, along with her underwear, clothes and shoes. I dusted any surface that I might have touched. I dressed near the door and then I took my coat and the garbage bags out to the car. I got my vacuum cleaner out of the trunk and went back to the house where I vacuumed every area that I had visited. Then I returned it to the car. It was pitch dark outside with minimal street lamp coverage and there was no one around to see my activities.

I went back one more time. I turned down the thermostat to the lowest setting, which would cool down Tamsin's body temperature considerably and keep her fresh for the police. It might also cause a bit of confusion over the time of death. I turned the lights off and locked the door behind me, using her keys. I threw them down a storm drain five miles away.

I took the garbage bags to three different Salvation Army depots and dumped them. I hoped that by the time the police figured out what happened, Tamsin's bedding, towels and clothes would either be washed and on sale or destroyed. I threw the gloves and vacuum cleaner bags into a trashcan in the middle of town. I flushed the condoms down a public lavatory by the University. I avoided the live cam monitors near Clinton Square and Marshall Street.

Tomorrow I would drive down to Ithaca and have the car valet cleaned, just to be on the safe side.

I went home, after switching cars at the airport. I took off all my clothes and lay on top of my bed, pleasantly cool and replayed everything that had happened that evening, but instead of Tamsin, it was Elene that I was seducing. It was extremely satisfying, to say the least.

I don't think that I need to write about what happened next.

ENTRY 51

THE VENUS OF URBINO:
The subject is a young beautiful naked woman lying on her back on a rumpled bed. Her head is propped up on two pillows and her face is tilted coquettishly towards the artist. Her dark golden hair tumbles down her right shoulder and her left arm is draped casually over her thigh, with her hand modestly protecting her sex. Her right arm is propped up on the pillows supporting her upper body. Her legs are crossed at the knee—the right under the left—and her toes are pointed in confident expectation. She is full of poise and quiet power, as only an immortal goddess could be.

My Venus Has The Following Additions...
I chose black as the first color as I thought it would create a more dramatic effect on Tamsin's fair skin.
On her abdomen, the following text concerning alchemy from Goethe's *Faust* is written in block capitals (which are very difficult to trace):
"There was a Lion red, a wooer daring, Within the Lily's tepid bath espoused, And both, tormented then by flame unsparing, By turns in either bridal chamber housed. If then appeared, with colors splendid, The young Queen in her crystal shell, This was the medicine—The patient's woes soon ended; And none demanded—who got well?"
On each breast, lovingly surrounding the aureole of the nipple is the sign for the Universal Seed in alchemy:

On her chest, I painted the mark of Venus, the sign for copper:

On the palm of her right hand, I painted the symbol for the Sun, the emblem for gold, the most precious of elements:

Never did she look lovelier than in death, because what is life but an eager rushing towards the terrible inevitability of oblivion? Death is the great peace and we should all embrace it with eager joy.

ENTRY 52

This morning when I woke up, the first sensation to hit me was fear. My stomach did a flip, my face burned and I felt a moment of utter panic. Jesus, the first killing was bad enough, but this time I had actually gone out of my way to murder someone. My heart was beating a mile a minute. What if the police knocked on my door right now? What would I say? What would I do?

Then another voice came into my head and said, "How will they ever find out? How will they ever know? Is your DNA on file? Do you have a criminal record as a sex offender? Have you ever been in trouble with the law before? Did you leave a messy crime scene? Were you noticed by anyone at the nightclub? No.

"You are way down their suspect list, buddy, if you are on it at all. So, relax and take a deep breath. Do not panic, because that's how all the dummies get caught. Blind, stupid panic."

I calmed myself down. I closed my eyes and I brought back the mental snapshot that I had taken of Tamsin before I left her in all her glory. She was stunning. More beautiful than any work of art that I had seen in a museum or a book. I wondered if I should take photographs of my goddesses before I leave them, to immortalize them for eternity, then I decided against it. The diary was bad enough. Anyway, I'm sure that the police would take plenty of pictures. All I can do is hope that I will see them one day.

I wonder if the authorities will eventually contact me about the investigation? Probably not yet, not after only one murder. However, I must eventually prepare myself and keep on the lookout for any surveillance. There is a small likelihood that I could become a suspect when it becomes a serial killer case. The police might target people with art backgrounds, although that would give them hundreds of suspects to wade through as far as the University is concerned.

I can relax for now. I have found the perfect hiding place for my journal, so when I finish writing this entry it will go back to its secret hole until the next thrilling installment.

ENTRY 53

I kept an eye on the papers. Nothing until Tuesday. Then just a small article, very discreet: "Syracuse Legal Secretary Murdered." No details were given out in the story.

So, it has begun.

The next day, I decided to see how Elene was doing. I went to the gym she visits on Wednesday mornings and there she was, working out. She looked so cute on the Stairmaster in her exercise gear, all sweaty and pink. She has a superb butt. I wandered through the gym, pretending to consider membership. Then I left. Seeing Elene made me feel oddly guilty, as if I had been unfaithful to her. I knew that I hadn't been, but my experience of the other night was so profound that it threatened to overwhelm my feelings for her. That bothered me. It wasn't fair. I wasn't supposed to take the others seriously, but making love to my little cat-like girl and Tamsin had been so sublime. I wanted it again soon, but I had to wait until the next conference of morons hit town and that won't be until after Christmas.

I do not want to get caught, but the compulsion is strong. The sensations were so overwhelming in their power and beauty that I long to experience them again, but the smartest thing I can do is let my sweet memories keep me warm.

ENTRY 54

I've decided that when the winter semester begins, I will go back to work. I talked to Professor Mandelson and we agreed that I would just start out with a couple of classes a week. I'm not looking forward to it, but it is necessary. At least for several hours a week, my mind will be concentrated on Art History and not Elene, sex, strangulation and death. It will be very relaxing, I'm sure. Also, I like the idea of having a good excuse for being on campus, rather than just hanging around hoping for a glimpse of Elene.

ENTRY 55

I am now a regular at Kahunaville, believe it or not, in my current disguise of a baby-shit green tracksuit and goofy glasses. (The better to fit in with rest of the zombies who shuffle mindlessly around the Mall.) Kahunaville is where Tommy Lee Shepherd takes Elene every Thursday. To my surprise, I've discovered that it's not that bad. The Bahi Bahi Shrimps are delicious and they do a decent Margarita with real lime juice.

Last week, they sat at the table next to mine, so I was able to eavesdrop on every word of their conversation. Tommy Lee's real first name is Frank. He sounds like a complete asshole to me: opinionated, testosterone-fueled and pig-headed. Why does Elene put up with it?

I think that they used to be an item, but are now just friends, keeping it going for the sake of their professional relationship. They say things to each other that you only do when you know someone intimately enough to really hurt them casually.

I was sitting with my back to them, thank goodness. I'm sure that my face would have betrayed me and they would have known that I could overhear them.

I am looking forward to listening in to this Thursday's chat. Will Frank mention the case? I'm sure he will. Maybe Elene has been consulted already. Maybe she has already gazed upon my handiwork and marveled.

ENTRY 56

I had another dream last night. It was a bad one.

In my dream I am—surprise, surprise—a serial killer. A super-hero serial killer with incredible powers. I am also a well-respected scientist. My laboratory is crammed full of bizarre, electronic, wiry devices that buzz and pop. It is all something to do with the Internet. I am incredibly handsome in my dream, tall with a face like Michelangelo's *David*—beautiful in almost a feminine way.

Elene is in my dream laboratory. She is my friend and I care for her very much. I have no desire to hurt her. She is the only person on the planet that I like.

A man comes to the laboratory. He is also very tall, with a beard and piercing, red-rimmed, gray eyes. He is dressed from head to toe in gray and he looks like a tramp. His face is shielded by a large gray fedora. He looks grim and disillusioned.

I offer to drive him home. Elene comes with us. We get to our destination and The Gray Man gets out of the car, thanks me and then grabs Elene and disappears.

I get out of the car and look for them, but I can't find them. Finally, I pass by some stairs that go down to a basement and there they are. The Gray Man is strangling Elene. I intervene, attempting to pry his large bony hands from her throat. Elene is also trying to fight him off, but she is losing her strength. As I struggle with The Gray Man, I see his face clearly for the first time.

It is the face of the Devil.

This realization gives me new strength. After all, I am superhuman. I tear his hands away from her throat and I catch Elene as she collapses. The Gray Man laughs demonically and disappears.

I look down at Elene, half-conscious in my arms, and a dark compulsion comes over me. I have to have her. I have to betray my friend. I lay Elene carefully down on the garbage-strewn ground. She is defenseless. Her tongue is just gently poking out of her open mouth, just like a contented cat. I lift her skirt and rip her panties off. She is trying to get up, but I push her down. I tear her blouse off and force her bra up over her breasts. I bite her nipples until they bleed and then lick her blood. She cries out. I take her. I penetrate her while she is still helpless and vulnerable and half alive.

Then I hear the sound of laughter. I look up and there is The Man In Gray, staring down at us with his penis in his hand. His cock is massive and it is made of rusty iron. For some reason, the sight of someone watching us makes me feel more turned on and I fuck Elene violently, but my eyes are riveted on the rusty penis of the Devil. I know that when I come, something horrible is going to emerge from that enormous metal cock.

I can hear Elene beneath me, but now she is moaning in ecstasy. She is conscious and her hands are on my face. She is begging me to look at her, but I can't. If I do, then the Devil will do something awful to us while our backs are turned.

All I can see are the Devil's eyes, red and burning. All I can feel is my penis banging into Elene, pounding, slamming, ramming into her to the hilt. She is screaming now with pain and lust. Her screams and his laughter are all I can hear. I have a revelation. I know now where all my superhuman powers have come from. HIM. I bargained my soul for them and now The Man In Gray wants my soul back.

Elene comes and then I come and then the Devil comes. A huge gush of foul black oily liquid spews out of his iron penis and covers us. It tastes bitter, like the disappointment of a thousand souls, and it starts to fill up the basement where I am fucking Elene. We are going to drown, but I can't move because I am still coming, she is still coming, the Devil—fuck him—is still coming. I look down and see Elene's face disappearing underneath the surface of the greasy black waters. It fills her open imploring mouth and for a moment, she disappears. I grab her and lift her up as much as I can, but I can't get up. I can't stop fucking her.

It is terrible.

Finally, the black waters rise above our heads. We're in total darkness, but I can still feel myself inside her. The blackness is suffocating. We are both cold now, both dead, but still fucking for all eternity. There is only one sound and that is the sound of the Devil's laughter.

When I woke up, it felt like my body had been electrocuted. I was shuddering uncontrollably and the sound of The Man In Gray's laughter was still echoing in my head. I had a bitter taste in my mouth, as if I had swallowed the foul black ejaculation from the Devil's unspeakable cock.

This was not a good dream. I did not feel like masturbating afterwards. I was horrified.

I lay there for quite a while. I looked at my clock and it said 4 AM, that special hour in the night when more souls depart this earth than any other time. It is almost as if our grip on the planet is at its most tenuous. We are completely defenseless and susceptible to dismal imaginings and repulsive fantasies. That's when the Devil rides out and it is his time when he holds sway. We forget logic and science, and really do believe in The Horned One. During the day, he recedes, evil falls back and lightness prevails. That is why it is so hard to believe it when someone gets murdered during the day. The shock that the following statement produces: "He was attacked in BROAD DAYLIGHT," is the shock of a rational person not believing that it is possible that anything bad can happen while the sun shines.

Maybe I am not making any sense. All I know is that I just had an extremely unpleasant dream. I suppose that I can't expect to go around killing people and not suffer some consequences. After all, a bad dream isn't the worst that could happen to me.

But that kind of dream can give you nightmares.

ENTRY 57

Today is Thursday. Tonight I will go to the Carousel Center and see Elene and Frank. It has been six days since I delivered my first Work of Art to the world.

The press coverage has been muted and I haven't read any in-depth reviews of my Venus, but I suppose that is to be expected. I can't do too much snooping around, as I don't want to bring attention to myself, so I will just have to wait in isolation and ignorance.

It is a strange feeling, having committed such a crime and not knowing whether someone is after you or not. I am fairly secure in the knowledge that I covered myself adequately, but there are still times when an icy stab of panic hits my guts and I break into a cold sweat.

That's when I can hear the laughter again. The Devil's laughter. It is so clear—a distinct auditory hallucination—and it's probably due to the front temporal lobe damage that I sustained in the Accident. When this happens, I have to make a heroic effort to calm myself, a mental clenching of the brain to throw off the fear. Then I feel at peace with myself again.

I never feel any guilt, only the dread of getting caught and that will not, cannot happen. I have thought this through completely and I have no intention of going to prison. If I do get captured, I will commit suicide. Suicide is the ultimate act of control, after all. One cheats the police of their arrest, cheats the authorities of their show trial, cheats the victims' families of their revenge. How sweet that would be.

But I don't want to look on the negative side. Deep down, I am an optimistic person and my fervent hope is that everything will work out for the best. I will meet Elene and help her with the investigation. She will fall in love with me and we will live happily ever after. Maybe we can even have children. That would be nice. I would like to pass on my genes to another generation. Just think what they could accomplish.

It is almost time to go to the Mall. I have to prepare my clever disguise. I have bought a different tracksuit, this one in a delicate shade of mustard yellow, as I don't want to be perpetually known as The Man in the Baby-Shit Green Tracksuit.

The price I have to pay for safety.

ENTRY 58

They mentioned me. They were talking about me over dinner.

They have a favorite table where they always sit, so I got there early and positioned myself so I could easily overhear them without them noticing me.

They came in, sat down and ordered their usual drinks: a Utica Club beer for him (yet another devastating indication of his taste bypass) and a glass of Pinot Grigio for her.

They were arguing, as usual, but Elene always gives as good as she gets. She's a feisty girl.

It went something like this:

Frank: "I think you're full of shit. I bet you five bucks that when we check the VIC out, she'll have some schizo ex-boyfriend in the wings and we'll have our man."

Elene: "How can you be so sure? This guy wrote poetry on her abdomen for God's sake. Look at the pose of the body: it is so odd, so...artistic, for lack of a better word. Disgruntled exes don't normally exhibit that kind of explicit behavior. This is the beginning of something, I know it."

Frank: "Oh, I see, the great psychologist is pronouncing her verdict after only a few days, eh? Jesus, what would I do without you, Doctor? Us poor dumb cops are just helpless in the face of your brilliance. I mean, am I supposed to base my conclusions on your gut instinct? Who do you think I am, fucking Steve fucking McGarrett, or something?"

Elene: "Button it, Frank. You know this is a weird one, or you wouldn't have called me in the first place."

Frank: "Yeah, and don't I regret it? You can be such a pain in the ass, Sheppard. You see psychos crawling out of the woodwork. I bet you're just desperate for it to be a serial killer, aren't you, so you can get on your forensic high horse and jabber meaningless psychobabble to us Neanderthal cops. And then, maybe you'll get a chance to take the stand and defend the asshole and say that he was misunderstood, or he had dysfunctional childhood, or his wife never gave him enough sex, or maybe he was abused as a kid, or even that he's brain-damaged, or something."

(Right on all counts, Frank!)

Elene: "Just let it go, Frank. I will be happy to hand this case over to someone else if you have a problem with me."

Frank: "No. I don't have a problem with you. I just have a problem with you jumping to conclusions. Until I have evidence otherwise, this is going to be treated as a probable domestic, understand?"

Elene: "You realize what you just said? The only evidence that will convince you is another murder with the same M.O."

Frank: "That is the official FBI definition of a serial killer, Doctor. Need I remind you? Two murders in a row with identical M.O.s."

Elene: "You are such an obstinate, narrow-minded..."

Waiter: "You folks ready to order?"

Well, they had to curtail their argument for the moment to look at their menus, but as soon as the waiter left, they went back to haranguing each other. Boy, I bet they had great sex when they were dating.

Anyway, the upshot was that Elene, being the perceptive individual that she is, thought that a serial killer was gearing up for business. Frank was leaning towards the idea that the murder was most likely committed by a former associate of the victim. The more I listened in, however, the more I realized that Frank was just indulging in wishful thinking. He was no dummy. He was probably being stubborn just to annoy the hell out of Elene. Also, serial killers are a cop's worst nightmare. If the perpetrator doesn't have any previous connection with the victim, how the hell are the police supposed to catch them? Sometimes the only answer is calling in the FBI, and local cops hate doing that.

It was a very entertaining evening. It really cheered me up. The Devil retreated back to his own private hell and I went home feeling safe that Frank and Elene were right on course, following THE PLAN.

I slept like a baby that night.

ENTRY 59

It has been a quiet time. Christmas didn't exist for me, except for watching the usual boring movies over the vacation period. I started teaching my little half-wits in January and I spent the rest of my time reading and working out. Occasionally, as a treat, I allowed myself to discreetly stalk Elene.

I went down to New York City again and bought another car, this time a Ford Explorer. I drove it home very late one night and put it in my garage next to Angie's BMW. From now on, I will use my most recent purchase to travel to the Venus Project Car and leave the BMW in the driveway, so the neighbors will think that I am at home. I suppose that I am being rather elaborate in my precautions, but you can never be too careful.

I am counting the days to my next outing. I keep tabs on the investigation every Thursday with my dinner date with Frank and Elene. (I've discovered that Kahunaville's Maui Teriyaki Salmon is magnificent.) I've had to invest in more camouflage outfits. I went to K-Mart and bought a few plaid lumberjack shirts, some cheap jeans and a pair of hideous sneakers. God forgive me, I even bought a baseball cap. Along with the goofy glasses and my unattractive hairstyle, I am now totally indistinguishable from the rest of the rabble.

Things are not going that well with the investigation. Frank has been laboriously checking out Tamsin's known associates and nothing much has shown up out of the ordinary. He does have high hopes for one ex-boyfriend called Gary Sharman, who sounds like a bit of an animal and who seems like first-rate prime suspect material. I was overjoyed to hear that Forensics had shown up very little in the way of any useful evidence. My meticulousness paid off, it seems. They are currently waiting for the FBI spectrograph of the magic marker, but they won't learn anything from that. I bought the most common brand that I could find.

They have nothing.

As I sat there, I felt a twinge of compassion for Frank and his little crew of investigating officers. Syracuse just isn't used to crimes like mine. It's singularly uninteresting when it comes to acts of violence. All the cops ever have to deal with is a few domestic- or drug- or gang-related killings a year, maybe a vehicular manslaughter or two, or the occasional rape of a student. Nothing too intense. The only case of note was that poor slob who attacked his wife a few years ago. First he bludgeoned her into a coma, but that didn't quite do the trick, so he finally did away with her with a dose of cyanide while she was recovering in hospital. Now, there was a man with a mission.

Well, I can't let my feelings of sympathy cloud my reason. I am pleased that they haven't got anything. Unfortunately, the more crimes I commit, the more evidence they will have—it is inevitable. I must remain vigilant.

ENTRY 60

Tonight's the night. I feel very excited, but I'm a little more nervous than the last time. I was so lucky with Tamsin. How will I fare with the lovely Katrin, I wonder?

It is the National Rotary Club Conference at the Sheraton, so the town is hopping with worthy Rotarians. I will dress more conservatively tonight, in brown. I have bought two new pairs of shoes, one brown, one black, that I will only use for The Project. I will keep them in the Project Car at the airport. I gave the shoes that I wore to Project Tamsin to the Salvation Army, as well as rest of the clothes I was wearing that night. There is nothing to link me to her.

ENTRY 61

I knew that the second time would be different. It was inevitable. How different, I couldn't have begun to guess.

I would have thought that the girls around town would have been on the alert since Tamsin's demise, but then the newspaper coverage has been pretty minimal.

Katrin showed up as expected at Awful Al's Cigar Bar. The joint was crammed with young professionals, students in plaid shirts, and rogue Rotarians. Katrin was wearing a red dress and looked truly appetizing. She was with friends, so I just sat back and observed. I was willing to wait to make my move.

She chattered away. She was very theatrical with her gestures, as any part-time actress would be, I guess.

Finally, Katrin went off to the ladies' room. I followed and lay in wait for her. On her way back, I accidentally on purpose bumped into her and spilled a little of my martini on her dress. I acted mortified and offered to pay her dry-cleaning bill. She was touched. I then invited her for a drink. Katrin accepted.

First level of communication with the victim achieved with ease.

We drank martinis. Boy, could Katrin put them away. I drank slowly and kept her well-oiled.

The dance began again, to a different tune.

Later, I made the same excuse to leave as the first time and offered Katrin a ride. She said, "Yes." My luck seemed to be holding.

I drove her home. Jesus, that girl could talk a mile a minute. My mind fast-forwarded to a silent

Katrin, transfigured into a quiescent, marble-skinned goddess.

I accompanied her to her door. We kissed. She was very responsive. I made the move to go. She invited me in. So far, so good.

Katrin took me straight to her room, no messing around in the living room. I was momentarily distracted by the display on the bedroom walls of commemorative plates depicting famous scenes from the movies. *Gone With The Wind*, *The African Queen*, *Casablanca*; they were all there in glorious, hideous Technicolor. It had to be one of the most-grisly manifestations of kitsch that I had ever seen.

Katrin instantly got on the defensive.

Katrin: "You're looking at my plates, aren't you?"

Me: "Well, you have to admit, it's hard to avoid them."

Katrin: "My mother bought them for me. She thought that I would love them because I want to be an actress. I can't get rid of them. She died last year."

In my opinion, Mom's death would have been a perfect reason to donate them to the local Home for the Terminally Tasteless, but I couldn't say that to the poor girl, could I? After all, I was just about to cut short her sweet little life.

We kissed some more on the bed, slowly removing our clothes. I felt a lot more relaxed this time. Katrin was a very sensual being. She liked being touched; she liked being undressed.

Sometimes, it scares me how easy it is to kill someone.

We fucked. She had already come a couple of times; I made sure of that. At the height of her third orgasm, I took her by the throat and snuffed out her life like a candle. She tried to stop me, but she didn't have a chance.

My orgasm was as powerful as the last time, if not more so.

Afterwards, I took her into the *en suite* bathroom. I washed her body, dried her, took her back into the bedroom and went to work. After a while, I finished with the painting and commenced the clean-up operation. When I was done, I moved my car around the corner. I don't know what possessed me to do that, but it must have been instinct. I paid one more visit to Katrin. I was in her room adjusting the room temperature, when I heard the front door open and shut.

My heart felt like it had stopped beating.

I heard someone bumbling around in the living room. Then a female voice calling, "Katrin?" I walked quickly over to the bedroom door and locked it. Two seconds later, the doorknob jiggled.

I took the bull by the horns and said in a deep voice, "She's got a visitor!"

On the other side of the door, I heard a giggle and an apologetic "Sorry!"

The sound of footsteps walking away.

What the fuck was I going to do now?

I was panting with anxiety. Then I calmed myself. This was just another problem to solve. So solve it.

I looked around the room. There was a large window by the bed. I went over to inspect it and the view. The window was big enough for me to exit and it wasn't that far to the ground, but I could tell that I would leave footprints in the mud around Katrin's shrubbery if I decided to go out that way.

I listened at the door. No sound. Perhaps Katrin's guest had gone to sleep. (I knew that she had to be a houseguest and not a roommate, because I had made very sure that all my girls lived by themselves.)

There was always the option of killing the guest and adding her to my pantheon of goddesses, but I felt uneasy about it. More time spent at the scene, more mistakes to be made because of the shock of the interruption, more possibilities of capture.

I turned off the bedroom light and waited.

After an hour, I carefully unlocked the door and opened it. The lights were off in the living room and I could hear gentle feminine snoring coming from the second bedroom.

I slid out of Katrin's room, shutting and locking the door behind me and made for the front door. I checked the neighborhood from the dark safety of the front porch before I strolled to my car.

After the disposal of the evidence in the usual manner, I was on my way to the airport, safe and sound. No one saw me. I felt almost sick with the fear of discovery. I didn't relax until I got home.

Lying on my bed, I did not relive my time with Katrin. I did not masturbate to sweet fantasies and memories of sex and death. I just wondered at my pure, unadulterated luck. A minute before or after and the guest would have spotted me. But she didn't. I was like a ghost, sliding in and out of my victims' lives and sucking their spirits clean and dry.

I had done it again. I moved amongst them like the shadow of death and no one knew, no one suspected. I had a close call, but I passed the test.

I am unstoppable. I am untouchable. I will succeed.

ENTRY 62

AN ALLEGORY OF VENUS AND CUPID:
The goddess Venus is presented to us in one of Bronzino's typically rigid, unnatural poses. She is not looking out at the viewer. On the contrary, her head is turned sharply to the right and she is gazing at the arrow that she is grasping awkwardly between her fingers of her right hand like a paintbrush—her pinkie finger extended as if she were taking tea with the Queen. Her legs are curled up at the knee and if she wasn't on her back, she would look as if she was kneeling. Her left arm extends down to her left leg, her fingers just grazing the surface of her porcelain calf muscle. The goddess is calm, regal, contained and controlled.

My Additions:

On Katrin's abdomen, I wrote the following lines that are an excerpt from *Cato*, a play by the English writer Joseph Addison (1713):

"The soul secure in her existence smiles at the drawn dagger and defies its point. The stars shall fade away, the sun himself grow dim with age and nature sink in years, but thou shalt flourish in immortal youth, unhurt amid the war of elements, the wreck of matter and the crush of worlds."

It had nothing to do with alchemy, but the sense of the poem was close enough to my themes of transmutation and immortality. I found it at www.cnn.com in an article about Edgar Allan Poe. Poe had published two secret messages in 1841 that had been puzzling scholars for years. This one in particular had only been decoded in 1992 and the reason it had made the news was that experts had recently decoded the second one. The joke was that although Poe had converted the messages into cipher, they weren't written by Poe at all, but by some other obscure writers. Always a practical joker that Edgar. All those scholars, for all those years, puzzling and calculating away, thinking Poe was leaving some meaningful message for posterity and all they got were some cryptic lines from a couple of unknown plays. What a laugh.

On Katrin's lovely left breast, I painted:

In alchemy, this is the sign for Nitre, which is a combination of Saltpeter and Potassium Nitrate. It is made by the extravagantly named process of lixiviation. A pile of soil rich in animal dung is exposed to the air (though protected from rain) and a crust of Nitre eventually forms on the windward side of the pile. When purified by recrystallization, this forms a white crystalline powder. It is a powerful oxidizing agent and when heated with Vitriol (sulfuric acid), produces the "Strong Water" Aqua Fortis. In other words, nitric acid.

On Katrin's right breast, I painted,

the sign for Salt, which alchemists think of as the Contractive Force in Nature. It symbolizes the processes of crystallization and condensation.

On her chest, I wrote,

the symbol for Aqua Regia, a mixture of one-part nitric acid (aqua fortis) and three- or four- parts hydrochloric acid (spirit of salt). It is called the "King's Water" because it is able to corrode and dissolve the king of metals, gold. Just as I corroded and dissolved Katrin's sweet spirit into the ether.

On the top of her right hand, I wrote,

depicting Sulfur, the Expansive force in Nature. It also symbolizes Dissolution and Evaporation.

On the top of her left hand, I wrote,

which represents Mercury, which is thought of as the Integrative Force, interweaving and balancing that of the Salt and Sulfur. It also stands for Circulation and Dynamic equilibrium.

The addition of the prop arrow was dangerous poetic license, but I felt compelled to do it for art's sake. It was a cheap, children's arrow, easily obtained at any Toys 'R' Us. I purchased it during my last shopping trip in New York. I made a point of buying it at a very busy time at the cash register, when the clerk would be too engaged to remember me.

If all this doesn't confuse them, then nothing will.

ENTRY 63

I made the papers, finally. I suppose that the police had to eventually spill the beans, because now there could be no doubt that a serial killer was at work. There were too many links between the two crime scenes to ignore.

It was fascinating reading. I felt very detached, as if I were reading about some other person. I wasn't capable of such awful crimes, surely. The newspapers certainly made me out to be some perverted psychopath, that's for sure. No mincing of words with the fine gentlemen of the Fourth Estate. "Psycho On The Loose" was one headline—admittedly from the more down-market Syracuse Sun.

Still, details in the press were sketchy except for a vague reference to a possible occult tie-in. Of course, they weren't going to give out too much information. This was to foil any fake confessions that always seem to be forthcoming in cases like these. Who is sicker, I wonder? The killer, or the loony-tunes who confess to crimes that they haven't committed?

The one thing the press did mention was Katrin's hapless houseguest. She was currently under sedation at Crouse Memorial for shock, grief and nervous collapse. It must be quite shocking to have had a conversation (albeit a brief one) with the murderer who strangled your friend without you even being aware of it.

Hopefully, I will learn more this Thursday during my dinner with Frank and Elene.

ENTRY 64

They weren't there. I waited a couple of hours, but Frank and Elene never showed up. For a while, I felt distinctly uneasy. Perhaps I had been noticed. Maybe they were watching me as I was eating my Teriyaki Salmon and wondering who I was.

Then I realized that they were probably working late on the case. On my case. They were probably in a dingy Incident Room somewhere, looking at crime scene photographs and dining on soggy, take-away pizza. And arguing. Always arguing.

I was disappointed, but I have to keep my cool. I have to remain fluid and adaptable. The more murders I commit, the more there is a chance of discovery.

ENTRY 65

The next week passed uneventfully. After the initial spurt, the newspaper coverage was surprisingly minimal, but that is usually the case with serial killer reportage. No need to panic the man or woman in the street. God forbid that we keep reminding people that there is a killer on the rampage. It might hurt the convention trade. University admissions might go down. And what about the tourists? (What tourists? In Syracuse?)

Tomorrow is Thursday and I hope that Frank and Elene are back at Kahunaville. I may even follow Elene to see where she goes after her five o'clock class ends.

Maybe Frank and Elene decided to change venues. Perhaps they tired of Kahunaville's menu of pseudo-Eastern Rim specialties. I hope not. I have just discovered their Riki Riki Rib-Eye Steak with extra hoisin sauce.

ENTRY 66

This morning I woke up feeling so paranoid that I was having heart palpitations. I had to spend at least ten minutes calming myself down, talking to myself, assuring myself that there wasn't a SWAT team poised to swoop into my house the minute I opened my door to get the paper.

It was very unpleasant.

I finally managed to get out and retrieve the Herald Journal. I read everything I could about Katrin, but there weren't any new developments.

I went for a drive into Manlius to pick up a quart of milk, but in reality it was just a test to see if anyone was following me. If they were, I couldn't spot them.

I worked out for a while, but it didn't help. I scanned the headlines on www.syracuse.com, but no relief there. I checked out the police scanner on the Internet as well, but nothing was happening except an altercation on Salina Street between two drunks. I turned on the TV for the lunchtime local news. Nada.

I sat at the kitchen table and tried to remember what all my research (including copious re-runs of *Law and Order*) had taught me about murder investigations. I wanted to calm my mind and give it something to do. What would Frank and his band of merry men be up to? How would they investigate the murders of two women, killed in an identical manner?

I imagined the crimes from their perspective. The first murder might perplex them, but not worry them unduly. As there was a nude female body involved, they would conclude straight away that this was a sex crime. It would be natural to assume that a boyfriend, family member or associate could have done it. They would interview all the victim's friends, relatives and work mates, paying special attention to the men in the victim's life. They would also interrogate the person who found the body and anyone who was in contact with her in her last hours.

I suppose that was the only real worry. Could someone place me at the Liquid Lounge? However, the club had been so crowded and my appearance so nondescript that I think I covered myself well, even as far as possible monitoring by the club's CCTV security cameras.

The police would then construct what they call a victimology: a precise chronicle of the victim's movements, habits, associations, hobbies and history. They would interview her neighbors to see if anyone suspicious had been seen hanging around her house recently. (I only checked out her place a couple of times over a month ago, so no problems there.) They would question her family to see if she had confessed to any worries about being stalked or threatened. They would ask her friends if they had seen anyone with her that night.

The police would have all forensic evidence found at the scene tested for DNA. They would do an autopsy and conclude that the victim had died from asphyxiation due to strangulation. They would ascertain that she had sexual intercourse before her death, because of the vestiges of the lubricant from the condoms left in her vaginal cavity. (Even with my careful cleansing of the body, I couldn't assume that they wouldn't find some trace evidence.) They would assume that the intercourse was consensual, as there would be no trauma to the genitals or evidence of anyone breaking and entering the house of the victim. They would analyze the magic marker to see what brand it was and then they would check the art supply and stationary stores in town, for all the good it would do them.

At first, they would be confident that they could probably catch the perpetrator. In a large percentage of these cases, the victim knows the killer and her friends were probably aware of him as well. Somewhere in her history there was a violent male who had come back to kill her. All the police had to do was look hard enough and they would find him.

The second murder would put a new spin on the investigation. There would be no way to deny that the crimes were linked, even though it would be revealed that the victims did not know each other. There were too many similarities: the pick-up, probable consensual intercourse, strangulation, the clean-up routine, the drawings and poems on the bodies. A serial killer had moved into the equation.

So the man was a stranger. A stranger to both victims.

After the first murder, the police probably filled in a VICAP form, as part of the FBI's Violent Criminal Apprehension Program. All the details from the case, including M.O., autopsy results and victimology would be sent off to the FBI to be fed into their computer. The information would then be matched to any other cases of a similar nature that had been committed in the United States. I can't imagine that they would come up with any hits, but if there were, that would work to my advantage. It would be wonderful if some killer in Salt Lake City got the blame for my crimes.

After a second murder, the FBI might be called in. They would attempt to profile the killer based on the evidence that he may have left at the crime scene.

Of course, Frank has already asked Elene to do a profile. I noticed from her records that she had attended some courses at the FBI's Behavioral Unit at Quantico, so she would be familiar with their techniques. What conclusions would they draw in a profile of my crimes? I wonder what Elene would think about my works of art. Would she be able to see their beauty, or would she be blinded by the ordinary perspective of "normal" people. Who knows?

Most serial killers share certain characteristics. Their behavior is a clue to their personality. By taking into account all the evidence, i.e., the crime scene photographs, victimology, the statements from witnesses, friends and relatives as well as the autopsy and police reports, the authorities would probably come to the following conclusions:

1. The killer could be an organized, sexual serial killer. They would probably conclude that he is a cunning psychopath who has the ability to con a woman into allowing him into her home after only a brief meeting. *(I don't know about the psychopath bit, but even I was surprised at the ease with which I picked up my ladies.)*

2. The thoroughness of the clean-up operation would point to a methodical person who put a lot of thought into the planning and execution of these crimes. Someone who might be familiar with police procedural and forensic science and who might also have an interest in art. *(Of course, anyone who has watched any of the CSI franchises or The FBI Files on the Discovery Channel would know about all that forensic stuff as well, but the police never seem to take things like that into consideration.)*

3. The killer would most probably be white as serial killers rarely cross race boundaries. He would be in his early to late thirties. (Younger killers very seldom leave such organized crime scenes, which is why the police would assume that the killer would be more mature.)

4. He may have a girlfriend, but it is more likely that he is divorced. *(Violently divorced, in my case.)*

5. He is most probably the oldest son of divorced parents and had some difficulty at school. (I didn't have any problems at school, unless you count that unfortunate incident with the fire hose.)

6. He is in a white-collar profession, possibly self-employed, and drives a late model car. *(This part of the profile would fit, as I am gainfully employed by the University.)*

7. He is a likable person and would be of medium to high intelligence. *(High intelligence, please.)*

8. There would be a strong probability that some incident or incidents of stress propelled him to murder on the evenings in question. He also may have been under the influence of alcohol. *(Not stress, but THE VENUS PROJECT. And, of course, there's nothing like a couple of martinis to get you geared up for a bit of mischief.)*

9. They would show particular interest in the fact that the killer was wearing a condom. Most men hate to wear them, yet the perpetrator was so aware of forensic techniques that he would rather lessen his gratification by wearing a condom than be caught by trace evidence. They may wonder if his DNA is on record somewhere. *(Luckily, my DNA isn't, but why take any chances?)*

10. They would have to deduce that the poses of the bodies and the paintings are part of the killer's scripted fantasy. The investigators wouldn't have a clue about the meaning of the drawings and the poems. Elene would probably recommend that the police consult an art expert or art historian from the University who might be able to understand the symbols painted on the victims. *(That's where I come in, hopefully.)*

11. Anyone consulted on these cases would have to be thoroughly vetted and their backgrounds checked, as the police would suspect that the perpetrator would try to insert himself into the investigation in some way. Officers would be posted at the funerals of the victims and the crime scenes, as this kind of killer likes to visit these scenes to relive his fantasies. (My background is impeccable, with nothing to link me to the victims. And with my vivid imagination, I have no need to attend the funerals. As for returning to the scene, that's how they caught Arthur Shawcross, the Rochester NY serial killer. A police helicopter spotted him in his car near a bridge over a river where he had dumped a body. They could even see the poor woman under the ice. Arthur was eating sandwiches and probably reliving his escapades. What is it about serial killers and sandwiches?)

12. They would wonder if anyone has ever escaped the killer. They would interview other nightclub-goers who were present on the evenings in question to see if some failed approaches had been made by the killer. *(I doubt if Carol would ever connect that nice guy who bought her a drink in Regina's with a horrible foul serial killer.)*

13. Approximately 75% of organized serial killers hide the bodies. As the killer didn't make any effort to do so and he made such a blatant staging of the scene, the authorities might draw the inference that the killer is egotistically flaunting the bodies as an open challenge to the police to find him. They would feel that he is a sensation seeker—one who is openly demonstrating his control over the victim, the crime scene, the police and the media. The police probably won't expect to hear from the killer in any other form than his works of art on the bodies. A high percentage of serial killers keep their mouths shut and there is no indication that this killer will behave

any differently. *(I am not exactly a blabbermouth. My secret is safe with me.)*

14. The police will pay particular attention to the known associates and neighbors of Tamsin, as the first victim often lives in close proximity to the serial killer. Seeing her every day could have triggered whatever motivated him to kill. *(All of my girls lived far from my base of operations, so no hope for the police there.)*

15. They will probably check the files for any unsolved murders of women in the past two years that may have some similarities to my crimes. The police would have to assume that the first murder was too well-planned and executed for this to be the killer's first crime. They might think that he may have had a "practice run" previously.

The first port of call would be to check on some of the recent murders of prostitutes, as they know that these women are in risky profession and would make easy targets. They will also check the files for anyone with a previous record for violent sexual assault. (I suppose the murder of my little cat-like girl might be studied, but there are enough differences between the cases to confuse the police: the use of bondage for instance. I noticed that there were some small bruises on my cat-like girl's wrists before I left her, which won't escape the notice of the police. Also covering her body with a sheet is considered a definitive act, often symbolizing the perpetrator's regret at his actions. Needless to say, "Non, je ne regrette rien.")

Of course, many of the above points could mark me out, but they also finger a few thousand other guys. Profiles are only one tool that the police use and, as romantic and magical as they seem, their usefulness is debatable. Narrowing down the field from millions to thousands isn't always that helpful when you have a limited amount of police officers working on the case.

Yes, they can profile their butts off, but they will never discover my real motivation: the love of a beautiful woman, Elene. She is the reason I am doing this. Not just some base sexual gratification—although that is fun, there's no denying—but the attainment of the perfection of Elene, my own personal Venus. I guess it's a bit extreme—dating by murder, that is—but then I am an extreme kind of guy.

I can't see how they could catch me. My anonymity is complete. I didn't attend the funerals of my victims. I haven't returned to the scenes of the crimes. I haven't returned to the scenes of the pick-ups. I haven't tried to inject myself into the investigation. I haven't written any notes to the press. I haven't kept any souvenirs (another serial killer trait). I have destroyed all evidence that could link me to the crimes. I have maintained a clean and tidy crime scene. I have used a different car than my own. I have used condoms and—the most important thing—I have stayed aloof and calm.

It is by sheer will power that I do this and will keep on doing it. It just takes concentration to keep the panic and fear at bay.

I feel a lot better already.

ENTRY 67

Today I did something that I shouldn't have done, I suppose, but I couldn't resist.

I audited one of Elene's classes. I chose one of the big ones, her five o'clock. I just joined in the crowd and headed for the seats in the back.

Elene came in. She looked wonderful. As soon as I saw her, my heart quickened.

She started talking and I tried to follow what she was saying, but I was constantly distracted by her face, her breasts, her legs, her lips. Then one of her students asked about the recent killings, can you believe it? My works of art. She obviously couldn't comment because it was all part of an ongoing investigation. She did say that she felt that the killings were definitely linked.

One student asked, "Dr Sheppard, why do you think there are more serial killers in the United States than any country?"

Elene: "That's a good question, Lucy. Why does America seem to have more serial killers than any place else? First of all, is this true? Let's look at the statistics: twenty years ago, the United States, with only 5% of the world's population, produced 75% of the world's serial murderers. So I guess we can safely say that even now America does have more serial killers at large than any other country.

"There are so many factors that make up the profile of a serial killer that it is difficult to narrow down the reasons to any single component.

"Here's one, for instance, a little theory of my own: the status of women in the USA is more elevated than most other places in the world. They have more equality, more money, more freedom, more mobility and more ability to choose. This means that men have lost their position of total dominance. Sexual frustration plays a huge role in the incipient fantasy life of a serial killer. If a man can't relieve his sexual tension, then he will resort to fantasy and pornography. Then, if the situation doesn't improve, he may take the step to violent fantasy, fueled by equally violent pornography. If he possesses elevated testosterone levels or low serotonin levels; if he has sustained front temporal lobe brain damage or abuse during childhood; if he displays the evidence of an anti-social personality disorder; if he has problems with the women in his life, then all these factors can lead a man down the road to serial murder."

(Wow, Elene, you hit the nail on the head. God, I love that woman! She is so smart; it's frightening.)

"All men have the capacity for violence. It is in their genes. Some are better than others in masking that capacity, but one only needs to look at the history of Mankind to see that violence is second nature to us all. It would be wonderful if we all could live in harmony, but it doesn't seem possible.

"I think society is too complex, and serial killers are too mysterious, for me to come up with a simple answer. By the way, don't let anyone try to tell you that serial killers aren't a puzzle. We—and by we, I mean law enforcers, psychologists, psychiatrists, doctors and prison officials—may try and fool ourselves that we have some handle on why these people kill, but, to tell the truth, we haven't got a clue.

"Since we do have so many serial killers at large in this country, why is it so hard to catch them? Well, one reason is the ease with which people can move from state to state, disappearing, making up new identities, always moving along when things get too hot.

"Then there is the ongoing problem of the lack of coordination between crime fighting agencies when it comes to solving interstate crimes. Sure the FBI's VICAP program helps, but it is still tough to connect the dots when it comes to crimes committed by one individual across several states.

"Back to motivation, another factor may be our great society of plenty that supplies everything you would ever need right there on the shelf, on the Internet, or on TV. This does nothing but engender deep dissatisfaction amongst the general population. 'If I can have a hamburger in 23 seconds, why can't I have that cute little blonde over there?'

"Maybe it comes down to the rapid degeneration of stable family life. In the USA, one third of all babies are born to single parent families. Thirty years ago it was 8%. You can't ignore the ramifications that these kinds of changes in the social fabric can cause.

"It could be that good old frontier mentality that we're so proud of. Perhaps serial killers are just the Wyatt Earps of our time. They are out there riding the range, killing for their own pleasure, doing their thing, man, without a care in the world for anyone else. Shit, ain't that just the great American tradition: one man and his gun, or knife, or ligature? We all have the right to bear arms. It's even written into our Constitution.

"Perhaps we should blame the media, that's always a good one. Nobody killed anyone until Oliver Stone filmed *Natural Born Killers*, or Quentin Tarantino made *Reservoir Dogs*. We love violent films and TV, the more vicious the better. We laugh when meteors pulverize the earth and when Godzilla eats Manhattan. We cheer on Clarice Starling when she is on the trail of Buffalo Bill, but when it comes to Hannibal Lecter, deep in our heart of hearts we are rooting for him to get away. Wacky guy, but he's an independent soul. Let's face it, we just adore Arnie kicking butt as the Terminator, but everyone secretly preferred it when he was the BAD Terminator, rather than the GOOD one.

"Perhaps we should blame the fashion industry for inventing miniskirts or the advertising industry for putting near-naked females on enormous billboards. Most men admire the female body on display in a healthy way. However, there are a few who would view these girls as candy that they aren't allowed to eat. They feel that they are being tortured by all beautiful, available-looking women. These men are convinced that if they attempted to approach a gorgeous girl, they would probably be rejected. Rejection leads to frustration, frustration to anger and anger to violence. But violence never really gets you what you want, so it's back to frustration again. The ultra-vicious circle. All you have to do is watch a movie, or turn on the TV, or read a comic book to realize that America is the only society to extol the beauty of violence."

My Elene. What a girl!

After that little speech the class went ape-shit. Some of the female students were enraged. I was surprised that she spoke so frankly, but she did look a little tired. I felt responsible. If only she knew that the guy causing her sleepless nights was sitting right there in her class room.

I left as discreetly as I could. No one noticed, because they were having a lively debate on whether women asked for it by wearing skimpy clothing.

The way I look at it, they all took a risk, from my little cat-like girl on down. In these troubled times, any woman who takes a strange man home with her is, if not asking for it, then at the very least taking a big chance. She has to expect that things may not turn out quite like she expected. Sex with a stranger may appear to be the ultimate high, but, like the mating rituals of certain insects, it can sometimes lead to death and destruction.

I went home and changed into my new costume of a blue and green lumberjack shirt, baggy jeans, baseball cap and glasses, preparing for yet another fabulous evening at Kahunaville. I hope that they were going to turn up this time.

ENTRY 68

Frank was already there. He didn't give me a second glance.

I took my usual table and waited with him. Ten minutes later, I was surprised to see another woman come in and sit across from Frank. She was tall and willowy, with black hair and Spanish good looks. After careful eavesdropping, I ascertained that her name was Salma and that she worked in the clerical department of the Public Safety Building.

I was disappointed and at the same time intrigued. I was missing out on Elene, but who was this delicious new girl? I thought it was typical that Frank, of all people, should have such a gaggle of tasty females to choose from, but then his kind of bastard always does.

Anyway, I lost interest while they were ordering. I was munching on my starter—Spicy Tuna and Shrimp Quesadillas—when my ears caught something relating to my works of art.

Salma: "So how are those murder cases coming along, Frank?"

Frank: (growling into his Utica Club) "Like shit. This perp is so organized, he should be running for Mayor. It's giving me a major pain in the butt. So far no obvious suspects have presented themselves. Unless he slips up by leaving some evidence behind, or unless a victim escapes him, I don't see how I can't avoid handing this over to the Feebies and that fucks me off."

Salma: "Well, the Feds do have plenty of experience with serial killings."

Frank: "And don't they love telling us about it. Damn it, I want this one myself. Nick Carlopolis over at the FBI thinks he's God's gift to law enforcement and he's already trying to muscle in on our investigation. I know it sounds fucking infantile, but I don't give a shit."

Salma: "It's okay. I understand how you feel." (...followed by more comforting noises.)

I could see right away that Salma was the opposite of Elene. She was supportive of Frank and was non-confrontational. Salma is more an ideal partner for the mercurial Frank than Elene, who is never afraid to speak her mind.

Elene, on the other hand, is the ultimate partner for me.

ENTRY 69

Yesterday, I saw an item on the *CBS News*. The anchor was trailing a *Sixty Minutes II* episode and he mentioned a puzzling case that caught my attention. The police had found some guy's DNA at the scene, but the suspect was in prison at the time of the crime. The big question was: how did the DNA get there? I missed the actual program, but the concept started an idea rolling in my head. Up until now, I have been supernaturally careful about not leaving behind any trace evidence at the scenes of my crimes. Maybe next time, I will leave some DNA—either a sample of skin, blood, sweat, semen, hair, saliva, dandruff or fingernail clippings—but the kicker will be that it won't belong to me.

Now the question is, where am I going to obtain this rogue DNA? Maybe I should go to the local gay hangout and scrape some semen off the toilet stall floor? Break into a barbershop and steal some spare hair clippings? Empty a few ashtrays from the local Bar And Grill? Grab any old Coke can from the garbage and leave it at the scene? No, I couldn't do that. I have to make sure that the sample was from a man. Scientists can now obtain DNA samples from tiniest amount of saliva on a cigarette butt or a coffee cup. They don't even need the follicle at the end of a hair sample, they can obtain the DNA just from a clipping. Unfortunately for the criminal, as soon as the suspect discards a cigarette butt or a Coke can, that evidence enters the public domain and the police don't need a warrant to take it and test it.

I guess the world is my oyster. There are so many possible places to obtain my traceable evidence that I am almost spoiled for choice. Maybe I should just raid a sperm bank and mix a little cocktail of semen to put up my next victim's vagina. Now that would confuse them. The police would have to come to the conclusion that there was a gang of serial killers on the rampage.

Maybe I should sneak into Charlie Landru's house and bag some of his DNA. What a laugh that would be. Such sweet, sweet revenge. Teach you to fuck my wife, buddy.

On the other hand, maybe I shouldn't mess around with a winning (hopefully) formula. Planting DNA could backfire and I'm having too much fun to screw things up now.

ENTRY 70

Susie Morton was next on my list and I saw no reason to deviate from the overall plan. I waited until the Syracuse Orange Men were playing Boston University at the Dome. The town would be packed with Bostonians eager to support their team.

Susie's patterns were pretty random, so on the off chance I decided to visit Viva Debris Comedy Club, on the assumption that she would probably go there first, then on to Sh-boom's for a nightcap.

Viva Debris was amusingly decorated with the detritus of a million garage sales. Wrecked cars littered the dance floor, manned by garishly dressed mannequins and lit by old fifties standard lamps. Not one item of furniture matched with another and the outfits worn by the waitresses echoed the decor. One girl might be dressed up as a sailor, the next as an extra from *Oklahoma*, the next as a naughty schoolgirl. The crowd fit right in, with businessmen rubbing shoulders with shaggy-haired students, nerds with pocket protectors dancing with cheerleaders and jocks flirting with nurses just off their shift from the nearby St. Francis' hospital. It was a crazy place, a perfect hunting ground, because a person could easily move amongst all the chaos and not be noticed as anything out of the ordinary.

Susie was propping up the bar and I was disappointed to see that she was already talking to some pea-brained, Adonis type. He was wearing a Syracuse sweatshirt, the sleeves pushed way up to show biceps that The Rock wouldn't have been ashamed of. I went up to the bar close to them, ordered my usual and kept an eye on the proceedings.

Susie was wearing an eye-popping, pink and green, low-cut minidress that had a very Sixties feel to it. I thought that it was a trifle young for her, but she had the body to pull it off, so why not? I noticed that her companion was a bit diffident and all was explained when another bruiser with a matching sweatshirt sidled up to him and brazenly gave him a full kiss on the lips right in front of Susie. They swapped spit and everything. I was a bit shocked. I was used to seeing such shenanigans at Trexx, Syracuse's primo gay hangout, but not here. But who I am to complain? Some guys fuck each other up the ass, some prefer to strangle girls. Different strokes for different folks. *Viva la difference*, I say.

Susie didn't look surprised, in fact she greeted Bruiser Number Two with affection. I hung back as the brawny pair went off to trip the light fantastic on the dance floor. Susie finished off her drink and then sat there looking thirsty. I made my move.

Susie eagerly accepted my offer of a drink and contact was made. We talked and danced, talked some more, drank some more. Eventually, I asked her if she wanted a lift home, and she said, "Yes."

I nearly blew it when I started driving to her place without asking her where she lived, but luckily she didn't notice and volunteered the address. We drove to her place and I felt strangely nervous and out of sorts. As much as I enjoyed The Project, my recent bouts of paranoia had made me feel edgy. I even wondered if there was any point to it all. Here I was driving home some strange drunk woman who I had every intention of fucking and killing. God, how weird can you get? I had to keep reminding myself that I was doing this for the attainment of Elene.

We got to Susie's house just after midnight. I kissed her goodnight, making it a nice long one. To combat my distraction, I thought about how much more beautiful Susie would look dead and that helped a lot. My penis hardened and I gently guided Susie's hand to it. She whispered, "Oh, baby, you're ready, aren't you?" I assured her that I was. She then apologized and said that she was on her period, but that she would be happy to suck my cock for me.

Ah, shit.

I contemplated throttling her anyway just for wasting my time, but decided it wouldn't be worth the time, the trouble and the energy. I made my apologies and left. What a bummer.

Dear little Susie will never know how lucky she was.

ENTRY 71

Today I got a phone call from the head of my department, Professor Mandelson. I picked up the telephone without screening the call through my answering machine, which is exceptional for me.

After the usual pleasantries, he got to the point.

Mandelson: "Michael, I've been working on a little project for the police for a few days and I'm not getting anywhere. I wonder if you might be interested?"

Me: "What project?"

Mandelson: "They wanted to consult with me regarding two murder cases they are investigating. The criminal psychologist who is working on the case is convinced that there is some kind of art angle and she called me in. But after a few days, I couldn't make heads or tails of it all and frankly I just don't have the time. She wanted a replacement and I thought of you. She teaches at the University. Her name is Dr. Elene Sheppard."

Me: (At the mention of Elene's name, my mouth went instantly dry, but I kept it together.) "What would consulting mean, exactly? I don't want to do anything that will interfere with my classes."

Mandelson: "Dear boy, you'll have the time. After all, we're not exactly overworking you. All I had to do was look at some rather gruesome crime scene photographs and give her my opinion. Not pleasant viewing, I have to tell you. Dr. Sheppard is convinced that the killer is trying to tell us something by leaving the bodies in certain positions. I couldn't make anything out of it. If he is using some kind of artistic template, then it would be more your field than mine. You possess a virtually photographic memory of paintings and works of art. I've burned out too many brain cells over the years with alcohol abuse to have much of a memory left at all."

Me: "Sounds like a left-handed compliment to get yourself out of something difficult and me in."

Mandelson: "You always could see through me, *compadre*. What do you say? It's not as if teaching at the University is unduly straining your health, you know, and Dr. Sheppard is a tasty little work of art herself."

Me: "I am shocked—shocked—Professor, that you would refer to a fellow colleague in such unprofessional terms." (I pretended to think it over for a few seconds.) "Oh hell, why not."

Mandelson: "I knew you would come through for me, my son. You've made an old man very happy. Those damn photographs gave me nightmares."

Me: "Great. Just what I need."

Mandelson: "It will be good for you. You have to admit, I have been coddling you. It's time to get out of your academic haze and back into the real world again. What better way to do that than by helping our brave boys in blue solve a series of dastardly murders?"

Me: "Well, when you put it like that."

Mandelson: "Fantastic. I'll call the luscious Doctor and tell her that you are eager and willing to help. I am sure that she will call you immediately, as she is such an enthusiastic creature. It's not every day that Syracuse has a serial killer to dinner. It's downright disreputable."

I always liked Mandelson, the clever old bastard. An ace manipulator, someone who would never do any more work than was absolutely necessary to get the job done, and yet was always considered a leader in his field. You had to admire someone like that.

I thought that my initial demure protests were fairly believable. I am sure that my voice didn't change when he mentioned Elene's name.

Elene is going to call me. She is going to call me soon. I am going to see my works of art again. It's too good to be true.

ENTRY 72

The call came when I was in the bathroom. I heard Elene on my answering machine. I was in the middle of having a tremendous shit, and the sensation of the excrement easing itself out of my body accompanied by the dulcet tones of her voice was orgasmic.

She wanted to see me. She needed me. She wanted to consult with me. She desired my help.

Oh, God. Oh, God. Oh, God.

The time is coming, literally and figuratively. I will meet her. Speak to her. Help her. Fuck her brains out onto the floor. Whoa, boy, slow down. One thing at a time.

I am beside myself. But I always was, wasn't I?

Yes, you were always beside yourself, Michael, from the time you were a little tiny boy.

Elation. Ecstasy. Euphoria.

ENTRY 73

I spoke to Elene. It took me two hours, but I finally screwed my courage to the sticking place and called her at the number she left on the machine. Her home number. My heart was hammering so hard in my chest that I almost thought that I would pass out.

She answered the telephone on the third ring.

Elene: "Hello?"

Me: "Hi. Is that Dr. Elene Sheppard? This is Professor Michael Friday."

Elene: "Oh, hi there, Professor. Thanks for getting back to me so soon."

Me: "Professor Mandelson already mentioned that you needed an art consultant for some murders in Syracuse, but I am still a bit confused as to why you would need my services."

Elene: "You may have already read about it in the papers: the so-called 'Painted Lady Killings'? There are some peculiar aspects of our current murder investigation that require some expert advice in the field of art. Professor Mandelson recommended you after he found he didn't have the time to help. The poses of the bodies are so unusual and so studied that they obviously signify something to our killer, so it is vital for us to find out their meaning. I can't be much more specific over the phone, as I am sure you can understand. If you are willing to meet with me and sign a Non-Disclosure Agreement then I would be able to give you more details about the problems we are facing."

Me: "It sounds intriguing. I'm perfectly willing to meet with you to discuss it at the very least."

Elene: "Do you mind coming to the Public Safety Building tomorrow at around 10:00 in the morning? Just ask for me at reception and they will show you up to Incident Room Number Ten."

Me: "No problem. I'll be there."

Elene: "Thanks so much for your help, Professor. See you tomorrow."

Me: "Goodbye."

Not exactly the out-takes from the love letters of Abelard and Heloise, but heck, it's a start. I couldn't believe how wooden I was, but as far as I am concerned, the fact that I didn't act like a babbling loon was a triumph. How will I cope tomorrow? I have to discipline myself. I don't want to give anything away to her.

I must prepare myself, mentally and physically, for the challenges ahead.

ENTRY 74

I was early for my appointment with Elene, so I sat in my car in the parking lot outside The Public Safety Building for about ten minutes. I stared blankly at the miserable February rain falling relentlessly on the windshield, my breath slowly steaming up the windows.

My heart was thumping in my chest again. It would be ironic if I had a heart attack right now and missed out on the chance to meet the girl of my dreams. I took a deep breath. Control. I needed to control my emotions before entering the lion's den. I had to keep reminding myself that they knew nothing. Their ignorance was like a comforting cloak I could wrap around myself like the armor of a great king. King Arthur. He was a great king. If he existed at all, that is. Didn't he screw his sister, Mordred, or was that the name of his son? I used to be able to remember things like that. No, it wasn't Mordred at all. Morgana, that was her name. A mind like a steel trap, that's me.

I had made an extra effort to make sure that I looked my best. I was wearing my favorite Armani suit, which in an obscure way made me feel more secure. That morning, all my clothing was a non-threatening shade of gray, to match my eyes, the weather and the storm clouds roiling in my brain.

I looked at my watch. It was just before ten. Time to go in.

I entered the building and went up to reception. The Desk Sergeant told me where to go and gave me a stupid little name badge to wear. I went through the metal detector without incident. I walked down the dismal industrial yellow corridors and they hardly knew I was there. All those cops running around like chickens with their heads chopped off looking for the nasty serial killer and there I was—in their very midst. I was killing myself laughing—on the inside. On the outside, all was calm, impassive, impressive. Maybe I should have gone on the stage—yet another talent wasted.

I looked around the incident room and I felt pity for the police again. They were so woefully unprepared. Upstate New York was hardly Serial Killer Central. How could they possibly cope with works of art as intricate as mine?

I could feel confidence starting to flow back through my veins. I calmed right down, no more palpitations. I was in control of the situation. I felt powerful because of my secret; the secret that no one else knew about.

Guess who came in first? Not Dream Girl—of course not. Frank poked his head in and inquired, "You the professor from the University?"

Me: "Yes."

Frank came in and plopped into one of the uncomfortable-looking chairs littered around the room.

Frank: "Dr. Sheppard said you were coming in today. She seen you yet?"

Me: "No."

Frank: "I'll warn you right now, she's always late."

He looked at me and, as it didn't occur to him to ask me to sit down, I just took a chair. I stared back at him with as much lack of interest as he was showing in me.

Frank: "I have to be honest with you, Professor. I think you and the Doc are barking up the wrong tree."

Me: "Well, I am not even sure why I am here, Officer. Dr. Sheppard said that she could only explain in full once I signed the Non-Disclosure Agreement."

Frank: "It's Sergeant. Right. Well, I'll see if I can scare her up. She's really running late this morning. Must have had an emergency patient with ants in his pants."

He left.

I thought it was a neat touch that I kept calling him Officer instead of Sergeant. He hadn't bothered to introduce himself, so how would I know who he was? What a clod.

Elene arrived. Flustered, beautiful, apologetic. She shook me by the hand and, for one absurd moment, I thought, "I'll never wash that hand again!"

Elene: "Professor, I'm so sorry I'm late. Have you met Sergeant Frank Bianchi yet? He's the officer in charge of the investigation. He was supposed to meet us here."

Me: "There was a Sergeant here, but he didn't condescend to give me his name."

Elene: "That sounds like Frank. You'll have to forgive him. The only way I can stand it is by imagining that he has warped in from another time; a kind of Clint Eastwood era where policemen were never required to be polite."

Me: "Right."

Elene: "Let me go through the agreement that you'll have to sign and then we can get to work."

So she took me through the paperwork. I studied it as carefully as I could, but I was totally distracted by the close proximity of HER. I caught a whiff of her delicious perfume. Chanel Number Five, I think.

I signed the agreement and then Elene told me what the police had so far, which wasn't much. She showed me photographs of the crime scenes. Detailed close-ups of the drawings. My drawings. Thank God I was seated at a table by this point, because, understandable in the circumstances, I began to get aroused. Perusing my works of art was so stimulating, especially in Elene's company. My goddesses looked exquisite. I desperately wanted some copies of the photographs.

Maybe the preceding paragraph makes me sound like I lost my cool, but I am sure that I was acting very "professional". I made few comments, and I even averted my eyes at one point and pretended to try to regain my composure. Elene put her hand on mine and said, "This must be very difficult for you, Professor. I realize that you aren't used to looking at photographs like this, but any help you could give us would be greatly appreciated."

I heroically pulled myself together. Robert de Niro couldn't have done it better. I studied the photos for a little while and finally said, "Dr. Sheppard, I can't give you any kind of intelligent analysis in so short a space of time. The poses of the bodies bring certain things to mind, but unless I have my research books in front of me, I can't assist your investigation."

Elene: "I'll see if I can get you some copies of the photographs. Then you can take as long as you need."

(Fantastic! Masturbation fodder for the next few weeks!)

Elene: "Any ideas about the signs and poetry on the bodies? The symbols look astrological."

Me: "Well, poetry isn't exactly my field of expertise, but the symbols are definitely familiar. I can research them as well, if you like."

Elene: "Oh, yes, please. We are short of manpower here and while the police do regard this evidence as important, they can't devote as much time to it as they would like."

Me: "Time is something I have plenty of, at the moment. I'm only teaching a couple of classes a week."

Elene: "Professor Mandelson told me about your accident and the loss of your wife. I'm so sorry."

Me: (looking deeply into her eyes) "That's all behind me now."

Elene smiled and it was as if the gods smiled down on me as well. The sun came out in my head. She is my savior. I know it.

Elene went off to get permission to give me copies of the crime scene photographs. From force of will I made my erection go away so I could stand up without embarrassing myself. It was made much easier by Frank's reappearance.

Frank: "Professor, just a friendly warning. If those photographs fall into the hands of the press, I will personally track you down and hang you from the nearest lamppost. *Capisce*?"

Me: "Of course, Officer, I wouldn't dream of allowing anyone else to see them."

Frank: "It's Sergeant."

He left without saying good-bye. What an asshole.

Elene came back with the copies. I had to sign another piece of paper to acknowledge receipt of them.

She accompanied me downstairs and our elbows touched in the elevator. I got another hard-on. Luckily, I was wearing my coat, so I don't think she saw anything.

At the door, Elene said good-bye and shook my hand again. She smiled at me once more and I was almost dumb struck, but I kept it together and managed to act fairly normal. I promised to call her if I got any bright ideas.

In my car, I had to sit and breathe deeply for a few minutes. I contemplated masturbating, but thought it would be too dangerous in the middle of the day outside a police station.

I drove home as fast as I could within legal limits, the photographs of my works of art snug in my briefcase.

I wanted to postpone the enjoyment of gloating over the pictures in private for a while, but I couldn't resist their allure. The desire was too strong.

Oh, they were beautiful. My goddesses looked divine. For some bizarre reason, I thought that the photographs would be in black and white, but no, the colors were bright and realistic. The only complaint I had was that the lighting was a bit harsh, but that's just quibbling.

I put a picture of Tamsin next to one of Katrin. I imagined them together, gently playing with each other, sucking each other's pussies, toying with each other's breasts. I undressed and scattered the photographs on the living room floor. I sat on the couch and I engaged in my solitary pleasure.

I fantasized about Tamsin and Katrin being in bed with me. Totally devoted to me. I pictured myself kneeling on the bed with Tamsin giving me a blowjob while Katrin gently probed my ass with her finger. I ordered them to stop. Tamsin lay on her back and Katrin straddled her face and lowered herself down on Tamsin's waiting tongue. I entered Tamsin while Katrin sensuously undulated on Tamsin's face.

I came. Then I came again. And again. My imagination ran riot. I spent hours reliving my time with Tamsin and Katrin and it was so good. I was exhausted by the end of it.

I took a shower and for one moment felt guilty that I hadn't done any research for Elene. Then I remembered that I didn't have to. I knew it all already. I had immersed myself in my role as art consultant with such enthusiasm that I was beginning to believe my own hype. Disconcerting, to say the least.

After my shower, I ate a hearty meal and took a nap.

ENTRY 75

As their souls were extinguished, they were totally mine. I possessed them utterly. I could manipulate their limbs and arrange them in any position I wished. I could caress their smooth cold breasts. I could playfully tweak their permanently erect nipples and fear no recrimination—no reproving hand would push mine away.

Have you ever seen a dead person just after their soul has flown off to whatever adventure awaits it? Their beauty is icy, pure, refined; their features are as immovable as a Buddha's and just as peaceful. All the suffering is over. All the worry. I have lifted my darlings to another level of existence. There is no doubt about that. I helped my dear sweet goddesses shuffle off their mortal coils, and I know that they are all grateful for my attentions. I saw it in their eyes as I coaxed their spirits from them. I helped them shed the dull chrysalises of their sad, little lives. They are no longer mundane prostitutes, or legal secretaries, or dental assistants. They are immortal. They are now officially "Victims of a Serial Killer." All because of me. They love me for it. I know they do.

ENTRY 76

Today I woke up so depressed that I could hardly breathe. The contrast from the day before could not be more different. The world outside my window seemed to be painted with various shades of gray— all the color leeched from the landscape. (And I'm surprised? It is Syracuse in February.) I felt caught, trapped...wondering how the hell I had got myself into a situation that was so wildly improbable. I had met Elene and that was great—big breakthrough there—but how could I hope to get closer to her on a romantic level? At the moment, it was all business with her. Maybe I should just sweep her off her feet and take her to Kahunaville—it obviously gives her a thrill. It is gratifying to note that neither Elene nor Frank recognized me from the restaurant. Yet another indication that most people walk around in a dense haze of self-absorption most of the time and never pay attention to what is going on around them. Surprising for a policeman to be so unaware, but Frank is always so engrossed by Elene when he is with her that he sees nothing else of the world. And I can't blame him for that.

I guess I just have to take the lows with the highs. The highs are stratospheric, but the lows are crippling. All the feelings of power I have when I am involved in The Venus Project seem to evaporate once the hideous reality of life comes barging in. It's as if black dogs are barking at my door, following me everywhere. Sometimes when I am driving around town, I think I hear them in the trunk of my car, snarling and howling and whining and baying for my blood. Then the sound turns into the Devil's own laughter and that's when I think, "Shit, am I psychotic? I'm hearing things." I suppose that if I have the awareness to ask that question, I'm not, but what if I'm just an extremely observant psychotic?

Maybe I'll ask Elene the next time I see her. Now, there is a charming opening gambit for a dating strategy: "Hi, Elene, would you like to have dinner with me tonight? Oh, by the way, in your opinion as a psychologist, do you think that I am suffering from a massive psychosis with delusional paranoid tendencies?" That's bound to get her interested. I'm sure that she'll just be desperate to leap into the sack with me. Yes, siree, Bob.

Angie always ate chocolate when she got depressed. I think that it had something to do with her period, but, hell, I am willing to try anything. I can't have a drink. If I start on the martinis before noon, I'll be a goner by sundown. Maybe a Milky Way Bar is all I need to perk me up.

Who am I kidding? I know what I want. What I really, really want is to commit another murder. To further advance The Venus Project to a higher level. I am getting bored with waiting. I am tired of pretending to be a normal person. I want to do it again. I want to feel the power. I want to take those girls—my goddesses—to a place they never dreamed of and leave them there in a state of grace.

I am going to the corner store now to get some chocolate. Hopefully the black dogs will leave me alone. Maybe I will put some chocolate in the trunk to appease them. Appease the God of the Black Dog.

ENTRY 77

I have an itch that I can't scratch. I need to have more contact with Elene, but asking her out on a date now would be premature. I am desperate to see her again, but I can't take the chance of following her, not now that she knows me. I suppose I could try stalking her in disguise, but what if she spots me anyway?

"Hi, Professor Friday, why are you wearing that hideous green track suit and those goofy glasses? Has Halloween come early this year?"

I can't afford to take that chance.

Maybe I should bump into her, accidentally on purpose. After all, we do work at the same University. In fact, it's incredible that we haven't met before. I know her routine. It would be so easy for me to "arrange" a meeting. Yes, I will do it.

What the fuck do I have to lose, anyway, except my sanity?

ENTRY 78

I feel like the Puppet Master of the Universe. People are so unaware, so unseeing. It is a dawdle for someone like me to manipulate them; to pull their strings and watch them dance. All it takes is the will. I realize that now.

I went down to Phoebe's on Tuesday just before the lunchtime crush. I knew that Elene, that adorable creature of habit, would arrive in about fifteen minutes, so I picked out a table with a clear view of the door. Not only would I see her when she came in, but she couldn't fail to notice me.

It was perfect. She walked in the door, exquisite as always, and looked around for a free table. When I saw her out of the corner of my eye, I pretended to study the menu, but I was fully aware of her presence as she came up to my table.

Elene: "Hi, Professor, how are you doing?"

Me: "Oh, hello, Dr. Sheppard. I'm fine. And yourself?"

Elene: "Hanging on in there. Are you making any headway with our cases?"

Me: "Some, but it's a bit of a puzzle, as you can imagine."

Elene: "Of course, but I hope you'll have a breakthrough soon. I am convinced this guy is going to strike again soon and we have to catch him before he has the chance."

At this point, the headwaiter came up and apologized to Elene for the lack of table space. He told her that the restaurant was booked up and that she would have to wait for about fifteen minutes. (Which is exactly what I told him to say. It's wonderful what twenty bucks can do, placed in the right hands.) Elene looked disappointed and that's when I came to the rescue.

Me: "Why don't you sit here? I mean, you're welcome to share my table if you want."

Elene looked a bit taken aback. I knew that she loved her little solitary lunches, but here was a free seat, ready and available.

Elene: "You're sure I wouldn't be bothering you?"

Me: "God, no. I'd love some company. I've been spending too much time on my own lately."

Elene smiled and sat down. I watched her slouch off her coat and get settled in her chair. At one point she leaned forward and I was awarded with a tantalizing glimpse of her cleavage. It was bliss just observing her and chatting to her like a normal person. Although there is a great pleasure to be gleaned from stalking someone, there is nothing like actual contact. It makes one feel less like a pervert and more like a regular human being. Odd to think that she knew only the barest facts about me and I knew virtually everything there was to know about her. It made me feel a little bit more confident, a little bit more in control.

Unfortunately, that confidence did not translate to my conversational skills. They were desultory at best. I was so afraid to make a mistake, to reveal too much. Hopefully, I came across as deep and mysterious rather than slightly retarded and tongue-tied.

Fortunately, like most women, Elene was happy to keep the talk flowing with very little help from me. I let her words wash over me like a veritable waterfall of conversation. She loved to talk. She loved using interesting and archaic words. She loved telling little stories.

My one beef was that Elene made the mistake that all women do at least once when they are getting to know a new guy, whether she is romantically interested in him or not. She eventually got onto the subject of Frank and proceeded to tell me what a bastard he was. Not that I minded hearing that my instincts were right and that Frank was a turd. However, nothing is more certain to put a man off a woman than the woman droning on and on about her ex. In disparaging someone else, the complainer is diminished, in my opinion. This was the first warning sign to me that maybe getting to know Elene on a personal level was not such a hot idea. What if I found out that my Venus had feet of clay? That would be very disappointing. Perhaps she should just continue to live up there on my fantasy pedestal, never condescending to mix with mere mortals.

After a couple of hours, Elene bustled off to her next class and I stayed at Phoebe's and had a martini. I considered the possibilities:

1. Do I ask Elene out and see if the relationship develops? On the down side, the consequences could be devastating for my fantasy world. My love object could turn out to be just as neurotic and desperate as Angie and others of her ilk. On the other hand, Elene could turn out to be an angel in real life. We might end up wildly happy and get married and have kids and I could give up being a horrible foul murderer and go back to being Mr. Nice Guy. I would learn to be content with having a normal sexual relationship and my sick fantasies would recede to a deep, dark, spidery cavern in my mind.

2. Do I pull back and keep it on a professional level and continue to live in my sick fantasies? That would be fine, I guess, but since it might be unwise to hunt at the moment, I might get very frustrated.

3. Do I kidnap Elene and take her to some out-of-the-way spot and make her my sex slave? That might be very gratifying. But unrealistic. The police would inevitably check me out, as I've had some

contact with her. It would be quite embarrassing to be discovered in a log cabin in the woods somewhere with a naked Elene chained to a wall, sucking my cock. On the other hand, I am not ruling this possibility out. Hey, I should work on that log cabin fantasy. Sounds promising.

ENTRY 79

Last night, I couldn't sleep. My mind was a nest of wasps, all buzzing with evil little songs of betrayal, insecurity and hate. I felt like Hamlet's father—someone was insidiously dripping poison into my ear while I slept.

The lyrical content was, "Who Are You Kidding?" with "Do You Really Think You Can Get Away With Murder?" a close second. They went something like, "Do you really think that Possibility One could work? Do you really think that you can retire from serial killing and play happy families with Elene? You have fallen too deeply into The Project. You can never go back to being a normal person. You are never going to give up all that power and control. We will never let you go. You like your work too much. You will continue to kill until you go mad or get caught, whichever comes first."

The wasps buzzed and zinged their tuneless melodies until I felt like I was lying in a bed of stinging nettles. I got up and had a drink. And then I had another one and another until oblivion came and smothered me with a warm alcoholic blanket.

The next morning, I woke up with a bitch of a headache. As a punishment for my stupidity, I taught my morning class without the benefit of painkillers. It was torture, but I had to prove to myself that I had the determination to conquer my pain and function normally. I can do anything if I really want to. I know that now. I have to triumph over the Mind Wasps and the other evil thoughts crowding my brain. Those thoughts are my greatest enemies, not the police, not Elene, not even God.

Between the Devil, the Black Dogs and the Mind Wasps, I have a hell of a pest problem in my brain.

I need to call an exterminator. A Mind Pest Exterminator. If there was such a thing, can you imagine how much money he would make?

Some worrisome thoughts about the state of the global economy? "No problem, sir, I can get rid of those in a jiffy."

Nasty niggles about your creditors baying for your blood? "I've got just the thing, sir, just let me insert this tube in your ear and your predicaments will be hydraulically sucked out in no time."

Maybe they could get rid of those annoying floaters in my eyeballs at the same time. Perhaps they should just suck out my entire being, give it a good scrub and then insert it back into my flabby outer husk. Now there's a charming thought.

I only hope that I can hold it together. Hold off the Devil and the Dogs and the Wasps long enough.

ENTRY 80

The lunatics are taking over the asylum and death is overwhelming the world.

Last night, I stayed up until 3:30 in the morning watching TV. Even in the middle of all this activity, I am still a television junkie. CNN was made for people like me. Every item on the news justifies my course of action. My crimes are small potatoes compared to say, the shenanigans going on in the Middle East. Where in the Middle East you might ask? Name it, say I. What a carnival of fools: they kill each other, they kill their children, they kill their politicians—with no thought of the future.

What new idiocy will be committed in the name of Allah, or Jehovah, or Jesus, or Shiva next, I wonder? What fresh travesty of justice will be wreaked on a suffering people? What blunder of stupefying proportions will be perpetrated yet again by an uncaring government with no one left accountable? I think that of all the rationalizations that people use to kill each other, surely religion has got to be one of the most puerile. To believe in a God is irrational enough as it is, but to kill in the name of your all-knowing, all-seeing, all-loving God is the height of inanity. But of course, these people aren't killing in the name of their God. They are killing because, secretly, they love it. Yes, they love every moment of the thrill of the chase, the sound of broken bones, the screams of pain, the look of agony on their victim's face, the final death throes. They don't kill in the name of their faceless Gods or because somebody stole their rotten little parcel of land that their ignorant families have scratched out some pathetic living on for the last few centuries. They kill because that is the only thing that they know how to do well. They kill because it is the only creative thing they can do: kill and be killed. Such a wonderful legacy to leave their children, who they now send out to do their fighting for them. Teach the children to fight, fight for God because "God is on our side." Oh, is he now? Well, hey, guess what? I've got some news for you. God is on the other guy's side, too. Ain't that a laugh?

God doesn't give a flying fuck what we do. He sits up there, tearing out what is left of his hair and despairing of us like any other exhausted parent about a child who has gone wrong. And he probably thinks, "Fuck the human race. I'm going to send an asteroid their way to wipe them out and start all over again. This time I'll give cockroaches brains instead of monkeys. It's got to be an improvement over the last bunch."

Good riddance to all of them.

ENTRY 81

What am I going to do? I need to create. My urges are becoming overwhelming. They are so pervasive that I can't even face seeing Elene again. I need a release.

I have thought long and hard about this. I know that it might be dangerous, but it could also be an entertaining way of distracting the police.

I am going to take a little trip. I am going to visit the old stomping grounds of serial killer extraordinaire, Arthur Shawcross. Arthur, as I have mentioned before, cruised the highways and byways of Rochester, New York, where he killed a number of prostitutes for his pleasure. Rochester is only eighty-six miles west down the Thruway, a quick little trip. I checked out some hot nightclubs on the Internet and found a hunting ground that sounds perfect: The KonTiki Klub.

Tomorrow night I will go to there and see what I can sniff out. I know that it is dangerous. I know that things could go wrong. I know that I am deviating from my carefully planned operation, but what can I do? I don't want to take the chance of committing another murder in Syracuse. It's just too risky. I feel too exposed.

I know that if I just do one more—just one—that I will feel so much better. I will feel calmer and I will be in control again.

I am getting excited about it already.

ENTRY 82

This time, I am going to go in a new disguise. No longer as Mysterious Out-Of-Town Businessman, but as Baby-Shit Green Tracksuit Man! Yes, I think that he deserves a shot. The last time I was in Rochester, I was struck by its lack of sophistication. I think that M.O.O.T.B will stick out too much, while B.S.G.T.M. fits in everywhere.

I may just pick up a prostitute. I feel like an easy time of it. Doing the whole gentlemanly, buying drinks, having a chat number is so exhausting. Also, I'm in the mood for a little bondage and there's no way a non-prostitute will go for that kind of kink on an initial pick up. If she's smart, that is.

Jesus. I just had a thought. I am creating two different serial killers, with two different M.Os. There's Businessman with his paintings and poses, and Geeky Bondage Guy. How intriguing for the police.

Maybe next week, I'll head farther West to Buffalo as Lumberjack Shirt Man and commit yet another murder. Then three different police forces will be looking for three different serial murderers. Now that would be fun. Except I would have to kill the Buffalo girl in a different way and I don't want to do that. Strangling is so sensual. I can't imagine using any other method. Stabbing someone is so messy and gruesome.

When I was doing my research, I discovered that three out of four serial killers employ strangulation (with or without a ligature) as their preferred method of causing death. Next is stabbing, then way down the scale is shooting. I guess we like to get up close and personal with our victims. We need that "hands on" approach.

Personally, I find the sensation of squeezing the life out of a beautiful woman erotic in the extreme. The way they struggle. The way their tongues poke out between their lips. The way their eyes widen and bulge. The way their pelvises bang convulsively against mine. The way they ineffectually try to pry my hands from their lovely pale throats. I look into their eyes and I see the light die. I see their souls go away to another place. As they go, I come. I shoot my seed into their hot little pussies at the same time as their spirits disappear on their final journeys.

Can you get sexier than that, I ask you?

ENTRY 83

Last night didn't exactly turn out as I planned. It seems that even with serial killing, there is something like beginner's luck. My first murders were so easy, as if they were preordained. I should have known that I would have a miserable time in Rochester.

After the usual change of cars at the airport, I left Syracuse around nine in the evening on Saturday, wanting to take the ninety-minute drive to Rochester at an easy pace. The place was as dull as I remembered it, like most one-company towns. I headed downtown and moseyed around, taking in my surroundings and trying not to look too conspicuous. However, yet again, no one seemed to notice me. I don't seem to resonate with most people. It's as if I carry some kind of nondescript gene. Not that I am complaining, as it has served me in good stead so far.

The only people that seem to notice me are my victims. Why is that, I wonder? Is it because I am noticing them? I suppose any woman likes the fully undivided attentions of a man. Pity that they don't have a clue about why I am so interested in them.

I arrived at the KonTiki Klub and parked around the corner. One of my pet hates (I have so many of them now) is the way people misspell words on purpose. I blame Prince (The Artist Formerly Known As The Artist Formerly Known As Prince). He started using unconventional spellings for the titles of his songs years ago: *Nothing Compares 2 U* is a prime example. Now, it has grown out of all proportion, with every rap artist worth his salt misspelling the life out of perfectly good words. What kind of example is this giving to our numskull kids, I wonder, who have difficulties enough spelling their own damn names, let alone more complicated words like two and you? I gritted my teeth and entered the bowels of The KonTiki Klub, squashing a desire to climb up to the sign and change the K in Klub to a C.

It was as if I had never left Kahunaville. The place was like an immense version of the restaurant, only more so. Verdant plastic foliage sprouted from every crevice and the cocktail waitresses were wearing fetching turquoise mini-sarongs and leis. Fake palm trees, colorful murals and stuffed parrots completed the South Seas image and, in a florid way, it was quite restful.

The place was bustling with prey, young lovelies on the make. In the end, I had chickened out wearing the Baby-Shit Green Track Suit. It was just too awful and I don't think I would have made it past the dress code of the club. Also, I wanted to feel confident tonight and I wouldn't be able to do that looking like a sack of shit. I was dressed casually in an expensive gray sports jacket and black jeans, with my tinted glasses and different hairstyle. I looked innocuous but not out of place.

I made a bargain with myself. If I couldn't pick up a girl in couple of hours, I would drive to the seedier part of town and snag a hooker.

I bought myself a drink, perched on a bar stool and observed for a while. I soon zeroed in on a girl by the bar that seemed unattached. She was pretty, with black hair and green eyes. Sensational figure. Purple velvet mini skirt and a green, tight, low-cut top. Great tits, no bra. I observed her for about ten minutes. She occasionally glanced at her watch, so I deduced she was waiting for someone. That someone was very late and I was amused at how angry she got as each moment passed.

After fifteen minutes, I made my move. I walked up to the bar next to Waiting Girl and ordered another martini. It was like standing next to a pressure cooker. Any minute now steam would be coming out of her ears.

Me: "Excuse me, I couldn't help noticing, but are you waiting for someone?"

Waiting Girl: "Yes, I am, and the bastard is half an hour late. I am staying five more minutes, then I'm blowing this pop stand."

Me: "I don't blame you. The man must be crazy, keeping a pretty girl like you waiting. May I buy you a drink?"

She was so angry, she hadn't noticed me. Now, she looked at me for the first time. She smiled and said with a certain reckless abandon, "Sure, why the hell not."

Her name was Nancy. The bastard's name was Jerry. Nancy liked Piña Coladas. She worked for RiteAid as a pharmacist's assistant. I heard all about Jerry. He worked at Marine Midland Bank and thought he was God's gift. Her friend Diandra had warned her about Jerry, but Nancy had thrown caution to the winds and now she was ruing the day she'd ever met the guy. Nancy had been an idiot to get involved with such a jerk in the first place. Blah, blah, blah.

She glugged down three Piña Coladas in twenty minutes. I was starting to congratulate myself on a successful entry to stage one of the pick-up, when a not-so-gentle prod in my back turned me around.

That's when I met Jerry, who—considering he worked for a bank— was very tall, very wide and very muscular.

Jerry: "Who the fuck are you?"

Me: "Uhhhhhhhhhhh..."

Nancy: "Don't you talk to him like that! Who the hell do you think you are, turning up this late?"

Jerry: "Beat it, Jack. This is between her and me."

Me: "Ummmmmm..."

Nancy: "Don't you tell him to beat it, you bum. I like him, so he's staying."

Me: "Eeerrrrrr..."

Jerry: "Listen, baby, I'm sorry I'm late. I just don't like the idea of some creep hitting on you, that's all."

Nancy: "That creep bought me three drinks. I could have died of thirst waiting for you."

Jerry: (turning to look at me in an ominous fashion) "Three drinks? Are you trying to get her drunk?"

Me: "No, um, not at all."

Nancy: "Don't change the subject. Why are you so late?"

Jerry turned to explain and I took it as a cue to melt away as discreetly as possible. They were still arguing as I got to the door.

I didn't feel like trying another bar. I walked around for a bit, to clear my head, and then I headed for my car.

Time for Rochester's red-light district.

I cruised down to Lake Avenue, keeping one eye peeled for the police. The houses along the road had all been built circa 1880 and looked as if they hadn't had a coat of paint on them since. It was starting to snow sporadically, but the cold weather hadn't kept those undaunted ladies of the night off the street.

Finally, I spotted a likely looking number. She was tall, honey blonde and in her late twenties. Most of the hookers in the area were a bit rough-looking, but she looked promising.

She was all by herself. I stopped the car and she came up to the window.

Street Girl: "Looking for a party, Mister?"

Me: "You bet."

Street Girl: "Ten bucks for a blow job, twenty-five bucks for straight sex. Hundred if you want anything kinky."

Me: "A hundred it is. Do you know a motel?"

Street Girl: "No problem." She got in the car. "What kind of kink are you into, Mister?"

Me: "A little bondage, maybe."

Street Girl: "Me or you?"

Me: "Sorry?"

Street Girl: "Who gets tied up, honey? Me or you?"

Me: "Oh, I see. You, if you don't mind."

Street Girl: "I don't mind, but that's fifty extra."

She directed me to a fleapit near the Thruway. It was a carbon copy of the first motel in Syracuse. We went through virtually the same routine. She got the key and I parked away from the lights so no one would notice my car or me.

We got to the room and I quickly came to the realization that I had made a big mistake.

She was a nonstop talker. In five minutes, I seemed to have more information about her than I'd found out about Elene in a week of investigation.

Her name was Gertrude, believe it or not. She was convinced that the reason she became a prostitute was because her mother had given her such a lousy name. I asked her why she didn't change it if she disliked it so much. She looked at me as if I were a moron. "It's my name," she said. "I can't change my name." Gertrude was from Watertown, near the Canadian border. Watertown was a dump. She was a high school dropout. She married some guy when she was sixteen and he turned out to be—surprise, surprise—an asshole. Gertrude found herself slinging hash browns in some greasy spoon up near the Mohawk Indian

Reservation north of Utica and decided to move on up in the world and "go on the game," as the English say. So the bright lights of Rochester beckoned and now she was happy as a pig in shit.

When Gertrude finally ran out of things to say, I managed to get a word in edgeways and told her what I wanted. She got undressed down to her stockings, garter belt, leopard-skin bra and panties, and lay on the bed. She was chewing gum. I told her to spit it out. She obliged and lay there.

I tied Gertrude up. I stood and looked at her for a while, but I couldn't get it up. She just didn't fit. It was not a sensual experience.

Gertrude got impatient: "Whaddaya doing? You're just standing there. You gonna do something? Jesus, hurry up or I'm gonna have to charge you double."

Me: "Shut the fuck up."

I stuffed something in her mouth. She started to struggle, but it wasn't any good. She didn't turn me on. She only made me feel exasperated.

What was I going to do? If I left her there, she might complain to the cops. Killing her would be a waste. It would be meaningless. Why take the risk?

I took the gag out.

Gertrude: "What the fuck did you do that for, you bastard? Untie me or I'm going to holler for the cops."

Me: "I don't think so, Gertrude. I can't imagine that you and the police are exactly bosom buddies."

Gertrude: "Ah, shit."

I apologized to her. I said that I suffered from a sexual problem due to an unfortunate logging accident. I was trying to rejuvenate my sex drive with kinky sex, because the straight stuff didn't do it for me anymore. Gertrude was amazingly sympathetic. She told me that a lot of her clients had problems. She asked me to untie her, so I did.

Gertrude got up, bent down to pick up her stilettos and then swung around and hit me so hard on the side of my head with her shoes that I literally saw stars. My knees buckled and I dropped to the floor.

Gertrude: "That's for gagging me, you prick. I hate that!"

Gertrude grabbed her clothes and marched out, still in her bra and panties.

I left as quickly as I could. I hadn't touched any furniture and I wiped down the doorknobs as I left.

I drove a couple of miles, then pulled over and held my aching head in my hands for a while. When my ears stopped ringing, I drove back to the center of town. I found an all night drug store and picked up some Extra Strength Tylenol.

What an evening.

That's what comes of deviating from The Plan. I deserved getting whacked in the head for my stupidity. It's a miracle that something more drastic didn't happen, like getting nabbed by the police for curb crawling for instance. The God of Serial Killers was definitely on vacation last night.

ENTRY 84

Another night, another dream.

In this dream, I am Frank, God knows why. I have been called to the scene of a multiple homicide. I'm accompanied by my partner, who bears an uncanny resemblance to my friend Jerry from the KonTiki Klub. We are walking from room to room of a house that is scarily reminiscent of Norman Bates' home sweet home in *Psycho*. We're trying to analyze what has happened. The scene of the crime is dreadful, with huge Jackson Pollock-like splashes of blood dripping down the walls. In my dream, I seem to have the uncanny ability to decipher the bloodstains and ascertain the order in which the murders occurred, which is crucial to the investigation.

Then I wander into the bathroom and see a vision that sears itself on my dream retinas. Three people are tipped over headfirst into the bathtub: a woman and two children. Their hands are tied behind their backs. As I peek over into the tub, I see that the backs of their heads have all been blown off. Blood is dripping everywhere. Some Picasso has written on the wall in blood, "Fuck You Gertrude." I back out of the bathroom, calling for my partner, but he has disappeared. I look everywhere for him, as my feelings of apprehension grow. I can't find him anywhere in the house. I go outside and all the other police cars have left. There is no one around and I am in complete darkness. I stumbled around, calling out for my partner, but there is no reply.

There is nothing weirder than dreaming about being in complete darkness. It is as if I had been struck blind.

Then I get the distinct feeling that that I am no longer alone. My partner has reappeared. I suddenly realize with absolute certainty that he is the murderer. I am totally vulnerable. I am in a black void, seeing nothing, hearing nothing, feeling nothing. I sense his presence right behind me.

I willed myself to wake up. I knew I was dreaming and I had to get out of there, but I was suffering from sleep paralysis. It felt like I was at the bottom of a deep black lake and I was slowly struggling to the surface. I finally managed to open my eyes, but I felt so groggy that it was as if some evil force was trying to drag me under the surface of the water again. I had to slap myself in the face to get out of it.

I got up and had a cup of coffee. I didn't want to go back to sleep for fear of returning to the void. It was too similar to the evil black flood from the Devil's cock from my earlier dream.

Some people say that Freud is full of crap and that your dreams don't mean anything. They say that dreams are just the random firings of a dormant brain chewing over the events of the previous day. Well, I think I can safely say that my dreams are a true indication of my disturbed mind. There aren't any hidden meanings, it's all there in plain sight...lying right there on the surface. Death isn't a symbol for anything. It is just death.

Sometimes I feel so tired, that I just want to give up. The anger dissipates and I am left feeling empty. Back to being the Zero Man. Mr. Nonentity. As I write that phrase, Zero Man, I can feel myself getting angry again. I want to feel full again. I demand to be filled up and if the only thing that fills me up is murder, then so be it. I am not afraid of death. I am not afraid of dealing death. I am only afraid of being a Zero Man.

ENTRY 85

Elene called this morning. I was still bleary-eyed from my sleepless night and I probably didn't sound very coherent. She asked me if I wanted to come over for a meal and discuss the case further.

This wasn't in my game plan. I needed time to reassess my feelings for her. I needed time to find out what I really wanted from her.

She was so insistent that, in the end, I decided to go along with it, but I was scared that more contact would destroy her as a Venus in my eyes.

How strange to feel like this. To retreat so thoroughly from my previous position. I still want her, of course. I want to possess her, but I no longer want a relationship with her. I just want to own her. No give and take. No arguments. No petty discussions about who is going to take out the garbage. Fuck that. Just outright possession.

ENTRY 86

I decided this morning not to go over to Elene's house tonight. I called her up and made an excuse. She sounded disappointed. I told her that something had come up and that it would be more convenient if I met her at the Public Safety Building on Tuesday morning.

I need more time to think.

ENTRY 87

Sometimes the voices in my head are so loud that I am positive that I left a television set on somewhere in the house. I go around looking for it, but nothing is on. Boy, is that scary, or what? I know that if I listen too closely to the voices then I am lost, but luckily they are quite indistinct. The doctors told me to expect the occasional auditory hallucination, but this is fucking creepy. Maybe there is a perverse gnome living in my basement, coming out to torment me by turning on various TVs around the house, then switching them off when he hears me coming. That's a marvelous concept, isn't it? Black Dogs, Mind Wasps, the Great Gray Devil and now Perverse Gnomes. It's getting kind of crowded around here. Even the Mind Pest Exterminator would have a problem with all the shit that's flying around my head.

I better forget about the gnome idea. It's just an auditory hallucination. I can live with brain damage, but I can't live with gnomes. Gnomes remind me of the finale of the Nicholas Roeg film, *Don't Look Now*, when a red coat-wearing, gnome-faced lady dwarf skewers Donald Sutherland on the banks of The Grand Canal in Venice. Jesus, that image gave me nightmares for weeks. No gnomes.

ENTRY 88

It is 9:00 AM, Tuesday morning. Elene just called. She said that I didn't need to come in to the police station, as an arrest of the serial killer is imminent. An arrest is imminent. She said that she would love to get together soon to hear my conclusions, as they could be valuable when the case goes to court.

Me: "You really think that they've got the right guy, then?"

Elene: "Frank seems very positive, but he didn't have time to give me any details. He was on his way to arrest the suspect."

Me: "Oh. Well, just give me a call when you have the time."

Elene: (warmly...at least I thought that it sounded warm) "You can count on it."

So, at this very moment, the police are on their merry way to arrest a suspect in the killings. Will that suspect turn out to be me? Maybe that's why Frank didn't give any details to Elene. Maybe she told him that we had lunch together.

I don't feel as scared as I thought I would be. What could they possibly have on me? I will just have to wait it out.

ENTRY 89

Elene called again. The police have arrested a plumber called Lonnie Snarldon. A prostitute was found strangled last Saturday and the forensic evidence and witness reports point right to poor old Lonnie.

Now, why would they link my crimes to his? Okay, the basic M.O. was the same, but other than that there are no connections. I never left any forensic evidence at my crime scenes. Maybe the police think that the serial killer got careless. It does happen. A lot of them lose it near the end. They seem to run out of steam and want to get caught. Even Super Serial Killer Ted Bundy lost his concentration at the end of his career. But not me.

It is almost insulting that the police think that some bozo plumber named Lonnie had the wit, ingenuity, artistic talent, nay—genius—to commit my crimes. Lonnie is going to get all the credit, all the fame and all the publicity. It will be his name that goes down in the Serial Killer Hall of Infamy. How irritating. Not that I care about such fripperies, but in a strange way, my pride has been wounded.

On the other hand, maybe I should just shut up and be grateful—be very grateful—that they suspect someone else.

I certainly seem to have the luck of the damned.

ENTRY 90

I spoke to Elene again. She seemed to be quite eager to get together to discuss things. She wants me to come over to her place tonight. I decided to go. I need all the information I can get. I have prepared my presentation to her about the poses of the bodies, just in case she wants to hear my conclusions.

I feel more nervous about seeing her tonight than I did going out on my date with Tamsin.

ENTRY 91

Making the great leap.

Driving to Elene's house, I tried to analyze my confused feelings: fear, anticipation and doubt. At the bottom of the cesspool of my swirling anxieties thrashed the Great White Shark of Libido—ravenous for a taste of Elene's flesh, but on my terms. Half of me was determined to have her this evening. The other half was reluctant to break the barrier, to leap the chasm and dive into some form of intimacy with her. Intimacy? Who was I kidding? I wanted Elene. I wanted her completely. I wanted her to surrender to me so I could conquer her body and soul. That is what lovemaking is all about to men. If they admit it to themselves, most men know that to make love to a woman is to subdue her. Books are written about it, popular songs are composed, plays scribbled, movies made. If you are a stalker, all you have to do is look at popular media to see that if you are persistent enough, you will always get the girl. All the lessons are there if you want to see them, such as never taking "no" for an answer. How many women say "no", when they mean "yes"? Women say "no" because they want to make their surrender into something special. It's a little treasure they give to you: "I said 'no', but now I mean, 'yes yes, yes,' because you are the man who I am willing to break my strict moral code for. You are the man worthy of my love. You are THE MAN."

I got to Elene's around 7:30 PM. Her place was tastefully furnished: white walls, lots of books, minimal furniture and just a few framed, black and white Brassai posters on the wall. The usual female clutter must have been relegated to the bedroom. She greeted me at the door wearing a low-cut, blood red dress. The color suited her. The dress was mid-calf length, but she was in her bare feet, which I found very appealing. Perfect little pink toes, painted carefully with ruby red nail polish. Elene was wearing Chanel Number 5 again. I shed my coat, scarf and gloves and walked into her warm and cozy sanctuary. I immediately felt at home.

I sat on the modern gray leather couch and Elene poured drinks. She made me a passable vodka martini and she had a Ricard, the traditional French aperitif. We talked about the weather, then I opened my briefcase and gave her my conclusions about the positions of the bodies and the artwork. Of course, I had a distinct advantage since I committed the murders. I pretended that it had been quite difficult to trace the poses of the bodies to various works of art with the goddess Venus as their subject.

Elene was impressed by my efforts, I could tell.

Elene: "Professor, would it take a great knowledge of art to obtain this information? The reason that I am asking is that our prime suspect, Lonnie Snarldon, isn't exactly an Einstein from what I can gather. He went to Onondaga Community College and got a Bachelor's in Business Studies, but his grades were only average."

Me: "Well, I think if the desire is there, then it is possible to find out anything. If Lonnie is obsessed by images of Venus, then it would be simple enough to access the paintings off the Internet, for example, or any popular art book from the public library."

Elene: "I see. I have to be honest with you, Professor, I think the police have overstepped the mark on this one. There is plenty of forensic evidence to point to Lonnie as the murderer of Vivian Miller, the prostitute who was strangled on Saturday. There was also a witness who saw Lonnie pick up the victim in his car, but I don't think that they have a very strong case for him committing the 'Painted Lady' serial killings. I can't imagine someone like Lonnie having an obsessive 'Venus Complex'—for want of a better description. These are elegant crimes, committed by someone who put a lot of thought and planning into their execution. Lonnie doens't strike me as a thinking/planning kind of guy."

(Oh, Elene, you are so intuitive. "Elegant"—I like the sound of that.)

Me: "Other than strangling the girl, what additional evidence do the police have?"

Elene: "Frank would probably hate me telling you this, but you're assisting with the investigation anyway, so what's the difference? He wrote on the dead woman's body."

Me: (I couldn't believe my luck.) "Wow. Really? That sounds conclusive to me."

Elene: "He didn't write anything poetic. All he wrote was, 'Fuck You Vivian'."

(Echoes from my dream of the other night. Although I guess writing "Fuck You" is hardly original.)

Me: "Oh."

Elene: "Not what you would call lyrical verse."

Me: "Maybe if you're a rap artist..."

Elene: "There is something else that is bugging me. I know that I have to be aware of the professional pride aspect, but Lonnie just doesn't fit my profile of the serial killer and that, to be frank, annoys the hell out of me. Okay, he has a certain amount of rage against women and his relationships with the opposite sex are bumpy, but I just don't think he fits the bill."

Me: "What does Frank say about that?"

Elene: "Frank thinks that I am just sore because I missed the boat. He hates the idea of outsiders being involved in investigations at the best of times, even though I have been helpful to him in the past. He thinks it's hilarious that I pulled a boner on this one. In his jaded eyes, it serves me right that I got it so wrong."

Me: "Frank won't entertain the idea that HE might be wrong?"

Elene: "The police have a suspect that they think fits the bill and it will take a hell of a lot of evidence to the contrary to convince them otherwise. How they are going to prove that he committed the other murders may be a challenge, but believe me, they can make it stick if they want to bad enough. Poor old Lonnie is tailor-made for Death Row, I'm afraid."

Me: "Any previous convictions?"

Elene: "Two as an adult. One for assault in a road rage case and one for sexual assault. And his juvenile record isn't sterling either. Two B and Es and one Grand Theft Auto."

Me: "Things don't sound so good for Lonnie."

Elene: (taking a swig of her Ricard) "No, they don't."

Elene went off to finish preparing our meal and I chewed over the latest facts. Lonnie was looking good. He was looking real good for the murders. What a break.

We ate dinner. Elene was an excellent cook. We had an appetizer of baked green peppers garnished with anchovies, olive oil and black olives, which tasted better than it sounded, followed by roast chicken stuffed with parsley accompanied by rice and homemade ratatouille.

We drank a Bourgogne Aligoté white wine that complimented the food perfectly.

After dinner, Elene and I retired to the couch, listened to music (Chet Baker's *Greatest Hits*) and talked some more, mostly just personal stuff. I was only paying attention on the most superficial level. All I could think of was making love to Elene.

Touching her skin. Breathing in the scent of her flesh. Penetrating her and watching her face twist into that mixture of agony and ecstasy that women do so well.

Then something Elene said broke through...

Elene: "You seem a bit distracted, Professor."

Me: "I'm sorry. I keep thinking of those poor women getting killed and the police not catching the right guy. It's infuriating."

Elene: "I know. I think we should do something about it."

Me: "We should?"

Elene: "There must be a way that we can catch the right man."

Me: "Well, we don't exactly have the resources. After all, that's what the police are there for. Anyway, Lonnie will have legal counsel."

Elene: "Yeah, some crappy public defender."

Me: "You never know, this is bound to be a high-profile trial. Perhaps some hotshot lawyer will take on the case for the publicity."

Elene: "I know a good criminal lawyer in New York City. I might be able to persuade him to get involved."

Me: "Maybe you should give him a call sometime."

Elene jumped up and walked briskly to the telephone while I silently cursed myself. Why did I have to mention Lonnie again and get her all steamed up about the injustice of it all? I should have just told her what was really on my mind: ravishing her body.

Elene called her friend in NYC. He was interested, but, thankfully, he was extremely busy. He wouldn't be able to take the case. He promised her that he would give it some thought and call her back with the names of some other lawyers that he could recommend.

Elene returned to the couch. She was passionately fired up and she kept prattling on about poor Lonnie and how brazenly the police were going to stitch him up. I contemplated making a move on her, but something stopped me. I felt too exposed, too vulnerable and, frankly, too irritable. The security I had initially felt in her house evaporated. All this talk of Lonnie was killing my libido, which was remarkable in itself. Interesting to think that my potential savior was coming in between Elene and me, but there you go.

We broke up the party around eleven, as Elene had an early class the next morning. I went home and masturbated myself to sleep, accompanied by daydreams of ripping off that red dress, with all its connotations of red flags and bulls. Red, the color of blood, the color of sex, the color of her lips—open wide, begging for mercy, begging for more.

ENTRY 92

The news seems to engender the most depressing thoughts. I watch it daily and all I feel is despair and contempt for the human race. The things we do to each other beggar the imagination. I'm just a talented amateur compared to the maniacs running loose out there. All the incredible innovations of the 20th and 21st centuries become meaningless in the face of the mind-numbing poverty, ignorance and stupidity that one is confronted with every day. And yet we go on and on and on. The horrors don't stop us. We keep on plopping out babies like there is no tomorrow, even though for many of them, there isn't.

The most powerful human instinct of all seems to be the one to procreate no matter what—to continue to churn out mindless multitudes of ignoramuses every day without pause. Meanwhile there is only a tiny minority of people born into this world who develop abilities that will further the progress of mankind. Is there a design fault at work here? It is almost as if nature's most important task is to hand out this procreation instinct, regardless of the quality of the product. One would think that natural selection—survival of the fittest—would preclude this abundance of dunces, but the question is: the fittest what? Is it the fittest body or the fittest brain? Once upon a time, the physically strong would logically be the ones to survive; now it is supposedly the smartest. Does that mean that the world will be full of Bill Gates clones in fifty years? It doesn't bear thinking about.

If there are around seven billion people on the planet and 5.1 billion people are living on the barest subsistence level, then what is the point of the human race? What are we here for? If only 15% of the population are the movers and shakers, does that mean that we could get rid of those pesky 5.1 billion souls and not notice? The world might be a cleaner, smarter, less poverty-stricken and disease-ridden place.

Hey, I have an idea. Maybe instead of forgetting the debts of the Third World, we should just nuke them. They are never going to solve their problems anyway; we know that. The will is just not there. We should just nuke the poor, misbegotten lot of them. Except for the nuclear fallout, the world would be a better place. There would be no depressive atmosphere of misery to bring down our Have A Nice Days. On the other hand, forget nuclear weapons. Too much radiation. Just use neutron bombs. They kill all the people and dogs and stuff, but don't destroy the buildings. The radiation disperses very quickly, so there will be less harm to the environment. Trouble is, what would we do with all that shitty Third World architecture?

I think that this is a dandy idea. I wonder how difficult it is to get hold of a neutron bomb? I bet I could pick up one cheap in the local K-Mart in Tehran.

ENTRY 93

Elene called me today to tell me that District Attorney Kulkinski has charged Lonnie with my works of art. I should feel like celebrating, but until Lonnie is in the clink for good, I am not home free.

Elene was furious about Lonnie being charged and she asked me to come over to her place again to discuss my findings in depth. I am not sure how I am going to take advantage of all that negative emotion, but I am definitely going to make a move tonight. After all, she keeps begging me to come over to her place. That must mean something.

ENTRY 94

Elene was beside herself when I arrived. I'd never seen her so angry. I tried to calm her down, but she wouldn't listen. All she could do was talk about Frank and what a bastard he was. She even forgot to offer me a martini.

Elene: "Professor, did you ever see that documentary directed by Errol Morris called *The Thin Blue Line*? The police stitched up this guy called Randall Adams for the murder of a policeman. Just because it was convenient. Just because he was in the wrong place at the wrong time. Just because the only other suspect was a sixteen-year-old local boy ineligible for the Death Penalty. Just because Adams was a drifter from out of town. A policeman pointed a gun in his face and Adams was coerced into signing a confession. His lawyer was so overwhelmed by the case that he let it slide. Adams spent years in prison until the documentary came out and the authorities were shamed into doing something about it."

Me: "You're not implying that Frank would shove a gun in somebody's face to get a confession, are you?"

Elene: "Why not? Since Lonnie's incarceration, no more murders have occurred. Why not have him go down for the whole kit and caboodle? Jesus, it means that Frank can spit in my eye, he can spit in the FBI's eye and he can spit in Lonnie's eye."

Me: "Calm down. They will need some evidence linking Lonnie to the other crime scenes, surely."

Elene: "Not if they do a deal. Not if Frank explains the finer points of Death Row living to Lonnie in gruesome detail. Not if the D.A. gives Lonnie a blow-by-blow account of what it is like to die by lethal injection. Lonnie will sign the papers, because he is stupid enough to do it, because his lawyer is inept and because no one gives a shit. All they want to do is tidy up the paperwork and have someone—anyone—go down for the serial murders. Lonnie did kill someone, so he's not exactly an innocent babe. As long as the real killer doesn't strike again, Lonnie's sunk. And if I were 'The Painted Lady' serial killer, I'd lay low, change my M.O. and signature style, and even move to another city if I had to. Jesus, the real killer is going to get away with it and there isn't a thing we can do about it."

Me: "I guess not."

Elene put her head in her hands and, for a moment, I felt sorry for her. I did adore her and her compassion for Lonnie the Loser might have moved me, if it wasn't so funny. I sat down next to Elene and put my arm around her shoulders.

Me: "You are getting worried about something that hasn't even happened yet. Let the judicial process do its work. It isn't that corrupt, you know. It's functioned pretty well up to now."

Elene: "Do you know how many estimated miscarriages of justice occur in the United States every year?"

Me: "Please don't tell me, it will only depress me. Anyway, I appreciate your passion for Lonnie's predicament, but he has murdered someone. The precedence has been set. Maybe you're wrong. Maybe he did kill the other girls. After all, you can't be completely sure. People's minds work in mysterious ways. You can't say that just because he killed a prostitute one time, it doens't preclude his murdering a legal secretary or a dental hygienist on another night. Just because he's a loser, doesn't mean that he can't have fantasies about art and Venus. You've told me yourself that profiling isn't the be-all-and-end-all. Even the FBI gets it wrong sometimes, they must do. They're not perfect and neither are you. All you can do is base your conclusions on what has gone on before. And unfortunately, the human mind is a constantly evolving, living machine, so in the course of things, a killer could pop up who doesn't match the common, run-of-the-mill profile, like Lonnie. You have to learn to be more flexible."

Elene: "To hell with flexibility. I know in my guts that Frank is wrong."

Suddenly, Elene jumped up, walked to the telephone and started dialing. I had a sinking feeling of déjà vu.

Elene: "Frank, it's me. I need to see you right now. I don't care what you are doing. We need to talk."

Elene had her back to me, which was fortunate, because I don't think that she would have liked the expression on my face at that particular moment.

She turned to me and said, "Professor, I'm sorry, but I have to talk to Frank about this. I'm not going to let some poor guy get framed for two serial killings that I know in my gut that he didn't have the intelligence to commit. Let's meet up next week, okay? I promise I'll make it up to you then."

Marvelous.

Well, what could I say? "I'm sorry, Elene, you have to stay here and become my sex slave." I escorted her out to her car and watched her drive off in a huff. Jesus, if only I could channel some of that misplaced passion for poor old Lonnie towards myself, I might have something going here. Maybe Elene secretly has the hots for Lonnie.

Fuck it.

I drove around for a couple of hours, fuming in my own special kind of snit and then found myself irretrievably drawn to Kahunaville. I knew that I was taking a major chance of blowing things, but I couldn't care less. They weren't there. Maybe Frank went wild and took Elene to Pizza Hut instead.

I am getting tired of this. I am rapidly coming around to the idea that Elene deserves to be kidnapped, tied up, tortured and raped by a masked man, then horribly strangled and perhaps her body violated after death. That would shut her up once and for all, that's for sure.

ENTRY 95

I saw some female being interviewed on Oprah the other day. This creature had written a book about how women should go about trapping and keeping a man. The author had, unfortunately for her book sales, just gotten a divorce and was trying to explain how her book still worked, regardless of her own situation. I was torn between utter surprise and total despair. Is the state of relationships between men and women so parlous now that we need books to tell us how to date? I guess so. After watching a few excruciating minutes of the program, I turned it off and turned on my computer. I went to Amazon.com and found hundreds of books about the subject. How sad. How pitiable.

I can just see all these high-flying career girls hitting their late thirties and then going into a biological tailspin. "Fuck! I've got the job. I've got the car. I've got the apartment. But I ain't got NO GUY! What's it all about, Alfie?" What a joke. What did the dumb numb little bitches expect? How can any male find a female appealing if she is playing the part of a man all day long? All that fake testosterone must take its toll eventually. I observe the way women act on TV and their manner has become so unattractive that a vast majority of them are completely repellent to me. And most of the ones I see are actresses and models. What about the rest of the herd? What a state they must be in.

Most American women seemed to have totally lost touch with the essence of their femininity. They are so intent on buffing their bodies by aerobic exercise that they have forgotten how to walk like a girl. They are so obsessed with dieting that they have lost their girlish curves, except for the fake ones they have inserted at great cost. They are so bedeviled by the impossible ideal of "having it all" that they have lost it completely.

American women have even forgotten how to talk. Women from the forties and fifties had beautiful, melodic, educated voices. Now we are treated to strident-voiced harpies, who, if they can manage to string a coherent sentence together, use words like "empowerment", "personal space" and other buzzwords that make me puke.

It seems to me that the Sister's Struggle for Women's Liberation hasn't made any of the gaggle of emancipated ladies any happier—just more stressed out.

I see female singers waggling their asses in front of the camera on Youtube and I wonder what goes on in their heads. Is this really female empowerment—the freedom to stick your butt in front of a TV camera like a bitch dog in heat? Girls insist on doing these kinds of shenanigans and then they wonder why men still treat them like shit. Of course, men want to see titsn'ass—an ordinary man can never get as much sex as he wants, so any vicarious thrill he can grab, he'll seize it with both hands. But when I see pop stars in bikinis writhing in the waves in time to their latest tune, or movie stars showing off their bony chests and erect nipples at the Oscars, it just demeans them in my eyes. They become female creatures, not women. Not goddesses.

ENTRY 96

They have scheduled Lonnie's preliminary hearing in a couple week's time. How strange it will be for me to sit and watch someone on trial for crimes that I have committed. I imagine that it will give a special piquancy to my acts. Everyone will be talking about this monster, this fiend who preyed on innocent women and I'll be thinking, "Shit, they must be talking about me!" But no, all the fingers will be pointing in another direction: at poor old Lonnie. It's going to be extraordinarily liberating. And the power! The power it will bestow upon me. Frankly, killing girls is nothing to having the power of life and death over someone in such a public arena. I can't wait.

I have a choice. I could be reaching a major fork in the road of my destiny. Do I keep my mouth shut, or do I dramatically leap to my feet at an appropriate moment and declare my guilt, Perry Mason-style? Declare my guilt and clear an innocent man. Ah, but he isn't innocent, is he? Lonnie may not be an atrocious serial killer, but he ain't Pollyanna, either.

I don't feel sorry for him for a minute. He was careless and he got caught and I don't care one iota for him. Let him go to his death and let his death absolve me. He can be the modern equivalent of the medieval sin-eater. He can consume my sins and then take them to the grave with his own.

I like that concept. I feel very comfortable with it. My crimes will be washed away by his execution and I can start life anew. How delightful.

ENTRY 97

I decided to take some time off from teaching to sit through Lonnie's preliminary hearing for the murder of Vivian Miller. It was fascinating stuff. Despite Elene's efforts, I didn't think his lawyer was very good. Elene told me that he was trying to plead an insanity defense, which seemed tenuous in the extreme to me. Maybe the lawyer was trying to lay down some groundwork for Lonnie's impending trials for my works of art.

Through newspaper reports and a chat on the phone with Elene, I was able to find out Lonnie's side of the story, which was predictably sad and stupid. After picking up Vivian Miller on South Salina Street, he had sex with her and then fell asleep. When Lonnie woke up, he discovered Vivian diving into his wallet for a bonus. He snatched back his wallet, and Vivian, obviously a soul sister of Gertrude, hit him in the head with her shoe. "It hurt like a sumbitch," to quote Lonnie. He remembered nothing else until he found himself sitting in his beat-up Mazda outside of his house in Solvay.

Poor schmuck.

Insanity is the hardest defense in the world to prove. Blackout or no blackout, Lonnie probably knew the difference between right and wrong, which is the major provision of the M'Naghten Rules—as the primary test for the insanity defense is otherwise known. Also, the fact that he wrote "Fuck You Vivian" on the girl's stomach while still under the effects of the so-called blackout would strain the credulity of any jury.

I wonder if Lonnie is going to try to use his blackout defense in the trial for the serial killings. That would be to my advantage if he does. You can achieve just about anything in a blackout, even murders such as mine.

Maybe Lonnie should have entered a plea of self-defense. Nobody knows better than I how much it hurts being hit in the head with a shoe.

So I sat there in court and stared at the back of Lonnie's head. For hours, it seemed. I was trying to bore through his skull with my laser vision and ascertain what kind of character he was, but I was not successful. Lonnie's skull was impenetrable. I also kept getting distracted by his bad haircut, which was eerily reminiscent of a German soccer player's hairdo in the good old Seventies, that glorious decade that saw a complete taste bypass on oh-so-many levels.

I bet Lonnie was wondering how the hell he managed to end up in Court Room Number Two. What wild set of circumstances had led him to face the music—heck, the Big Combo—right here and now?

From what I heard from Elene, "Born To Lose" should have been tattooed on Lonnie's chest, instead of "Lorraine." Elene had to admit that Lonnie did fit a certain profile for a killer, but more akin to the Albert De Salvo type, rather than the dazzling Ted Bundy. Lonnie was blue collar working stiff, a bright guy but a low achiever and he suffered from poor relationships with the women in his life, especially his mother. His father had also been a plumber, with a history of alcoholism and wife-beating.

The prosecution trotted out their evidence and called their witnesses. After her interviews with Lonnie, Elene had decided that she would not testify for the prosecution, but since she utterly disagreed with Lonnie's defense team opting for the insanity defense, she wasn't going to testify on his behalf at his Prelim either. She just didn't believe he had experienced a blackout, as he had no history of them before or since the murder. Elene's theory was that Lonnie got angry, lost his impulse-control and strangled the girl. But Elene would testify for Lonnie in the serial killer cases, as she felt that he just didn't have it in him to commit those crimes.

She was right, but I think it was highly ironic that my dream girl was fighting so hard to free my perfect fall guy.

Frank was the first prosecution witness up on the stand. He was pretty good, I have to admit: straight from Central Casting, the tough detective who had fearlessly tracked down the killer of Vivian Miller. The fact that Lonnie left a trail behind him that an inanimate object could have followed was beside the point. Frank ran down the catalog of evidence:

1. Lonnie's thumbprint was found at the scene. It was on the dead woman's belt buckle. Since it was the only full print found, it would seem to indicate that Lonnie busied himself after committing the murder by wiping the joint clean of prints, making his blackout story seem even more unlikely.

2. Lonnie's semen was found in a condom found floating in the bathroom toilet. This was confirmed by a DNA test.

3. A palm print and two fingerprints of the dead woman and 4 strands of her hair were found inside Lonnie's Mazda.

4. A friend and "associate" of Vivian Miller, Lois Jorgenson, had seen Vivian go off with a man matching Lonnie's description on the night in question and then never saw her again. The two women had an arrangement to always keep an eye on each other and make a note of any dubious customers.

Next up on the stand, we had a forensic DNA scientist telling us all about Lonnie's DNA and that the odds that the semen in the condom came from someone other than Lonnie were a whopping 7.6 billion to one.

Then we had the fingerprint expert talking about Lonnie and Vivian's swirls and whirls. We had another forensic specialist talking about the similarities of Lonnie's handwriting to the handwriting on Vivian's body.

Finally, Vivian's friend Lois came to the stand. Crowned with a mop of shocking red hair and very questionable taste in what was appropriate to wear in a courtroom, Lois was quite a broad and very entertaining in her own way. It turns out that she and Lonnie had been intimately acquainted, as Lonnie habitually frequented the ladies of the night. Lois didn't like him much, because, in her immortal words, "A lot of times, he smelled like a goat," which caused considerable amusement in the courtroom. Lois said that one time, Lonnie got mad at her and socked her in the jaw. The defense attorney leaped to his feet and asked whether Lonnie had ever tried to strangle her. When Lois said, "No", he sat down with a satisfied expression on his face, which just goes to show what a numbnuts he really was.

The prosecution's case was wound up and the defense began by putting Lonnie's Mom on the stand, a strategy that baffles me to this day. I would have thought that it would have been poor salesmanship, but the defense obviously thought that the tales of woe from Lonnie's childhood might sway the judge.

Mrs. Snarldon, whose first name was the impossibly romantic Claudine, told us that Lonnie was a good boy, but that his dad, Carl, was a drunken, abusive bully who beat everyone in the family to within an inch of their lives every damn day. "I can't remember a day when me and Lonnie didn't get beat," Claudine said eloquently. The happiest moment of her life was when Lonnie got old enough to whoop the shit out of Carl. "I was so proud of him, I went over and hugged him," she said.

I glanced up at the judge and I could see that Claudine was losing her audience. Whaling the tar out of Dad at fifteen was not exactly the character reference they were looking for. Claudine went on to talk about the petty crime, which was always everyone else's fault but poor Lonnie's ("he just got in with the wrong crowd") and the indifferent grades ("bad teachers") and the divorces ("Lonnie just can't keep his hands off of trashy women—it's like an addiction with him") Finally, Claudine left the stand and I could tell that everyone in the courtroom was mightily relieved.

The defense then brought forth Lonnie's best friend, who made Claudine look like a rocket scientist. Doug Clutter was supposed to be another character witness, but it seemed like he was one of the bad crowd that Claudine was talking about.

At last a professional witness made an appearance. A forensic psychiatrist by the name of Dr. Ronald Butler took the stand and proceeded to go into a detailed explanation of what may have caused Lonnie's black-out. It turned out that when Lonnie was ten, he was carelessly playing on the monkey bars of his swing set at home and subsequently fell on his head. Unfortunately, Lonnie's Dad had moved the swing set to the patio because he was planning to mow the lawn, so instead of falling onto the cushioning grass, Lonnie tumbled directly onto concrete. This could have caused front temporal lobe damage to Lonnie's brain, which in turn may have precipitated the aforementioned black-out. The head trauma might have impaired Lonnie's primal neurological circuit functions and hence induced behavioral seizures, which could also have resulted in incidents of rage beyond Lonnie's control.

The D.A. made short shrift of this testimony. He got up and asked Dr. Butler if Lonnie had ever experienced any blackouts immediately after the bump on the head or in the intervening nineteen years until the night of the murder, or since the night of the murder. Butler said that Lonnie had experienced the blackouts twice before the night in question, but the D.A. cut him off, suspecting that Lonnie's lawyer was laying the groundwork for some kind of diminished responsibility defense in future trials.

In redirect, the defense asked Butler if Lonnie's previous attack on Lois could have been a result of some kind of behavioral seizure and the Doctor said it possibly could. Again, the defense sat down with a smug look on his face, but no one was buying it.

The judge didn't take much time to decide that the prosecution had produced enough evidence to prove that there was probable cause to continue onto trial, i.e., he felt that a reasonable jury would be convinced that the defendant committed the crime. Since he'd never made bail in the first place, Lonnie went back to his cell to await his trial.

ENTRY 98

I just heard from Elene that Lonnie's lawyers have persuaded him to cop a plea, i.e., to plead guilty to not only Vivian Miller's murder, but to the "Painted Lady" serial killings as well and therefore avoid a death sentence. So, no trial, no sensational press coverage, no potential Perry Masonesque moment of truth for me. I am a little disappointed, but somehow not surprised. New York State hasn't executed anyone since 1963, but why should Lonnie take a chance? He is already in for life. Hell, if I had been in his shoes, I would have probably confessed to the Kennedy assassination after being locked in a small windowless room with Frank for a few hours.

I wonder how Lonnie managed to explain the poses and the poems on the other victims. Perhaps the police gave him a helping hand to remember all the details of the murders. Maybe the police did just what Elene predicted and typed out the confession and gave it to Lonnie to sign. I guess that's why confessions are considered to be unreliable as the only evidence. Too many chances that corrupt policemen would take some short cuts and force a suspect to sign away his life. Unfortunately for Lonnie, no one gave a shit about him and since he was already going to go down for one murder, why not the others? The fact that the serial killer hadn't struck again after he had been arrested was also a major factor in the authorities wanting to believe in Lonnie's guilt.

I was a bit disappointed that Elene didn't mention inviting me over for our missed meal after all this time. I was also surprised that she didn't seem that interested in the fate of poor old Lonnie any more. Maybe Frank managed to persuade Elene that he had the right guy after all. It seems very unlikely though, but I suppose you can only contain that amount of hurt pride and righteous anger for so long. Although I seem to be holding onto mine with a firmness unto death.

ENTRY 99

I was watching the anti-globalization protesters on the tube last night. My first thought was, "Don't these people have jobs to go to?" Obviously not. They are happily collecting welfare and leeching off the state before they jet off around the world protesting against something that no one can stop: progress. I wonder how all the poor people in Africa and elsewhere feel about these selfless moronic knights in shining armor, championing their cause without a thought to the real issues in the case.

If I were living in a mud hut in Swaziland, I would be begging for more globalization. Please, more McDonald's, more laptops, more Nike trainers, more cell phones, more DVDs, more Shell Oil—fuck it—more hot pants. Please let me pour the black water of American Imperialism, AKA, Coca Cola, down my parched throat so that I, too, may feel that delicious jolt of sugar shock syndrome. Please lift me out of this grinding poverty so I can experience the joys of rampant capitalism. Spare me the ministrations of these brainless hippies who want to prevent me from tasting the illicit pleasures of the Yankee Dollar.

It makes me laugh when I see folks despairing of the passing away of the "culture" of some of the poorer peoples of the world. What culture are we talking about here? The culture of hunting with a bow and arrow for hours, when you could walk out and fell a deer in a few minutes with a high-powered rifle? What's so wonderful about bows and arrows? What is so cultural about living like your ancestors did ten thousand years ago? That's virtually the Stone Age. They did some pleasant wall paintings back then, but the life style was a bit harsh, to say the least. If the children of the Bushmen of the Kalahari, or the children of Amazon Basin tribesmen, or the children of some rice farmer in China had a choice, I am sure that they would rather be happily ensconced with a Playstation than spending every waking hour trying to find something to eat, or worrying about the myriad bugs and dangerous animals you had to avoid on the way to your stinking outdoor toilet. Yup, I bet those kids, if they had televisions, which of course they don't, would watch the protesters in despair. They would wonder why all these middle-class white kids want to keep their poorer browner brothers in ignorance and poverty. Why would they want to preserve a culture that—just picking some quaint customs randomly out of the air—still allows the brutal sacrifice of young children to some all singing, all dancing jungle god? Or orders by law that if you steal a loaf of bread to feed your starving family, the authorities have the right to punish you by cutting off your hand? Or believes that drinking rhinoceros horn tea or sautéing a tiger's testicles will make you more virile? Or believes that marrying your daughter off to a donkey will give you good luck? Or believes that it is perfectly okay to machete up to a million people to death, just because they weren't a member of your tribe? Oh, I could just go on and on. All culture and tradition stand for are just yet more ways for one segment of the population to keep another segment down.

On the other hand, maybe all that repression isn't such a bad thing after all. Maybe the worst-case scenario would be if every person on the planet had total individual freedom. It would mean utter chaos. It is almost as if man needs to be enslaved to the ideologies and cultures created by "The Few."

The best recent example is Yugoslavia. For years, you have a reasonably unhappy country limping along and doing nothing more infamous than churning out the disreputable Yugo automobile. Suddenly, with the demise of its leader Tito, it turned into a place where tribalism reigned and virtually every little farm in the country was demanding independence.

Soon we will be back to the system of the Middle Ages, where every city is a sovereign state and the no man's land in between is ruled by a robber baron of the week.

Refugees streaming out of the world's poorer countries will be in the same boat that they are in now, but worse. It will be just like that film, *The Masque of the Red Death*. All the rich and decadent people will be partying up in the castle with Vincent Price, while the hoi polloi scrabble around for the odd potato in the barren fields outside. But the Red Death is around the corner for them all. There is no escape from the deadly viruses that now plague mankind: envy, malice, blood lust, ignorance, religion, patriotism and stupidity.

What people don't seem to realize is that true freedom means having to use your brain. To take responsibility for yourself and your actions and not blame others for your troubles. To forget the past and think only of the future.

A while ago, I heard that Africans are attempting to get compensation from the European nations who were responsible for the propagation of slavery three hundred years ago. That is going to be a tough one, because how can they ignore the fact that there was a segment of the so-called Dark Continent's population who were responsible for the slaves being captured in the first place? There's the glory of culture again for you. Taking slaves is a fine old tradition of African tribal warmongering. (And the pathetic thing is, it still is to this day.) The white Europeans just took advantage of an already existing situation.

Some Afro-Americans are even demanding their forty acres and a mule that they were promised at the end of the Civil War. At today's land values, this would add up to roughly $1.2 million per person. I think that if this compensation were paid, then they would have to deduct all the money that person and his ancestors stretching back to the time of the Civil War earned as a benefit of living in the most prosperous country in the world. After all, the average yearly salary of a person living in the United States is $32,788 while the average salary of someone from a Western African nation (where most of the slaves came from) is $391 a year. Frankly, I don't think that most Afro-Americans want to go back to their roots that badly.

If this compensation thing spirals out of control (and with our litigation culture, anything is possible), then other downtrodden peoples might get the same idea and we'd all be sunk. They will have to compensate all the Slavic peoples in the world, because before Africa was exploited, the Slavs were the most enslaved race on the planet. (They even took their name from their unfortunate status.) Since it was the Romans who did most of the enslaving, it would be fun to see how the Slavs would squeeze their compensation out of modern-day Italy. Of course, Irish Americans could demand reparation from the British for starving them out of their country during the Potato Famine, and what about the decimated Indian populations of Mexico and Peru? I bet they would love to receive a cash bonus from the Spanish on behalf of their aggrieved Aztec, Mayan and Incan ancestors. Oh, hell, why not just sue all of Christopher Columbus' descendants and have done with it?

Why don't people forget about it? Why can't they just get on with their lives? Isn't there enough racism and hate going on right now without having to dredge up the past and its horrors? I think that some people enjoy wallowing in the past. It gives them a feeling of having some kind of history. Otherwise what would be the point of their and their ancestors 'meaningless lives?

That's the real problem. Most people have no purpose in their lives, which is why they are so dissatisfied. They long for something to believe in. That's why they're such suckers for the above named viruses, like religion and patriotism. Take that away from them, and they become the ants that they really are, only dreaming of being something important and never realizing their goal.

ENTRY 100

This is very difficult to write about. I have been betrayed.

I had been wondering why I hadn't heard from Elene for a while. Wondering, fuck, I was consumed with a kind of furious curiosity. I threw caution to the wind and drove to Elene's neighborhood in my Venus Project car. I parked a safe distance away and hung around. It being a Thursday, I assumed that Elene and Frank would have their usual date. I didn't have to wait long. They arrived at around 10:30 PM. Frank walked Elene to the door. They stood and talked for a while. He made some remark and she laughed. Then he kissed her in mid-laugh. He kissed her, just like that. She let him kiss her for far too long. They talked some more. Then he kissed her again. He kissed her and she kissed him back.

I was seething. I felt like leaping out of the car and running over there, but to do what? To cry out, "Unhand her, sir!" They spent at least ten minutes outside, oblivious to the rain, kissing and really getting into it. And then—I can barely write this—and then they both went inside her house.

I waited there for another hour. It was obvious what was going on. He was fucking her. He was fucking MY ELENE. And she was letting him. I thought about sneaking around to the back of the house and peeping in the window, but decided that was insane. I wanted to see what they were doing, but if I did, I don't know what I might have done. Kill Frank? Rape Elene? Fuck.

Frank got in there before I even had a chance. All I managed to do was rub her damn elbow in the elevator.

What the hell is going on and how long has it been going on for? The last time I saw her, Elene told me that she thought Frank was framing Lonnie to take the fall for the serial killings. She thought that Frank wanted to spit in her eye and prove that her psychological profile was wrong. She was infuriated by him a while ago and now they are fucking?

Something must have happened between them during the investigation into my serial killings. Now there's irony for you. Incontrovertible proof that God really does shit in your shoe whenever he wants. Did I bring them together again by creating my works of art? I wanted her for myself. This whole thing was meant to bring us together, Elene and me. Frank wasn't part of it.

This is devastating. I am trying very hard not to blame Elene. After all, what was she supposed to do, wait for me forever? While I have been dawdling around, stuck in a morass of wretched indecision, Frank walked in and took her. And I helped. If it weren't for The Venus Project, they probably wouldn't be screwing each other right now.

Maybe it started up again that night she went over there in her passionate fury over Lonnie. Maybe he calmed her down and gave her a couple of drinks and then made his move. She went to give him a piece of her mind and ended up giving him her body.

I bet Frank is an animal in bed. He's banging her right now, I know he is. I bet she's screaming with pleasure. I wonder if he has handcuffed her to the bed. Is she going down on him right now? I can just imagine her mouth around his big policeman's cock. I hope that she chokes on it.

Oh God, I am driving myself crazy. This is unbearable.

Elene is with someone else. What am I going to do now?

ENTRY 101

I woke up this morning feeling fine, then I remembered last night and I felt sick to my stomach.

I got up and had a cup of coffee and reasoned it out.

Every woman, given the chance, will betray you. It's in their nature. Not that men are shining examples of purity either, but I think that promiscuity must be built into our genes. Although I can't blame Elene, because she didn't know that I wanted her. She didn't knowingly deceive me.

What I am trying to say is that maybe if I had entered into a relationship with her, it would have ended badly anyway. Maybe she would have gone crawling back to macho man Frank in the end, and I would feel even worse than I do now.

So this is a blessing in disguise. I can see now that the object of my desire has feet of clay. To go for a guy like Frank, I mean, Jesus, all her taste must be in her mouth. The guy is right down there with pond scum.

The only women I can rely on are the goddesses that I made with my own hands. They can't betray me. They can't run away from me. They live in the shadowy halls of my mind: forever young, forever beautiful, forever mine. A real relationship with a woman—at this point in my diseased life—is impossible. She would kill my feelings for her by complaining about my socks, or picking her nose, or farting in bed. Now that I have tasted what it is like to be with my own personal Venus, a mere woman just isn't good enough.

I will have to create some more, I guess. As dangerous as it is, I will need more soul sustenance soon.

I almost wish I could take Elene. It would be so easy to drive by one day and offer her a lift to Phoebe's. Hit her over the head and take her somewhere and do anything I want with her. But I know that would be fatal. I have been in contact with her and I would be questioned. It is very frustrating though, because my fantasies about Elene are getting more and more detailed. Maybe when I am stronger in my mind, when I am not feeling so vulnerable, I will write them down. Spew them out on paper, where I can admire them in all their glory.

I hate the world again. Nothing could have prepared me for this shock.

I am very, very angry.

ENTRY 102

I haven't wanted to write down some of the fantasies that I have about Elene before this. Maybe in some atavistic way, I felt that writing them down might somehow diminish them. It is similar to how some primitive peoples feel about cameras capturing their souls. However, now I feel ready to commit my darkest Elene fantasies to paper. Those masturbatory waking dreams that have been keeping me warm at night. Even before the other evening, they were getting more and more violent. Maybe I knew something was up on a subliminal level. Maybe I could sense that something wasn't quite right with my Love Object.

Well, here goes...

The Elevator Fantasy

Elene and I are in an elevator. We are total strangers to one another. Suddenly the elevator judders to a halt. The lights flicker and then it goes completely dark. We hear a sound that is like the end of the world, and I realize that it is the sound of the elevator slipping on its cables. Then we go into free fall. I turn to Elene, grab her and kiss her, thinking that if I am going to die, then I may as well die in the arms of a beautiful woman. She kisses back and I know that she is as turned on by the thought of imminent death as I am.

Then the noise comes back, an unbearable shriek. The elevator comes to a jarring halt and the door opens. We scramble out just before the elevator continues its fall towards the basement.

We look at each other. People are surrounding us, trying to take us somewhere where we can get over the shock, but we don't care. We just want to go somewhere to celebrate that fact that we are still alive.

We rush outside. I have a limousine ready. Elene gets in and I follow, telling the driver to take us home. The partition between the driver and us slides up and when we are alone, I turn to Elene and kiss her. I put my hand underneath her blouse and play with her breasts. She falls back on the wide leather seat, her arms above her head, giving her body to me.

I reach up and rip off her panties and she cries out in surprise. I tie her hands to the door strap with my belt so she can't interfere in my taking complete pleasure in her body.

Then I suck her pussy—I fuck her in the missionary position—I untie her and she gets on top and rides me, screaming with delight—she sucks my cock. We come and come and come.

Finally, I open the electric window. I tell Elene to stand up and put her head out the window. She obeys me without question. I kneel down and eat her pussy from behind, at the same time inserting my left forefinger up her ass. She is at the point of orgasm as I press the button with my right hand and slowly put up the window, throttling her. Her legs kick at me furiously, but she can't save herself. I continue to suck her pussy as she dies slowly.

I've always liked the idea of fucking a woman in a limousine. Maybe one day.

The Angie/Elene Fantasy
Sometimes I pretend that Elene is in the car with me at the time of the Accident instead of Angie. It is just after the crash, and I have crawled out, miraculously unharmed. The only light is from the flames that are consuming the car. I find Angie/Elene lying unconscious on the ground. I am so angry with her

that I rip off her clothes and fuck her on the hard ground, the pebbles grinding into her back. She comes to and begs me to stop, but I won't. I hit her to make her shut the fuck up. I see blood on her lips and I bend down to lick it off. I pinch her nipples until she screams for mercy. I bite her on her neck like a vampire and I lick her blood. I keep telling her to shut up, but she continues to cry out. Finally, I just strangle the life out of her. I shake her by the neck. Her body is contorting beneath me and I am squeezing so hard that Angie/Elene's head pops right off. It shoots off into the night, but her body is still alive, still responding, still undulating passionately. The blood is gushing from her neck and I put my face into the fountain and drink her blood. And then I come.

That one isn't as good as the elevator one, but it does have a neat revenge angle to it. Although I always feel absurdly guilty about fantasizing about hitting Elene. I don't feel guilty about fantasizing about hitting Angie though, so what the heck.

The Dominatrix Fantasy

This is a good one. Elene is a dominatrix. She is wearing a sexy black plastic outfit, topped off with fishnet stockings and spiky heeled, patent leather stilettos. She is carrying a whip. I am visiting her dungeon, which is located in a beautiful apartment in New York City on East 55th Street. The room looks gothic in the extreme, with that perennial Inquisition favorite, the Rack, on prominent display. Chains and other implements of medieval torture decorate the room.

I walk in and Elene orders me to undress completely. She then ties me to the rack and painfully stretches my body so it is impossible for me to move. She puts clamps on my nipples that are excruciatingly uncomfortable. I get a hard-on, because she is so beautiful and she is being so mean to me, but she gets annoyed that I have an erection. She takes her riding crop and hits the bottoms of my feet, a particularly tender area of my anatomy. I tell Elene I want to fuck her. I tell her that I will rape her if I ever get free, but then she whips my thighs, telling me that a dominatrix would never condescend to have straight sex with a client. Then Elene whacks my penis, which hurts like hell. I get very angry and I find the strength to break the ropes that are tying me down. Now, the shoe is on the other foot.

Elene is scared and she tries to run from the room, but she can't run fast enough in her fancy stilettos. I catch her and wrestle her back to the rack. I tie her down and stretch her out on the rack until she begs me to stop. I get some scissors and slowly cut off the black plastic outfit, threatening to do the same to her nipples if she doesn't behave. I take an enormous black dildo off the wall and gradually insert it up her pussy. She screams and struggles. I fuck her violently with the dildo and I can tell that it is hurting her, but she is also enjoying it. Of course, she would like it both ways. A little "M" with her "S". I take the riding crop and lightly smack her breasts until they are pink and angry-looking. All the while, she is groaning and cursing me, ordering me to stop, then sighing with ecstasy.

I get up on the rack and I enter Elene. I stick the dildo in her mouth so she can't scream. I can tell that she is panicking. She can't breathe. So I take it out and stick my tongue down her throat. I fuck her and she can't do anything about it.

Finally, I untie Elene and order her to get down on her knees. I tie her hands behind her and order her to suck my cock. After a while, I get hold of her head and pinch her nostrils shut. She can't breathe.

I smother her to death and she dies sucking my dick. It serves her right for hurting me.

*

There is a common theme in the above fantasies and it's not a particularly surprising one. I like my women helpless and, in the end, dead. Don't need to be an Einstein to figure that one out.

The question is, what to do about these feverish thoughts of mine? Do I let them consume me, or do I use this dreadful mental energy to try to expand The Venus Project? Do I branch into something more challenging, more exhilarating? More important?

And at the same time, do I seek revenge on those that have betrayed me, whether they knew they were betraying me or not?

I have heard nothing from Elene since she telephoned to give me the latest about Lonnie. She no longer needs my expertise. I am no longer any use to her, so she has ejected me from her life.

Fine.

ENTRY 103

All that a man wants from a woman—when it comes right down to it—is a fuck, pure and simple. A man realizes that, because of society and civilization, he has to go through the elaborate mating rituals of the human animal such as the lunch date, the first dinner date, the movie date, etc., before he can make his move. But all that cash outlay only has one purpose and it isn't a pleasant chat and a steak from Sardino's. It is a fuck. Men spend a ferocious amount of brainpower on plotting how to bed a woman. His most basic instinct is to spread his seed, then move on. Settling down for a man is a kind of nightmare and the sooner women realize this truism the better.

Around five years ago, there was a book out dealing with the controversial theory that man has the biological imperative to rape. That rape (i.e., one violent unprotected sexual encounter) was not necessarily just an urge to wield power over a woman, but it was also primarily a sexual urge as well. I saw a study published on the BBC website that posited another theory that rape was much more successful at implanting a man's sperm (thereby leading to pregnancy) than normal intercourse.

That made me pause and think. What kind of Creator would think up that fucked-up scenario? If this was true, if rape was the most efficient way of perpetuating one's genes, then why bother with all those steak dinners at Sardino's?

Of course, feminists were up in arms about both the studies, as if getting mad was going to change the scientific data. Why can't rape be a sexual urge as well as being a power trip? Why can't women understand that when a man rapes a woman, it could be that he is profoundly sexually frustrated?

Most modern men want sex and can't have it. They want success and never get it. They want money and never earn enough. Everybody has desires and nobody—except the psychopathic few— has the guts to go out and just take what they want.

Maybe the Marquis de Sade was right: the world is shit and a man has an absolute duty to do exactly what he wants and damn the consequences. Of course, de Sade was advocating anarchy and, like some big obscene child, he wanted his every wish to be satisfied. Unfortunately for him, his society wasn't prepared to give him his heart's desires, even when that society was taken over by the very anarchists that he supported.

People who know what they want and are prepared to do whatever they can to get their desires fulfilled are considered by the establishment as menaces to society. They don't want to toe the line and live the miserable little lives that their so-called betters have mapped out for them.

The ruling class likes to keep us ignorant, so we can't question their decisions. They keep us fat, serving us portions at restaurants that would choke an elephant, in order to wedge us into our couches so they can send out more pernicious messages of infernal stupidity through the airwaves to clog up our minds. They keep us amused by selling us new gadgets that take up hours of our valuable time to comprehend. They keep us poor, draining our savings to pay for obscenely expensive bombers and computers and guns to protect us from enemies that probably wouldn't hate us so much if we spent a fraction of our war chest on food and medicines for the unfortunates of the world.

They don't tell us the truth, but what is the truth anyway? My truth is so different from the guy next door. My truth is different than anyone else's in the world.

I no longer have any doubt that what I am doing is right or wrong. If the world is a deceit, then why shouldn't I take my pleasures where I find them? If I believed in heaven or hell, in redemption or the burning pit, then I might pause for a moment. I might reflect that I will be punished somehow, somewhere. But I don't believe in anything anymore.

If I have no fear, only desire, then I am unstoppable.

I have no regrets for what I do. I do it for myself alone. Elene doesn't come into it anymore. She was a smoke screen, a blind, someone to make me feel better about myself, to feel that I had a goal. She was a bright shiny love object and soul mate that I could cherish. But Elene turned out to be a deceit as well. She is part of the world and the world is a corrupt nothing, so she is nothing.

It pains me to write these words, but it is also liberating. I can't be tied to any one thing or person. I must be a free agent, free to pursue my goal.

If that means that people must die, then so be it.

ENTRY 104

What is my most effective weapon? What is the thing that gives me power, that gives me the energy to go on? My anger, that's what. It is cool, it is crystal and it allows me to see so clearly what needs to be done. I have a tendency to forget how my anger makes me feel. It makes me feel good. Ironic that something so bad can make me feel so good, but hey, that's life.

ENTRY 105

I know now that creating my goddesses was only a warm-up exercise for The Next Phase. Up until now, I killed in the hopes of acquiring Elene and, to be honest, for my own sexual pleasure. But so what? That kind of thing is insignificant in the grand scheme of things. But now...now I have an idea that will really put me on the map.

To have contempt for one's fellow human beings is not enough. You have to do something about it. I thought that somehow I was making a statement. That, like the Unibomber, I was going to force people to sit up and listen, but killing ordinary women isn't important enough. I need a bigger target.

To truly feel like a god, one must assassinate someone with godlike power, like a president, or a pope, or a captain of industry.

I remember seeing this TV documentary about the largest, most poisonous spider in the world. This unpleasant creature lived in the Amazon rain forest and spent most of its time snuggled in a burrow in the ground, coming up only to kill and devour the occasional equally deadly serpent. Inter-cut with the spider shots were sequences of happy native people worshipping the spider. This involved telling spider stories, wearing stylish spider hats, singing spider songs, having spider dreams and explaining in detail how their love for the spider protected them from ever being bitten by their arachnid god. Then the happy natives decided to go on a spider expedition to show the camera crew the intricacies of their spider ritual.

Now, I had a bad feeling as I was watching this documentary, because I knew in my heart how it was going to turn out, but I couldn't change the channel out of some kind of grotesque fascination. The happy natives finally arrived at Spider Central. They captured the spider, which was as big as a man's hand, tied his legs together, wrapped it in leaves and then...threw it on the fire for a little barbecue. Yes, the happy natives consumed their god, which they assured the gagging film crew tasted just like shrimp. (How would they know? They lived in the middle of the jungle.) This act of deicide made them even happier. It made me want to puke, but it also made me think. By consuming their god, the happy natives became godlike in their own right. As I shall—when I pick my next target. Forget pretty women as victims, which I chose only for my base sexual pleasure. Successfully targeting a rich, famous and powerful person who really matters, now there is immortality in the making for you. That is doing something important.

I already know that it is absurdly easy to kill someone. All you need is the desire and the will. That, and the time to do the proper research on your subject and to figure out how to get away with it, which is a very important consideration in the scheme of things.

As the first stage of the Next Phase, I've decided to move to California, "the land of fruits and nuts," as dear old Dad used to say. The anonymity of the Los Angeles sprawl will provide ideal cover and it will give me a good base for my activities. It was either LA or Washington DC and I decided to opt for a place with good weather for a change. There are also plenty of targets for me out there—an embarrassment of riches.

ENTRY 106

Before I transform the Venus Project into my new Project of World Rage Assassination, I may do something. Something spectacular.

Here's a possible scenario. Picture this: Frank goes over to Elene's one night and they are fucking like rabbits. You can't get a situation where two people are more vulnerable, can you? While they are going at it totally oblivious to the world, I break into Elene's house. I kill Frank, something that would give me an enormous amount of personal satisfaction, and then I'd do exactly what I want with Elene.

From my point of view, Frank is the ideal victim. He is a policeman, so he has many enemies. There would be a vast pool of potential suspects. It would never enter the investigators' heads to suspect me. I'm just a quiet art historian who gave a minimum amount of help in one investigation out of a thousand that Frank has been involved with over the years. As for the rape and possible murder—I haven't decided yet—of his girlfriend, well, the police would probably consider that just collateral damage. Elene got in the way of a revenge killing gone haywire.

This is sweet. I like this idea. I am going to spend some time developing it. Meanwhile, I have approached the Art History Department of the College of Letters, Arts and Sciences at the University of Southern California in Los Angeles to see if they are interested in employing me. I have already told Professor Mandelson that I need a change of scene. He told me that he would be sad to see me go, but he was sympathetic. He said that he might be able to pull some strings to facilitate a transfer.

If the job comes through and hell, even if it doesn't, I will sell the house and ship everything out West. Say my good-byes and then leave Syracuse forever. Then I will surreptitiously return for my big finale. Oh, this is going to be good.

ENTRY 107

I've begun to do some research on my next Project. I was almost spoiled for choice. Forget about the scores of books available on a wide range of potential targets, the depth and variety of information about the rich and powerful on the Internet is almost spooky. Courtesy of MapQuest, I could print out directions and maps from the airport to their homes. I even could, if I wanted to, take virtual guided tours of their houses in Cyberspace.

It just goes to show that privacy really is dead in this country. It's not just the government who wants to know all your business, but scattered all over the country, nodules of computer nerds are compiling your address, your telephone number, your credit card ratings, your criminal record, your Social Security Number, the state of your health (courtesy of your HMO), where you went to High School, where you work, where you travel, where you shop on the Internet, where you eat and where you take your dog to get spayed. All in the name of free enterprise, no doubt.

The only way to fool them is to keep moving, keep changing, keep metamorphosing. Switch identities, pay with cash, get a couple of different driver licenses, watch *Day of the Jackal* a few times so you know how to get all the different IDs that you might need. Avoid being on the Electoral Register, because that's a sure way for THEM to find you. Be paranoid, very paranoid.

ENTRY 108

I have worked hard in the last couple months on my new Project. Writing letters, making phone calls, networking like crazy. I am going to lose out on my tenure at Syracuse University (like I care), but I am now going to be gainfully employed by USC as a Professor of 18th Century Art History. I start in September. I put my home on the market, instructed the real estate agent that I wanted a quick sale and got rid of it in record time. I flew out to L.A. for a few weeks and bought a nice, unremarkable-looking house driving distance from the University. I paid Mayflower to come in and pack everything up and ship it to the new place. Professor Mandelson had a little farewell cocktail party for me, with some of my old friends in attendance. It was a very pleasant way to say good-bye.

I called Elene. I hadn't heard from her in a while. I told her that I was moving out West. She sounded sorry, but she didn't offer to have me over for that rain-check meal that she had promised me all those months ago. She was probably too busy with her blossoming relationship with Mr. Loverman.

So officially to all my friends, neighbors and countrymen, I left the environs of Syracuse for California on July 4th, Independence Day, very symbolic. In reality, I drove thirty-nine miles west from Manlius to the bustling little town of Auburn. I checked into the poetically named Whispering Winds Motel on Genesee Street.

This will be my greatest challenge yet, but I feel mentally prepared for it. It is a necessary cathartic step so I can move on up to greater things.

ENTRY 109

It's Thursday night, that magical time when Frank treats Elene to a fancy dinner at Kahunaville. I wonder if they are keeping to the same regime now that they are a regular item. I hope so. Every extra day that I stay in New York State makes things more awkward for me.

All is ready. All is planned. I hope it works out, because I would really like to leave Syracuse with a bang, in all senses of the word.

ENTRY 110

In the evening, I drove back to Syracuse, stopping off at the airport to pick up my stalking car. I had made arrangements to sell it when the deed was done. I drove to the University and parked by the Sheraton Hotel and briskly walked the mile and a half to Elene's house. I was dressed casually in dark, nondescript clothes.

I walked past Elene's house at around 10:30 PM. I knew they would be coming back soon. I stood under a tree, in near total darkness and reconnoitered the area. The street was deserted. I slipped between the houses like a ghost, sticking to the hedges and trees for cover.

I was in Elene's back yard. I scuttled around to the kitchen stairs. I put on my gloves and went up and gently tried the doorknob. It was locked, of course. I nervously looked around, but her back yard was shielded from the view of the neighboring houses by a fair number of shrubs and trees, so I realized that I could relax. I went over to a basement window. It was big enough for me to crawl through. I used a glass-cutter (previously bought for this very purpose) and cut a small hole in the bottom of the window, quietly removing the circle of glass with a suction cup. I reached in, jiggled the lock and in a few minutes I was safely ensconced in Elene's extremely messy basement. I used my pocket flashlight, found the stairs and walked up to the first floor. I gently opened the door to the kitchen. It was dark and quiet. No one was home yet.

I couldn't imagine why either Frank or Elene would want to open the door to the basement, but just to be safe I went back downstairs. I sat on a couch that had seen better days and waited patiently for their arrival. I could see that I had left footprints from the muddy back yard on the floor, but I didn't care. I'd bought my sneakers with cash at a K-Mart in New York City a couple of months ago, so tracing them would be problematical. I'd also purchased a .22 caliber pistol from a nervous-looking man in Brooklyn during the same trip. The serial number on the gun had already been filed off. The man had also, at a great price, sold me a silencer.

Twenty minutes later I heard them. They were talking to each other. Surprise, surprise, it sounded like they were arguing. What a couple. They came into the kitchen and messed around for a while, probably making drinks. I heard music. It seemed like an eternity, but eventually I heard them go to bed.

I crept up the stairs, so slowly it was agonizing. It was surreal how deliberately and quietly I moved. Every creak of the stairs made my heart leap into my mouth. Finally, I got to the top and opened the door. The kitchen was dark and I could hear them. They were doing it. I heard Elene making sounds, like an animal. He had turned her into an animal. I could hear him too. Grunting like the pig that he was. They were hot, boy, they were on fire.

I moved towards the bedroom. How the bed put up with the abuse they were giving it, I'll never know. I peeked through the doorway and I could see them. There were candles everywhere. It made a very pretty picture.

All I could see was Frank's wide muscular back. His ass was covered by the sheet, but I was mesmerized by its pumping motion. He was like a drilling machine, never stopping for a moment, boring into her relentlessly.

I could hear Elene. She was loving it. I couldn't see her face. I was desperate to, but I didn't dare reveal myself at that moment. I wanted to see her, as much as I knew that it would hurt me. I knew that if I saw her face, like that, with him, it would make everything justifiable.

I stepped back out into the corridor and put on a Stomatex Neoprene Balaclava hooded face mask, which had a particularly gruesome aspect. I took out my gun and stuffed the flashlight into my jacket pocket.

I peeped around the corner again. The ass was still in action. Then Frank stopped suddenly and I thought that they might have sensed my presence somehow, but no. He kissed her and they rolled over. It was Elene on top now. I could see her beautiful back, her tousled hair and her perfect pert butt. I almost lost it. I almost walked over to them right then and there. I could have pushed her down on top of Frank and thrust my cock up that beautiful ass of hers and then she could have had both of us fucking her at the same time.

But I didn't do that. Too risky.

I waited. Elene came. Her cry of ecstasy broke my heart. I should have been the one to make her do that. It should have been me. It will be me. As soon as Elene came, Frank flipped her on her back and went back to the oil fields of Texas.

Finally, fuck-face Frank had his orgasm. They both moaned a while. I expected Frank to fall asleep immediately, as he seemed the type, but I heard him ask her if she wanted a drink. I scooted out to the kitchen and hid behind the door to the basement. A few minutes later, I heard Frank come in and open the refrigerator. My moment of truth had arrived. I opened the door. There was Frank—buck naked— bending over and looking into the fridge. For a split second, I entertained the notion of shooting him in the ass, but I instantly disregarded that as not life-threatening enough. I slid up behind him and said, "Frank?"

He whipped around and I shot him pointblank right between the eyes. He didn't even have time to get surprised. There was a small muffled explosion, more of a "pfffft" than a bang. I hoped that Elene would just think that Frank had farted. I caught him and lowered him to the floor, as I didn't want any additional noise to alert Elene.

I looked at him lying there, dead as the proverbial doornail. At least it had been quick. I put the gun back into my coat pocket and moved off in the direction of Elene, my ultimate prey.

The candles were still alight. She was lying on her stomach on top of the covers, her face pointed away from the door, fortunately for me. She was snoring ever so delicately. I shed my clothes and the gloves in the corridor. I was as naked as Frank now, except for the mask. I put on a condom and padded into the bedroom, my cock getting harder with every step closer to my goal, my Elene. I had five silk scarves in my hand, which I dropped by the side of the bed.

I got into bed with her. I was in bed with Elene. My fantasies finally realized. I reached out and stroked her ass, smooth and rounded. My body was electrified by the very touch of her. I moved closer and lay right next to her. I smelled her sweet sweat, a mixed whiff of alcohol and Chanel. I put my hand between her legs and touched her pussy, still wet and ready. Elene woke up a bit. She mumbled something under her breath. I caressed her gently. Her head still buried in her pillow, Elene responded to my touch. I snaked my other hand around her to grab her breast. I was almost lying on top of her now. She couldn't have lifted her head up to see who was on top of her if she wanted to, but why would she even suspect that it wasn't Frank coming back for a second course? Anyway, I could smell alcohol on her, so she was probably befuddled by drink and sex.

I tweaked her nipple and continued to tickle her pussy. Elene opened her thighs and I moved in between her legs. I slid my cock inside her and she seemed to groan from the bottom of her very being. I fucked her slowly, sensually, taking my time; each thrust long and leisurely, the opposite of machine-gun Frank. Elene liked it. She encouraged me. She told me that she loved it like that. She called me, "Baby." She said, "Oh, yeah, Baby. That's good." I lifted myself up a bit and she opened her legs even wider. I put my hand around and fiddled with her pussy from the front. She liked that a lot. I breathed in her ear, careful not to let the rubber material of the face mask touch her skin. I was surprised that she didn't notice that I smelled differently than Frank, but maybe she was too far gone to notice. Also, I had made a point to not wear any distinctive after-shave or deodorant.

Soon, probably because she had already been primed by Frank's vigorous fucking, Elene came. Yes, I made her come. I heard her cries of pleasure and they sounded different to me. I knew that it was because of me that she was having an orgasm, not Frank. I slowed up a bit and leaned over the bed and picked up a scarf. I took one of Elene's arms and brought it up behind her. She asked me what I was doing, but of course, I didn't answer. I took her other arm and tied her hands behind her back. She started to laugh, can you believe it? She said, slurring slightly because of the booze, "What do you think you're doing, Frank?" I took up the other scarf and using both hands, slid it down the pillow.

As soon as it came in contact with her forehead, Elene lifted her head to look at it, which is what I was waiting for. I pulled down the scarf to mouth level and gagged her, quick as a wink.

Well, that caused a violent reaction. Elene tried to squirm around, but it didn't do her any good.

She thrashed her legs, but I didn't budge. I was still deep inside her and she was pinned down on the bed. I put my hand on the back of her head and squashed her face into the pillow. Boy, did her legs kick then. I waited a minute, until the fuss died down a bit and then I let her up for air. She was trying to say something but I couldn't understand her, for obvious reasons. That's when I started to fuck her in earnest again. She still couldn't see who was on top of her. I wonder if she had an inkling. Maybe she just thought that Frank had gone a bit crazy. I fucked her and she came again. She couldn't help herself.

After a while I wanted a change, but I had to make sure that Elene wouldn't escape. I grabbed another scarf from the floor and then slowly withdrew. I was still on top of her, so she couldn't kick me. Then I slid down her body, keeping her immobilized. When I was low enough, I pinned her ankles together and tied them up. Then I could finally get up and look at my masterpiece.

She rolled over on her back and for a moment, didn't compute what the picture was. What had happened to Frank? Had he gone berserk? Who's this guy in the mask? I could see in her eyes that she still couldn't comprehend what was going on. She tried to scream, but it was useless with the gag in her mouth.

I got back on the bed and straddled her waist, my cock standing proudly at attention. I bent down, putting my hands on either side of her head and whispered in her ear, my voice low and unrecognizable. I said, "Your boyfriend's dead and so will you be if you don't do exactly what I say." Elene went very still then. Her eyes filled with tears and she shook her head, not believing what was happening to her or what had happened to Frank. "Let me show you," I said.

I got off her and stood up. I leaned over and dragged Elene to the edge of the bed. Then I picked her up in my arms and took her to the kitchen. The fridge door was still open and the light showed Frank splayed out, cold and lifeless on the floor—an ever-widening pool of blood surrounding his head like an infernal halo. Elene took one look and started screaming behind the gag. I said to her, low in her ear, "Do you want to join him?" She shut up.

I took her back to the bedroom and tossed her on the bed. I whispered, "You behave and do everything I tell you to and you just might survive the evening. Do you understand?" Elene nodded. I said, "Your boyfriend annoyed some people, but they don't have a beef with you. If you talk too much, if you say anything to help the police, then you will end up as dead as him. Do you understand?" She nodded again. She was crying and moaning. I didn't care and I was amazed that I didn't care. It felt good. It felt like I was in control again, that Elene had finally come down to Earth. Venus had landed and I was the powerful one now. I was the god. Mere mortals beware.

I tied Elene's ankles to the legs of the bed and then just stared at her. Stared at her wide open and helpless. I just stood and stared for a good five minutes, drinking in her complete vulnerability. Then I walked around the bed, continuing to just look. I think that got her more scared than seeing Frank dead. She was groaning, but not with pleasure. Finally, I got on the bed and just caressed her. Gently, to allay her fears. After all, I wanted something from her and I wanted her to give it to me willingly. I traced her nipples with my fingertips, barely touching the surface of her skin. I fondled her most delicate areas with utmost sensitivity for a long time. Then I lifted the mask away from my mouth so my lips could have free reign. I spent at least twenty minutes on each nipple: playing with them, licking them, teasing them and tenderly biting them. I kissed every inch of her body. By this point, Elene was reacting in spite of herself. I sucked her pussy. (But not before cleaning her thoroughly with a washcloth to expunge any Frank residue.) I spent a lifetime down there, because I was aching for her to come. I knew that if I could make her have an orgasm in these circumstances then I would have triumphed over her. I would have conquered her utterly and completely.

I laughed when she finally came. I could hear her behind the gag and she was in seventh heaven. Elene had an orgasm with the stranger who had just murdered her boyfriend. Analyze that, Doctor Sheppard.

I desperately wanted to hear her cries of pleasure. I whispered in her ear again, "If I remove the gag, you have to promise not to scream. If you scream, I will hurt you. Can I take out the gag?"

Elene nodded. I took out the gag. She started to say something, but I put my hand over her mouth. "You have to understand that I am in control here. Don't speak unless you are spoken to, okay?" She nodded again. I didn't want to give her a chance to bewitch me with any of her voodoo psychobabble.

I took my hand away. She looked at me, but could only see the grotesque mask. I said, "Tell me to kiss you." She obediently said, "Kiss me." How long have I waited to hear those words? I dived in, my tongue plunging deep down. She made little noises of sexy suffocation. I came up for air and looked at her. I never loved her more than at that moment and I never hated her more either. I hated her for the noises of passion that she had made with Frank and, at the memory of it, the blood rushed up to my face. I was glad that she couldn't see behind the mask.

I entered her again, this time with no grace, just with anger. She cried out and I was back in my dream with the Devil's rusty cock and Elene on the floor crying because I was hurting her, but I didn't care. I just stuck my fingers down her throat to shut her up and I fucked her. Elene bit my fingers, which I liked in a perverse way. She was always a feisty girl. I took out my fingers and kissed her again.

I stopped after a while and withdrew. Elene was panting. She called me names, none of them "Baby." She was disobeying me, but it didn't bother me. I untied her legs and, luckily for her, she didn't try to kick me. I helped her up and made her kneel on the bed, sitting back on her heels, legs wide open. I knelt behind her and fondled her breasts with one hand, fiddling with her pussy with the other and nibbling the back of her neck at the same time. She loved it. She lost herself.

Elene was the ultimate slave girl: arms still bound behind her, breasts sticking out, chest totally exposed, captured, her mate murdered, but forced to fornicate with her conqueror. She looked just like a detail from French Romantic artist Eugène Delacroix's famous painting, *The Death of Sardanapalus* (1827).

Now it was time for the pièce de résistance. I gagged Elene again, picked her up and took her out to the dining room, that very same place where only a few months ago I had enjoyed that charming little meal with her. I placed her in a chair while I cleared the table. I hadn't bothered to tie her legs up, but she was too exhausted and frightened to run away. After the big table was cleared, I laid her out, tying her arms out as well, so every limb was tied to a table leg. I brought the candles in from the bedroom and placed them around her.

There she was, the perfect vision. A veritable banquet of sexual goodies. On cue, Elene started to

WRITHE against her bonds. Well, it had to happen, I guess. Maybe it's just an instinctual girl thing. I admired her for a few minutes more and wondered, "Do I really want to do this? Do I want to kill my love object? Do I really want to fulfill my ultimate fantasy? Because if I do, then where do I go next?"

So, I didn't. I didn't kill her, although I was sorely tempted. I was content with teasing her with the carving knife that I found in the kitchen, tracing the sharp point across her skin, her body trembling with dread and anticipation. I enjoyed dropping hot wax on her nipples and genitals and watching her squirm with pain and delight. I relished sucking her toes, sucking her pussy, sucking her tender nipples. I was happy to torture her with exquisite and dangerous sensuality. I was gratified by the muffled noises of ardor I heard, by the lascivious undulations of her sweating, shining body, by her multiple orgasms. I licked the perspiration sheen from every part of her body, reveling in her flavor, the taste of passion and fear. I took her again and again. I was a glutton at the feast.

For hours, I fucked Elene without allowing myself to come. It was agony, but I had to do it. I had to prove to myself that I could be the depraved high priest to her fallen Venus. I pleasured her until I couldn't stand it anymore and then I allowed myself to explode inside her. How desperate I was to shoot my sperm into her unprotected pussy, to leave a new bad seed for posterity, but this wasn't the time to be careless. It was bad enough that I was leaving her alive.

I longed to mark her in some way: to tattoo a love poem on her thigh with the knife perhaps, or to bite her and draw blood. I wanted to leave something for her to remember me by, but self-preservation again stepped in. The greatest satisfaction of all was that I knew that she would always remember me.

She would never forget our evening together. It would live in her mind until the day she died. That is a kind of immortality, I guess.

When I had my fill, when I had taken everything that I could from her, when I had drained her life force from her to the point that she was as limp as a wet noodle, I took Elene into the bathroom and immersed her in a full bathtub. This brought her back to life again and prompted some spectacular struggling and splashing, as she no doubt thought that I was trying to drown her. I was only trying to get rid of any trace evidence, but I wasn't going to tell her that. I dried her off and took her back to the bedroom, where I tried to make her as comfortable as possible, considering she was trussed up prettier than a Christmas present.

I leaned down and whispered to her, "Don't forget what I said. You don't want to end up like your boyfriend. Oh, and thanks for the memorable night. I'll never forget it. Neither will you, I'm sure." I blindfolded her, shut the door to the bedroom and left Elene to her thoughts.

I cleaned up, as always, with a thoroughness that I am sure that my ex-wife, if she were alive today, would have wished I had exhibited during our marriage. I made a special effort to clean the wooden floors in the bedroom, kitchen, dining room, bathroom and adjoining corridors, as I knew that one could be identified from footprints as easily as fingerprints.

I left the house at 3:30 AM. I was sure that Elene would be missed sooner rather than later, so I wasn't worried that she would starve to death. I could safely never worry about her again, unless I wanted her to star in my fantasies. But that's unlikely now. I think that I need a new love object. Someone who won't betray me.

I drove to the airport, switched cars and then went back to the Whispering Winds, dropping the gun in a handy storm drain on the way. I will take a little nap and then leave at around ten in the morning. I intend to pay my bill in cash so there will be no credit card trail. Then I will drive westward, ever onward, ever upward.

ENTRY 111

I spent a leisurely week traveling to California, my next port of call for my new Project of World Rage Assassination.

Just as an experiment, just to see if I still had the magic touch, just to see if I could maintain the tricky proposition of keeping two Projects going at the same time, I picked up a prostitute named Tanya in Rapid City, South Dakota. I easily performed my miracles on her. I changed my M.O. slightly by not exhibiting her indoors at the fabulous Dunworth Berdell Motel on Neck Yoke Avenue, where I had decided to rest my bones that night. Instead, I left Tanya beautifully displayed in a woodland glade off Lafferty Gulch Road within spitting distance of the Mount Rushmore Monument. I felt so patriotic as I left, having added enhanced beauty to the surroundings of the stirring, grandiose, granite sculptures of our most notable Presidents. The tender ministrations of Mother Nature would work their wonders and change Tanya into something more than just a woman. Mother Nature and I would make her into a new Venus, one of many goddesses and gods to come.

I am a tiny soul lost in a sea of other tiny souls,
Like the stars in the Milky Way...
So many stars that it hurts your eyes.
What does it matter if a few twinkle and fade out to
oblivion?
There are always millions more to take their place.

Michael's favourite paintings and works of art
can be viewed at:

www.barbiewilde.com/paintings.html

BIOGRAPHY

Barbie Wilde is best known for playing the Female Cenobite in Clive Barker's classic British cult horror movie, *Hellbound: Hellraiser II*. Before moving to the UK, Wilde attended Syracuse University in the United States, majoring in Drama and Anthropology. She continued her education in London, studying Drama, Classical Mime and Art History, before joining Britain's largest classical mime troupe, SILENTS.

Wilde also was a vicious thug in Michael Winner's *Death Wish 3*; robotically danced in the Bollywood blockbuster, *Janbazz*; and played a drummer in an electronica band in *Grizzly II: The Concert* (finally completed after 37 years and released in 2020 as *Grizzly 2: Revenge*), which starred then unknowns George Clooney, Laura Dern and Charlie Sheen. She featured in 16 TV different shows in the 1980s and 1990s, such as *The Morecambe and Wise Show*, *Rebellious Jukebox*, *Pukaski: The TV Detective* and *Hale and Pace*.

In the early 1980s, Wilde sang and danced professionally at the top nightclubs and rock venues of New York, London, Bangkok and Amsterdam with her music and dance group, SHOCK. SHOCK released 2 singles on RCA Records and supported Gary Numan, Ultravox, Depeche Mode and Adam & the Ants.

Wilde also featured in 14 pop videos for various artists such as Ultravox and Simple Minds. Wilde wrote and presented 7 music and film review TV programs in the 1980s and 1990s, interviewing such artists such as Iggy Pop, The Sisters of Mercy, Black,

Wet Wet Wet, The B-52s, Johnny Rotten and Cliff Richard, as well as actors Nicolas Cage and Hugh Grant.

In 2009-2021, Wilde contributed short stories to 16 different horror or crime anthologies and publications. Her 2009 Hellraiser-inspired short story, 'Sister Cilice', made it to the top of the list of Dread Central's 8 Most Gruesome Hellraiser Stories Told Outside the Movies: "This is a messy, viscera-soaked, disturbing story that's also lurid and steamy in a way that would make Barker proud."

Wilde's illustrated collection of short horror stories, *Voices of the Damned*, published by SST Publications in 2015, was called, "sensual in its brutality" and "a delight for the darker senses" in a starred review from *Publishers Weekly*. Each of the 11 stories is introduced by a full color artwork and-or illustration created by some of the most imaginative artists in the genre: Clive Barker, Nick Percival, Steve McGinnis, Daniele Serra, Eric Gross, Tara Bush, Vincent Sammy and Ben Baldwin. *Voices of the Damned* was nominated for the Best Horror Story Collection Award by This is Horror, 2015.

Wilde's most recent short story is 'Liaison' (theme: Lust), which features in the horror anthology, *Circles of Hell*, inspired by Dante's Inferno and published by TK Pulp.

Wilde is collaborating as co-producer and co-screenplay writer with ex-Fangoria Editor-in-Chief and director Chris Alexander (*Blood for Irina*, Parasite Lady, etc.) on the feature length horror movie, *Blue Eyes*.

Wilde returned to acting in the Amazon Prime horror series Dark Ditties Presents... in the episodes *The Offer* (2017) and *Dad* (2022), as well as playing a high society cannibal queen in *Body Horror: Eating Disorders* (2024).

Barbie Wilde is the proud recipient of the Texas Frightmare Weekend Lifetime of Torment Award 2018 and the Cine-Excess Innovator of Horror Award 2023.

The Venus Complex is also available as an audio book, narrated by the "King of Pain" himself, Hellraiser's Doug Bradley.

STEPH SCIULLO – ART

Steph Sciullo's work has been called grotesque, dark, disturbing and visceral. She is a self-taught visual artist from Pittsburgh and works across a wide variety of mediums including sculpting, painting, drawing, printmaking and assemblage. Steph uses a variety of materials in her work including wax, wood, clay, acrylics, inks, stains, and found objects.

Steph shows in various galleries and sells work not only online, but at various curiosity shops and horror conventions throughout the country.

"Steph's work is challenging and highly original: grotesque, beautiful, twisted, funny, demented and downright fucked-up!"
—Doug "Pinhead" Bradley

"I'd buy her whole collection if I could!"
—Sid 'Captain Spaulding' Haig

"Stunning, sensual, unique, controversial, gore-geous: what's not to love about Steph's work?"
—Barbie Wilde, Author (*The Venus Complex*, *Voices of the Damned*, *Sister Cilice*) and Actress (Female Cenobite *Hellraiser II*)

Steph Sciullo at Etsy:
https://www.etsy.com/shop/stephsciullo/
Average item review: 5 out of 5 stars (283)

Steph Sciullo on Instagram:
https://www.instagram.com/stephsciullo/

ADRIAN BALDWIN (COVER DESIGNER)

WINNER of INDIE NOVEL OF THE YEAR 2016 (Readers' Choice) at Underground Book Reviews

Adrian Baldwin is a Mancunian now living and working in Wales. Back in the Nineties, he wrote for various TV shows/personalities: Smith & Jones, Clive Anderson, Brian Conley, Paul McKenna, Hale & Pace, Rory Bremner (and a few others). Wooo, get him.

Since then, he has written three screenplays, one of which received generous financial backing from the Film Agency for Wales. Then along came the global recession to kick the UK Film industry in the nuts. What a bummer!

Not to be outdone, he turned to novel writing - which had always been his real dream - and in particular, a genre he feels is often overlooked; a genre he has always been a fan of: Dark Comedy (sometimes referred to as Horror's weird cousin).

BARNACLE BRAT (a dark comedy for grown-ups), his first novel won Indie Novel of the Year 2016 award (see above) - his second novel STANLEY McCLOUD MUST DIE! (More dark comedy for grown-ups) published in 2016, and his third novel: THE SNOWMAN AND THE SCARECROW (another dark comedy for grown-ups) published in 2018.

Adrian Baldwin has also written several dark comedy short stories, some of which he has published himself, whilst others have appeared in anthologies published by a variety of indie publishers.

His latest project, DEVIL'S ACRE, is a horror/sci-fi/period drama; it's basically Victorians vs 'aliens' vs zombies! What's not to like. The unfolding story will be released in a series of novellas/novelettes – with Episode 1 The Great Stink already out there.

Adrian cites his major influences as Kurt Vonnegut, Monty Python, Stephen King, David Bowie, Christopher Moore, David Mitchell, Robert Rankin, Galton & Simpson, Colin Bateman, Bruce Robinson, Jasper Fforde and Irvine Welsh.

For more information on the award-winning author, check out: www.adrianbaldwin.info (*You can read the beginnings of all his works there.)

DEMAIN PUBLISHING

To keep up to-date on all news DEMAIN (including future submission calls and releases) you can follow us in a number of ways:

WEBSITE:
www.demainpublishing.org

TWITTER:
@DemainPubUk

FACEBOOK PAGE:
Demain Publishing

INSTAGRAM:
demainpublishing

www.ingramcontent.com/pod-product-compliance
Lightning Source LLC
Chambersburg PA
CBHW030421180626
46812CB00005B/2117